—THE **SHADOWS** OF **MISKATONIC**—
BOOK TWO

Thin Places

BARBARA COTTRELL

ISBNs:
979-8-9865938-2-1   Thin Places   Trade Paperback
979-8-9865938-3-8   Thin Places   E-book

DEDICATION

To H. P. Lovecraft, who created the world.
And to Lance, who encouraged me to chase the dream.

"All my life," he said, "I have been strangely, vividly conscious of another region—not far removed from our own world in one sense, yet wholly different in kind."

—Algernon Blackwood, *The Willows*

In the universe, there are things that are known, and things that are unknown, and in between them, there are doors.

—William Blake

Chapter One

If something lurked in the woods, Victor Ramsey would find it. He had no other choice. With only six months left in his senior year, he needed a thesis topic. Fast. His advisor was growing impatient.

That's what made the stranger's sudden arrival so remarkable. Just when he reached his lowest point, when Victor was about to abandon his dreams and pursue a more traditional major, his spiritual guide appeared. Sure, the guy was weird. Clad in a buckskin coat, threadbare shirt, and stained leather pants, he looked like a character out of *The Last of the Mohicans*.

Victor didn't care.

He was desperate.

Even the darkness seeping into the Pine Barrens didn't bother him. He grew up in the backwoods of Maine, home to some of the densest wilderness in North America. Victor could navigate using only the trees as his guide. It took a lot more than a scraggly New Jersey forest to bother him. But the moment he stepped off the main road, his inner compass spun out of control. The Barrens confused him. It seemed like the Barrens *wanted* to confuse him. Victor didn't like to give nature a human face. Nature deserved better, a lot better, but this place . . . A dark presence lived here. A dark presence determined to hurt him. Tree branches grabbed him as he passed. Stones wobbled beneath his feet. Birds chirped in the twilight, eagerly plotting his demise.

Against you, a voice whispered. *They're all against you.*

Victor stopped in his tracks. He dug into his jacket pocket and pulled out an EMF detector. Almost immediately, the machine beeped. He stared in disbelief as the number registered: 206. A reading you'd expect from an electrical fault. A *dangerous* electrical fault.

"That would explain the paranoia," he muttered.

His guide turned and looked at him.

"What?"

"My electromagnetic field reader. The readings are through the roof."

"That is to be expected. This place is full of iron. Machines do not do well here," the stranger explained.

Victor followed the man deeper into the woods. The moon peeked through the narrow spaces between the trees. After a few feet, the forest closed on the moon, and its cold light vanished.

He stopped again.

A voice screamed in his head.

Leave! Leave, leave!

"Are you coming?" his guide demanded.

Victor knew this moment would forever define him. He could crawl away like a coward—his father's favorite name for him—or he could prove himself once and for all. He could prove he had what it took to graduate from Miskatonic University. And if he didn't? Victor saw his life spread out before him, as flat and empty as his father's.

He dug into his backpack and put on a pair of night-vision goggles.

It bathed the world in a sickly green hue.

"Yeah, coming," he called out.

Victor studied the man walking ahead of him. His guide was in his mid-thirties, handsome in a rugged sort of way, but his eyes held a darkness far beyond his years. Faint scars lined his skin. The patterns suggested some kind of tribal initiation. What bothered Victor the most was his face. It was rigid. The man held it like it was a mask about to fall off.

They hiked for most of the night. Victor's wristwatch beeped every hour, reminding him of the world beyond the forest. The Garden State Parkway was only a few miles away. He read that you could see the lights of the Empire State Building from the top of one of the hills.

He hoped they were headed there.

He longed for a glimpse of civilization.

The EMF readings continued to climb. Victor's dread rose with it. Shadowy forms danced on the edge of his vision. Up ahead, he could hear his guide talking to himself. Victor tried to catch a few words, but the wind carried them away.

"Are we close?"

The man gestured to the top of the hill. "Do you see that ridge? That's where we're headed."

Victor gazed at the desolate, windswept peak. He knew he should be unpacking his equipment. He needed to take some measurements at the base of the hill. But excitement outweighed common sense. Victor scrambled up the summit, leaving his guide behind.

He gasped when he reached the top. Everywhere he looked, there was wilderness—miles and miles of dark, unbroken forest. And sure enough, he could see New York City twinkling in the distance.

"Oh my God," Victor breathed.

"God does not live here, my friend," the man said as he pulled out a piece of chalk. He began to scribble on the granite slab where they stood.

A chill stiffened Victor's spine. "What did you say?"

The man bowed his head and smiled.

"God does not live everywhere in your world."

"In my—"

Victor watched as the man filled the stone with figures and marks. The young student shuddered.

His guide stared at him with cold, sharp eyes. "You sure you want to go through with this?"

"Positive." Victor surprised himself with the firmness in his voice.

"Then you must prepare."

Victor took his time arranging his cameras. He hated the sloppiness of most paranormal investigations. Whenever something exciting happened, equipment always failed—it was out of focus or unsteady or, worst of all, broken. He was determined to capture the evening's events from every conceivable angle.

His guide devoted the same care to his drawing. He scribbled on the rock, then, like a mathematician pondering an equation, stood back to appraise it. Occasionally, he made small adjustments. Victor was impressed by the man's ability. Even the most seasoned investigators at Miskatonic relied on books to write spells. That this man could do it from memory strengthened his resolve. Being on top of the hill helped, too. The air was clearer here. Less oppressive.

The man drew an open pentagram around his work. He straightened, finally satisfied.

"Are you ready?"

Victor moved in front of one camera and rattled off information. "This is Victor Ramsey. I'm in the Pine Barrens of New Jersey. With me is—" He gave the stranger a questioning look.

"My name is not important, friend. Like you, I am merely a seeker," the man insisted.

The guide kept his back to the camera. He motioned for his companion to enter the circle, and Victor stepped through the opening. Once they were inside, his companion closed it.

Victor shivered when he heard the rasp of chalk on stone.

"Should I be doing anything?" he asked in a trembling voice.

The man looked up. His expression was a blend of pity and contempt.

"Sit down in the center of the pentagram. And stay still," he ordered.

"Should I cover my eyes and count to three?" Victor knew it was a childish thing to say, but he couldn't help himself. It made him feel like he had some control.

The illusion shattered the moment the incantation started. Victor was familiar with the spell, having studied it for countless hours in the Miskatonic Library. He'd wrestled with the words, trying to free them from a leather-bound book. This man had no trouble. They flowed out of him with cold, fluid grace. Victor closed his eyes, letting the words wash over him. They were hot, and they were cold, and they . . .

Tickled.

Victor giggled, even though it felt wrong.

The man's words came back to him.

God does not live everywhere in your world.

Your *world* . . .

His eyes flew open. He struggled to focus on the guide he'd followed so blindly into the forest. The man whirled around the circle in a blur. Or was it the circle that moved? Victor looked at the ground, hoping to regain his balance.

The man stepped forward and struck him.

Victor fell backward, his head smashing into the stone.

That's when he saw it.

A creature fell from the sky. Victor watched helplessly as it descended on him. Enormous wings. Pointed tail. Long arms and spindly legs. And claws. Outstreched. Razor-sharp. Reaching out for him.

"No," he wailed.

He flipped onto his stomach and tried to scurry away.

The thing pounced on him, sending a shock wave of pain through his body.

Victor screamed as the monster sunk its claws into his spine.

"Damn. You're not the one," the man announced sadly.

His spiritual guide said nothing more. He turned and walked away.

Chapter Two

"**I**f there's anyone here, would you please give us a sign?"

Ellen Logan pointed her microphone into the darkness. Even though it was the dead of winter, the attic was warm and musty. But there was no oppressiveness, no feeling of being watched. Not a single sign the house was haunted.

She turned to her partner. "Are you getting anything?"

"I don't like the way Greg looks at you."

"What?"

"Greg," Phil Marcus said, referring to the expedition's leader. "I think he's interested in you."

"Oh, for God's sake." Ellen tore off her night goggles and sat down on the couch. The cushions let out an exhausted woof. "You think everybody's interested in me."

"That's because they are," Phil insisted. He was Ellen's current boyfriend, a blond-haired, blue-eyed surfer from Redondo Beach.

She thought a relationship with a guy like him would bring some much-needed light into her world.

She was wrong.

"Are you getting any readings?"

"Nah. EMF is flat." Phil sat down beside her. "I don't get it, Ellen. Why do you do this?"

"What do you mean?"

"The ghost hunting. You've put in the hours Miskatonic requires of students. Why do you still do it?"

Ellen shrugged. "Because I like it."

That was only half the truth. The real reason? Ghost hunting was all she had left. Already in the middle of her junior year, Ellen still hadn't been asked to join Miskatonic's advanced program. And without the university's special training, she could never be a serious paranormal investigator.

Her window of opportunity wasn't just closing.

It was collapsing.

"Well, I don't think you should be doing this. Especially now," Phil insisted.

"What do you mean?"

"Jeez, Ellen, haven't you heard? There's a serial killer on the loose."

Ellen rolled her eyes.

"There are always serial killers on the loose around here. I swear, there should be a major in serial killing at Miskatonic."

"I'm serious. They've found bodies scattered all over Arkham County."

"Ours is a dangerous profession."

"Profession?" Phil frowned at her.

"Yes. *Profession*," she shot back.

An awkward silence filled the room.

"Do you think this place is haunted?" he asked.

"Well, there's always the possibility we're here on an off night."

"Yeah, yeah." Phil motioned for her to get to the point.

"I don't think there's anything here. Even if it were an off night, I would feel something. Some residue or—"

A sudden impact rocked the house.

The roof above their heads bulged and buckled, and a fine layer of dust rained down from the rafters. Ellen looked at Phil. He stared back, his mouth hanging open.

She rose and grabbed her walkie-talkie.

"Greg, this is Ellen," she barked into the receiver, calling down to the command post on the ground floor. "Is anyone on the roof?"

"I was just about to ask you the same thing. What the hell is going on up there?"

"Maybe a bird hit the house," Phil offered.

"Have to be a flying dinosaur to make that kind of racket," Ellen muttered. Flying dinosaur or not, she knew what she had to do. "I'm going to take a look."

"Are you insane?" Phil spluttered.

"We have to find out what it is."

"We don't have to *do* anything," he insisted.

Ellen stared at him until he wilted.

"I can't stop you from going out there, can I?"

"No."

He hissed and shook his head. "Then for God's sake, please be careful."

"I will," she promised.

The attic was in one of the towers, at the point where the strange angles of the house converged. Ellen crawled out of a window and made her way to the widow's walk.

As she inched closer, she heard a wet, gurgling wheeze.

A man's face appeared between the railing posts of the widow's walk; it was mangled and bloody. As she got closer, she realized he was impaled on one of the iron spikes.

Ellen stabbed the button on the walkie-talkie. "Greg, there's somebody up here. He's hurt. Call 911!"

The battered man motioned for her to stay away.

"No, don't. It's a trap," he rasped, his torn lips making him slur his words. "Get away . . . It's watching . . . It's watching." The man spluttered blood.

"What's watching?" she asked.

She tried not to look at him. The sight of the man made it hard to think. Every time he breathed, his chest bubbled. And his hands—there were no fingers left. They had been ripped off. Even the bones were gone.

Ellen closed her eyes and swayed. For a moment, she thought she would lose her grip.

"Will somebody *please* get help?' she screamed into the radio.

The man looked across the roof.

Ellen followed his gaze.

She saw nothing except a large stone gargoyle.

"Just hold on. Help is coming," she reassured the broken man. She listened for the sound of emergency vehicles. Only the wind rattled through the trees.

Phil stood in the street below, along with the rest of the ghost-hunting team. They gawked up at the house. Phil was filming her.

Enraged, Ellen yelled to her boyfriend, "Where the hell is the goddamn ambulance?"

"Ellen, *move!*" Phil shouted.

"What are you doing? Don't just stand there! Call 911!"

"Ellen, move. *Now.*"

She heard a crisp snapping sound, like the flapping of a sail. Except it sounded raspy. Leathery. Loud. She looked up. A monstrous creature hovered over her, its huge bat-shaped wings unfurling in the winter air. Ellen's words came back to haunt her. *Flying dinosaur.* With its huge wingspan and long spiked tail, the creature filling the night sky did look like a dinosaur. But the shape of its body was all wrong. It was sleek. Humanoid. It had arms and legs. A torso. A head. Ellen paused. But no face. No eyes, no nose, no mouth. Nothing that connected it to the world as she knew it.

She was so transfixed she didn't see it swoop down on her. Only the cries of her friends snapped her out of her stupor. She rolled to the side as the creature punched through the roof. The sudden movement sent her sliding down the wood-shingled slope. *This isn't real,* she thought as her hands fluttered, searching for something, anything to stop her descent. *This can't be happening. I'm going to wake up. Any sec—*

Her feet caught on a storm drain. The old metal split from the house, rocking under her weight. The rain gutter held just long enough for her to swing her body through the attic window. She tumbled onto the floor—her breath hard, her heartbeat thundering in her ears.

She looked up at the roof.

The creature was still there. It toyed with the broken man clenched in its talons. Ellen knew she should be running. She should be racing downstairs to the safety of the group. But she couldn't move. She was trapped by it, by the mere fact of it, and by a single, terrible thought.

I've seen a thing like this before.

She closed her eyes and shook her head.

"No. No, no, no, no," she chanted.

A moment later, Phil burst through the door. The rest of the team followed, enveloping her in a cloud of noise.

When she looked back out the window, the creature was gone.

"Jesus, are you okay?" Phil rushed to her side. When he saw she was uninjured, he babbled like a hyperactive child. "I can't believe it! I can't believe what we . . . I got some incredible footage. It's a little out of focus, but I think we got it. I think we got that thing! We couldn't quite see what it was messing with, though."

"It was a man."

A shadow passed over Phil's face. His enthusiasm evaporated. "*What?*"

"The creature was 'messing around' with a man," she repeated, loud enough for the others to hear.

A hush fell over the group.

"The guy was hurt. Bad," Ellen whispered.

"Did you recognize him?" someone in the group asked.

She shook her head.

It was only then that the full significance of what happened hit her. She started to tremble. Pain shot through her body. She could feel bruises forming from her rough ride down the roof.

If it weren't for that storm drain, I'd be dead. Smashed on the driveway like a pumpkin.

An ambulance wailed in the distance.

"We need to call our advisor and let him know what happened," Ellen said.

"But he said to call only if it was an emergency," Phil protested.

"And you don't think this qualifies?!"

He looked at her, stunned.

"Um. Yeah. I guess it does."

He unlocked his phone and called for help.

Chapter Three

"Do you have any idea how much this is going to cost?" Ellen watched as the owner of the house raged at the university spokesman. She didn't like public relations people. No one at Miskatonic did. PR always seemed to get in the way, demanding safeguards and guarantees to protect the community. Their requirements made serious paranormal investigation almost impossible.

Still, she was glad the PR guy was there.

The owner of the house was mad. Not just mad. Livid. He planned to open the house to the public in a few weeks. Now, with the damage to the roof, his schedule would have to be pushed back. The official listened to the owner's complaints, trying to placate him in a gentle, soothing voice.

Ellen strained to hear what the man was saying, but she was too far away. And the paramedic kept harassing her. She asked the same basic questions, just to make sure Ellen didn't have a head injury. Ellen gave up trying to eavesdrop. She'd have to rely on Phil for information. Her boyfriend stood next to the official, absorbing the abuse that should have been hers.

"Are you sure you're okay?" the paramedic asked for what seemed like the hundredth time. As she turned to answer, Ellen noticed the woman was distracted.

So that's why they're staying so long on the scene, she thought with a smile.

"His name's Phil Marcus," Ellen offered.

"No, I was just . . . just . . ."

"Really cute, isn't he?" she teased.

"Is he available?"

"No. Sorry. He's with me."

The paramedic turned as red as the lights on her vehicle.

"Oh God, I didn't mean—"

"I know." Ellen reassured the woman. "Am I free to go?"

"You'll have to sign some paperwork first."

"Fine."

The paramedic climbed into the back of the vehicle for the necessary forms. As Ellen waited, her eyes drifted back to her boyfriend.

A shadowy figure stood by the side of the house, only a few feet away from Phil. At first, she thought the man was a neighbor attracted by the commotion. But his clothes were too formal to be someone jolted out of his sleep. He wore a long jacket, lace-up boots. He looked like a mountain man who just stepped out of the wilderness.

And he wasn't watching the men.

His eyes were on her.

The stranger stepped into the light.

He smiled and raised a finger to his lips.

A voice swirled in her head, sweet and sticky.

There you are. I've been looking for you.

Come with me.

Ellen's body jerked. She rose to her feet and started to walk toward him.

A hand closed on her arm.

"Miss?"

Ellen blinked.

It took her a moment to focus on the paramedic.

"Yeah?" she blurted, if only to hear her own voice.

"Are you okay?"

Ellen glanced over the woman's shoulder.

The shadowy figure was gone.

Phil arrived a moment later, spewing obscenities. "Son of a bitch. *Fucking* bastard!"

The paramedic cringed and retreated. Ellen was glad. She didn't want to go through another round of "are you okay?" questioning.

"What's wrong?" Ellen asked.

"They're going to certify the house."

"What?"

"They're going to certify the house as haunted."

"But they can't," Ellen said. "There's no evidence. No documented proof—"

"It's a concession, Ellen. They're paying the guy off," Phil snapped.

His anger cooled when the paramedic interrupted them with paperwork.

Phil watched Ellen sign the release forms. "You sure you're okay?"

She looked at the spot where the mystery man had been. Nothing.

Tired, she told herself. *I'm just tired.*

"Did they find anything?" she asked Phil.

"No. Well, the investigator found some blood on the roof. They took samples, but since they don't know who—or should I say what—to compare it to . . ." Phil's voice trailed off.

"It's like trying to catch smoke," Ellen murmured.

"What?"

"Nothing. Just something someone said once."

Andrew Carter. The words came from Andrew Carter. Ellen didn't want to admit it, but as she tumbled down the roof, she thought about him. They worked on only one case together, but she felt a deep connection to the famous professor.

She wondered if he shared her feelings.

If I died, would he miss me?

"Uh, oh. Here comes the executioner," Phillip announced before she had a chance to think about it.

The university official shot her boyfriend a sharp glare, which he easily returned.

"Miss Logan, may I have a word with you?"

"Of course."

"I'm coming with you," Phillip insisted.

Ellen waved him off.

"I'll handle it. Just wait for me here."

The official seemed surprised by her willingness to go with him. As he led her away from the ambulance, she noticed his rumpled suit. Ellen could almost picture the scene that brought him here. Startled out of bed by the call, he grabbed the first thing he could find—all while his wife complained about the odd hours he kept. She imagined his wife nagging him about a lot of things. The Miskatonic bureaucrat looked haggard. His worn expression went well beyond sleep deprivation.

He paused at the edge of the property and pulled out a cigarette.

He offered one to Ellen.

"No thanks," she said as he lit up. "What's your name?"

The man's eyes narrowed, and he glared at her through a veil of smoke. "Why? You want to put me on the report?"

"No, I just want to know your name."

The bureaucrat continued to glower at her. After a few moments, he relented.

"My name's Calvin. Calvin Leonard."

"It's nice to meet you, Mr. Leonard," she offered.

He snorted at her attempt at civility.

"You won't think so after you've heard what I have to say."

Ellen crossed her arms, bracing herself for bad news.

"You're off the ghost-hunting team until further notice."

"You mean permanently." Ellen's eyes darted to her teammates. They were clustered around the back doors of the van, watching the video Phil shot. She had yet to see it. Between the paramedics and this guy, she had been unable to rejoin the group.

"That all depends on the results of the investigation." He dug into a leather satchel and handed her a thick stack of papers. "Write down everything that happened. Then I'll decide what action we're going to take. Do I make myself clear, Miss Logan?"

"Yes." Ellen reluctantly took the bundle. Miskatonic paperwork was a nightmarish blend of bureaucracy and madness. There were rumors that people committed suicide rather than having to fill out a report.

"I want this on my desk in two days. Two days." Calvin Leonard held up two fingers just in case she didn't understand. "I don't want to have to chase you down. You don't want me chasing you down."

"No. I don't, sir."

"I suggest you grab your stuff and get out of here. This guy's still mad," he said, nodding at the homeowner.

Ellen watched the man pace the front porch. He gestured wildly as he talked on his cell phone.

Probably talking to his lawyer about how many ways he can sue, she thought. "Fucking opportunist," she hissed before she could stop herself.

Leonard shot her a sideways look.

"On this point, you and I agree, Miss Logan." He flicked his lit cigarette onto the lawn. "Now, run along and let me clean up this mess."

"What happened?" Phil demanded when she returned to the ambulance.

"I think I'm on the Miskatonic version of administrative leave," she replied. When her boyfriend frowned, she told him the unvarnished truth. "I'm off the ghost-hunting team."

"*What?* That's crazy! You didn't do anything! She didn't do anything!" He shouted the last sentence at Calvin the Bureaucrat.

The man walked past them, pretending not to hear.

"It's called a concession, Phil."

Her partner refused to be swayed. "But it's not fair! You didn't do anything," he stammered with indignation. "I'm not going to stand for this. None of us will. We'll resign from the team, go to the press—"

She put her hand on his arm. "Don't. Please. You need to be on the team to graduate. I'm just a volunteer."

"But it isn't fair," he repeated with a vehemence as sweet as it was misguided. Phil had yet to be corrupted by Miskatonic. He still had principles, a clear sense of right and wrong.

God, never let him lose that, she thought.

"Look, Phil. I appreciate your loyalty. Really, I do. But you have to choose your battles," she advised. Even though he was only two years younger, she felt older. Wiser. "Besides, I don't think Calvin likes the owner any more than we do."

"Calvin?"

Ellen nodded at the university official.

"Oh, so the two of you are on a first-name basis, are you?"

"We won't be when I give him a big stack of nothing." She held out the pile of formal paperwork. "Please, tell me you know how to fill these out. I mean, you're a business major, right? You know how to write a report."

He looked at the papers as if they were something unclean.

"Not *that* kind of report."

They both fell silent.

Ellen chewed on her lip.

"I know someone who might be able to help, but I don't think he'll do it."

"Do we have any other choice?" he pressed.

Ellen sighed. She knew there were no other options.

Chapter Four

"**D**r. Carter? You *know* Dr. Andrew Carter?" Phillip whispered as they stood in the back of Carter's 9:00 a.m. class.

"Sort of," Ellen replied, trying to focus on the lecture. Even though she had taken Carter's class before, she was still interested in the material.

"Sort of? What do you mean sort of?"

"He's a friend of my uncle's."

Ellen wasn't going to tell Phil that she and Carter worked on a case together. In Phil's mind, a man and a woman working together meant only one thing.

A few minutes later, Carter dismissed class. Most students left, weighed down by the prospect of an upcoming midterm. But a small group lingered. Ellen and Phil took their spot in line. Ellen's mind drifted. She thought about the man in the shadows by the house. The way he lifted his finger to his lips. As if the two of them shared a secret. As if they were in on something together.

Come with me, his voice rasped.

A bolt of pain shot through her head.

Her boyfriend nudged her.

"Ellen? Earth to Ellen?"

Tired, she thought. *I'm just tired.* "Do you have a Red Bull or something?"

He dug into his backpack and handed her the familiar red and blue can. It was warm and tasted awful, but it worked. As she climbed the stairs to the stage, she felt ready to face Andrew Carter.

"Yes?" he demanded when she approached him. He didn't look up. He pretended to be absorbed in unhooking himself from the audiovisual equipment.

She saw no point in engaging in social pleasantries.

"I need your help, Carter," she announced.

He grinned into the podium.

"Why doesn't that surprise—" He looked up. The moment his eyes settled on Phil, his expression changed. A mild spring day turned into a deep freeze. "What do you want?"

"We had an, um, incident when we were ghost hunting."

"An, um, incident?" Carter mocked her.

Phillip jumped in. "We saw a—"

He shot her boyfriend a lethal glare. "Not another word. You don't talk about this in public."

Ellen deposited a stack of papers on the podium.

Andrew Carter let out a bitter bark.

"Oh, is that what you meant when you said you needed my help? You want me to do your paperwork for you?"

Ellen fought to keep her voice even. "No, I don't want you to do my paperwork. I want you to show me how to do it."

"When is it due?"

"In two days."

He fixed her with an incredulous look.

"Not a chance. Jesus, Ellen, how long have you been sitting on this?!"

"I got the paperwork a couple of hours ago."

Carter blinked.

"What?"

"I got the paperwork a couple of hours ago."

She saw something creep into Carter's eyes.

"What is it?" Ellen demanded.

"Look, I don't know what happened." Carter paused and gave her a long look. "But if it were me—"

"What?" she demanded when he hesitated.

"I think you're being set up."

"I knew it! I fucking knew it!" Phillip exploded, startling her before she had a chance to absorb the information.

"I've been suspended from the ghost-hunting team," Ellen informed Carter. "There was an incident at the place we were monitoring. I broke a rain gutter."

He continued to stare at her. "You don't get suspended for something as simple as property damage."

Carter glanced at his watch.

"I don't have time for this. I have a ten o'clock across campus."

"Yeah, well, thanks for the help, Carter," she said as she grabbed her papers and walked away. She felt like she was sleepwalking. *God, let this be a dream*, she prayed. *Please, let this be a dream.*

"Friend of the family, my ass. What's the deal with you and the professor?" Phillip demanded once they were outside.

"Not now. Please, not now."

The uneasiness Ellen felt was changing, blooming into full-blown anxiety.

You're being set up.

Carter's words and the man last night, waiting in the shadows, calling out to her with his sickly sweet voice . . .

There you are. Come with me.

Her hands began to shake.

"Seriously, Ellen. What is going on between you and Carter?"

The dam broke.

"I said *not now!*"

Ellen burst into tears. Right in the middle of Miskatonic University.

"Oh God, he's right. He's right. I'm being set up," she wailed.

Phil held out his hands. "Hey. Hey, hey, hey. You don't know that. He doesn't know that. He said he *thought* you were being set up."

"Carter was just being nice."

"Look, I know he's a friend of the family and all, but I don't think that man's capable of being nice."

Ellen said nothing.

"Look, we have a lot of options," he told her. "We have a recording of what happened. And it shows a lot."

"Does it show the man on the roof?" she asked, hoping there was enough to file a missing person report. Or better yet, launch a search party.

Phil's mouth tightened. "It shows a lot."

She was about to ask him more when her cell phone rang. Ellen glanced at the caller ID. It was Connie Blake. He was a member of the Eibon Institute, a private think tank run by psychics. Even though she wasn't sure she could trust him, she kept in touch. Besides Carter, he was the only psychic she knew. And unlike Carter, he had time for her.

"I need to take this," she said to Phil as she retreated. "Hi, Connie."

"Ellen, where the hell are you? You're late."

"Late?"

"You were supposed to be here half an hour ago."

The institute. She was expected to attend an event.

"Oh shit, I forgot! I completely forgot."

"Well, if it's not important to you—"

"No, it is. *It is* important, Connie. A situation . . . Please." She hated the desperation in her voice. "Could you give me the address again?"

"It's 1353 Haverbrook Drive."

She jotted the information on a scrap of paper.

As soon as she was off the phone, she turned to Phil.

"Do you think you could get me across town in five minutes?"

Her boyfriend flashed her a shit-eating grin. He loved showing off his state-of-the-art Japanese motorcycle. "You wanna bet?"

"How do dinner and a massage sound?" Ellen offered.

"Sounds like you're going to lose."

Chapter Five

Ellen pressed her face into Phil's back as they rocketed across town. The whine of the motorcycle pierced the stillness of the late-winter morning. She imagined the sound ripping though the houses, the insect-like buzz disrupting people's routines. Ellen tried to think of the last time she'd spent a leisurely morning at home, sleeping in, reading the paper. She couldn't remember.

Her life had become a blur of sleepless nights and endless cups of coffee. She'd hoped to grab a few hours of sleep between ghost hunting and classes. Then Connie called and reminded her of their meeting. She had no choice but to stay awake, at least for a little longer. She didn't mind. Not really. The prospect of seeing Connie Blake again perked her up. Or made her tense. She wasn't sure.

Phil slammed on the brakes.

There was a loud squeal and a cloud of burning rubber.

Her boyfriend took off his helmet and beamed at her triumphantly. "We're here. Four minutes and fifteen seconds. Get the massage oil ready."

Ellen barely heard him. The house at 1353 Haverbrook Drive was another old Arkham Victorian, almost identical to the place she shared with her uncle Joshua. The only thing different was the crowd milling around outside the gates. It wasn't a very large group—ten or fifteen people. Still, Ellen's heart thundered in her chest. The last time she met people from the Eibon Institute, they threatened her, forcing her to flee to the relative safety of Miskatonic University.

"Are you sure this is the right place?" she asked him.

"Yep, 1353 Haverbrook Drive. This is it," he replied after consulting the scrap of paper she gave him. Phil shared her misgivings. He frowned at the crowd who watched them. "I don't know about this, Ellen. I'm getting a Jim Jones kind of vibe—"

"Miss Logan!" a voice called out.

Connie Blake emerged from the crowd. He wore a crisp pinstripe suit that made him look steampunk. The rest of the crowd also dressed formally. Ellen looked down at her jeans and fisherman's sweater and tried not to panic. She felt completely unprepared.

"I don't know about this, Ellen," Phil repeated.

Connie paused on the other side of the street and waited for her to finish her conversation. He glared at her. And Phil.

"I'll be fine," she said. She was only half-convinced. There was something about the whole situation that seemed off.

"Then I'll leave you to it," he said as she returned his passenger helmet. "See you at the lecture tonight."

Ellen groaned. "Oh God, I forgot about *that*, too."

"Don't be so negative!" He scolded. "It's bound to be something interesting. Everyone at Miskatonic is expected to attend. Undergraduates. Grad students. Faculty. I wouldn't be surprised to see the janitors there."

Ellen smiled as she gathered her things. A mandatory assembly. She wondered how Carter felt about that. Put out, to say the least.

She moved in and gave her boyfriend a goodbye kiss.

"Thanks, Phil. You're a lifesaver."

"Remember, if you need me, I can be here in four minutes and fifteen seconds flat. Just call."

"I will," she assured him.

She watched him roar off down the street. Phil was heading back to the ghost-hunting team, to start the first of what would be many hours of data analysis. Ellen bit her lip. She wished she could be with them.

"Is that your boyfriend?" Connie asked when she crossed the street to join him. He posed the question casually, but she could feel the dark undercurrent.

"Is there a problem?"

"You're late." He stared at her coldly.

"I know. I'm sorry. I was on an investigation, and I was, um . . . detained."

"Well, at least you dressed up," he quipped.

The people behind him tittered.

"I wasn't aware there was a dress code." Ellen glared at him, then the crowd.

"Maybe this wasn't such a good idea."

"Maybe it wasn't."

She turned to leave.

A well-dressed older woman pushed her way through the onlookers. Ellen could tell by the way Connie straightened that the woman was in charge. She reminded Ellen of the British actress Helen Mirren. Gray hair cut in a no-nonsense bob, eyes that radiated intensity and intelligence. Ellen grew up alone, in a series of foster homes. She tried not to fantasize about her missing family, but this woman . . .

Ellen felt a twinge of longing.

I want my grandmother to look like this.

"Dr. Blake, we can't wait any longer for your . . . oh, is this the girl?"

"Yes." He looked away, jaw clenched.

Ellen stepped forward and extended her hand.

"My name is Ellen. Ellen Logan."

"Frances Cummings," she offered.

Ellen was relieved when the woman took her hand.

"I'm sorry I'm so late, Ms. Cummings, but I almost fell off a roof."

"Oh dear." The woman's hand fluttered to her throat in a way Ellen found both quaint and charming. "I hope you're all right."

"I'm shaken up. And a bit bruised. Other than that, I'm okay. I didn't have time to change, and . . ."

"Are you sure you're up for our little exercise?"

"I don't know. I have no idea what you're doing."

Ms. Cummings scowled at Connie. "Dr. Blake didn't tell you?"

"No, he just called and told me to show up."

"My, such loyalty," the woman murmured.

She took Ellen by the arm and led her past the gaggle of psychics.

Connie walked behind them.

"Well, Miss Logan, this is the Eibon Institute's version of an entry-level exam. Every student must go through this exercise. What we want you to do is walk through the house and see if you can pick up on anything."

"With all these people around?" Ellen didn't relish the thought of trying to sense psychic imprints with such a large group milling about. It sounded as promising as having a picnic on a busy highway.

"Oh, no. They've already been through the house. They're waiting for the bus to take them back to the institute. It'll just be you. Well, you and Connie."

Ellen wasn't sure that was any better. Living people polluted the surroundings, even after they left.

Jeez, if I go through this house after all those people, I won't need a Red Bull.

"Do you think you're up to it?" Ms. Cummings pressed her.

"I'd certainly like to try."

"Excellent." The woman dug into her purse and handed her a packet. Ellen cringed. *More paperwork.* "Here's the questionnaire. Go through the house and take notes on the rooms that speak to you."

"Mind if I take some readings?" She asked, nodding at the ghost-hunting equipment in her bag.

Ms. Cummings looked at her, shocked.

"Oh, no. No, no, no, my dear. We rely on our natural senses at the institute. We don't use machines."

"Then how do you verify your impressions?"

"We're not in the business of verification," the woman insisted, her lips curling in distaste.

Not in the business of verification? Ellen thought. *Then how do you separate fantasy from fact?*

"I don't understand." Ellen frowned.

"Of course you don't. They do things differently at Miskatonic, don't they?" Ms. Cummings gave her a sad look. "Well, never mind, just give it a try. Oh, and Miss Logan?"

"Yes?"

"Why don't you leave your backpack with Dr. Blake? That way, you'll be free to move around."

She clutched the bag to her body. "I'm good."

"I assure you, I have absolutely no interest in looking through your bag," Connie said. His words had an edge she feared was permanent.

She surrendered the bag rather than risking alienating him any further.

Ms. Cummings gestured at the house with a grand, sweeping motion that reminded Ellen of a real estate agent.

"It's all yours, my dear. The doors are unlocked. Feel free to spend as much time inside as you want."

Ellen felt naked without her bag. As she climbed the stairs to the house, she plucked at her sweater. She tried to quell her uneasiness by flipping through the questionnaire Ms. Cummings gave her. It made her feel even worse than the Miskatonic paperwork. The long form was full of strange phrases like "emotional coloring," "holographic sentience," and "thetic projection." *The secret language of psychics.* She felt a jittery, crawling panic. She wandered around the old Victorian, hoping to pick up on something, anything that would prove her abilities.

The house offered her nothing. It was empty. More than empty. The place felt sterile. Except for the well-worn paths in the hall, it was devoid of life. Ellen made a few circuits of the house before she settled in one of the upstairs rooms. She sat down in a window box and stared at the blank page. She prided herself on her ability to reason her way out of tight spots. She'd salvaged more than her share of tests by demonstrating just enough knowledge to get credit. But there was no writing her way around this test. Ms. Cummings's words came back to taunt her. *They do things differently at Miskatonic, don't they?* After a while, she wrote down the only thing she knew for sure. *I feel nothing.* Then she gave up and headed downstairs.

Connie Blake waited for her in the parlor. He'd shed his jacket and tie and was sprawled across an old leather chair. A book was perched on his knees. From time to time, he scribbled in it. She strained to read the title, but the light from the bay window was too bright. Ellen considered sneaking out. She had nothing to give him. But her bag sat next to his chair. She couldn't leave without it.

"Are you done, Miss Logan?" he asked without looking up.

"Yes."

He nodded toward a table piled high with questionnaires. "Leave your paper over there."

"Where's Ms. Cummings?"

"She went back to the institute with the others."

Ellen hesitated, unsure what to do. She'd hoped to have a word with Ms. Cummings, to ask for another chance. The long night of ghost hunting, the terrifying encounter on the roof, the mysterious man, Mr. Leonard and the Miskatonic paperwork . . . she had nothing left in the tank. *That's probably why I'm not picking up anything,* she thought, but a darker possibility lurked in the back of her mind. *What if psychic ability is a limited resource, like fossil fuel?*

"Is there a problem?" Connie Blake demanded as he rose from the chair.

Oh, if you only knew . . .

"If I only knew what?" Connie asked.

She blinked, startled by the intrusion. She'd forgotten what it was like to be around him.

"Nothing."

"Then turn in your paper. I'll look at it when I get back to the institute."

"Don't bother. There's nothing on it." She shifted under the weight of his stare. "I don't know what's wrong. I'm probably just tired. But the house doesn't feel right to me."

Connie tilted his head.

"What do you mean?"

"I'm not sure." She fiddled with the loose threads on her sweater. "Old places like this, even if they're not haunted, they should have some color. I mean, you have countless generations of people living, loving, and going through a whole range of emotions. You would expect to find *something* here. But the place feels cold. Bleached out."

"Bleached out?"

"Like a crime scene that's been cleaned up," she offered. She knew she sounded absurd. *You're clutching at straws,* a harsh voice whispered. "This place feels completely blank."

"It happens." He watched her as she gathered her things. His reassurance only made her feel worse. She wasn't used to failing. Especially at something that was so important to her. "Can I give you a lift back to Miskatonic?"

Ellen looked out the parlor window.

"Wait a minute. Didn't the bus just leave? How are you getting back?"

"I came in my own car."

"Oh." Ellen paused to consider the offer. "No. That's all right. You've wasted enough time on me already."

"Wasted time on you?" he echoed. "Jesus, why don't you just go home and flog yourself?"

"I can't afford a whip," Ellen replied.

Even though she meant to be serious, she laughed.

Absurd, she thought, *you're being absurd, girl.*

After a moment of stunned silence, Connie joined her.

Ellen felt the atmosphere in the room lighten.

"I so wanted to impress you," she admitted.

"Me? Why?" he asked. At first, she thought he was being coy, but he seemed genuinely surprised by her feelings.

"I felt bad about what happened. You know with . . . Maybe it's my fault. Maybe I was broadcasting or something that night when . . ." Ellen trailed off, unsure what else to say.

"I'm the one who snuck into that guy's head while you were making love to him," he insisted as he squirmed in his chair. "What I did was inexcusable. Completely against the

Eibon Institute's creed. Not to mention creepy. Really, really creepy. I'm surprised you're willing to be alone with me."

"What was in you before, I don't feel it anymore." She paused, working up the courage to ask the next question. "Did you think I was with *him* that night?"

Connie Blake frowned.

"I don't understand."

"Did you think I was with Andrew Carter that night? Is that why you . . . intruded?"

A strange, guarded look crept into his eyes. It wasn't exactly a wall. Still, she knew she'd reached the end of productive conversation.

"Never mind," she said as she grabbed her backpack. "I should let you go. You have a lot of grading ahead of you."

He stepped forward, blocking her attempt at a graceful exit.

"You want to go somewhere?"

"What?"

"I thought we might go somewhere and talk," Blake suggested.

Ellen glanced at her watch. Even though she had a crypto-zoology class in twenty minutes, she decided to ditch it. Her friend Martha Pickman was in the same class. Ellen could borrow her notes.

"I'd like that."

"Then help me with these papers, and we'll go."

Ellen scooped up an armful of questionnaires and followed him to his car. She peeked at some of the tests. There was no clear answer about the house. The observations were scattered. Some people's accounts even conflicted with each other.

At least I didn't miss anything obvious, Ellen consoled herself as Connie opened the car door. His vehicle was a generic sedan, the kind that screamed rental car. Or in this case, institute car. She carefully deposited the papers on the back seat. As she arranged the questionnaires, Connie tossed the book he was reading on top of them. Ellen expected something deep, an esoteric work peppered with phrases like "emotional coloring" and "holographic sentience." She smiled when she saw the title, *The Official Book of Sudoku.* Connie worked puzzles. She didn't know why, but it made him seem less intimidating. More down to earth.

He drove her to the edge of town, to a narrow spit of land that jutted into the Miskatonic River. Ellen tried not to smirk. McClellan Point was an infamous make-out spot. Anyone who wanted the privacy a dorm couldn't offer came here. They drank, they smoked weed, and they did all the wild things they couldn't do on campus.

As they climbed out of the car and hiked to the scenic overlook, Ellen wondered whether this was the place where Connie and Carter shared the woman. She caught a glimpse of their erotic encounter the first time she met Connie Blake.

When you intruded into his *head.*

Ellen blushed so hard, her skin crawled.

Is that the reason he brought me here? Is he suggesting something?

"That's not why I brought you here," Connie replied as he popped a cigarette into his mouth. "If you must know, I'm celibate."

"You are?" she blurted once she recovered.

"We all are."

"Is that something the institute demands?"

"Not demands. Strongly encourages," he insisted. "The institute believes that celibacy provides a purer connection with the spiritual world."

"Really? I think it would have the opposite effect," she replied.

"What do you mean?"

"If I were a ghost, I wouldn't want another spiritual connection. I'd want a physical one, one that reminded me what it was like to be alive."

A fierce look crossed Connie Blake's face.

"Have you ever fucked a ghost, Ellen?" he demanded.

His body might be celibate, but his mind sure isn't, she thought as she decided how to answer. In the end, she told the truth.

"Yes. At least, I think I did."

"You *think* you did?"

"I was, um . . . I was drunk at the time," she admitted.

He reacted the way she expected he would. He got mad.

"Jesus Christ, Ellen. One-night stands, possession, unprotected spiritual contact . . . you're the poster girl for bad behavior!"

Ellen looked out at the river. She closed her eyes. She suddenly wished she hadn't skipped class. It would have been nice to have a little normalcy in an otherwise crazy day.

"I'd like to be your teacher," Connie announced.

Her eyes flew open. "*What?*"

"You may be wild and a little unconventional, but you saw through the deception."

"The deception?"

"The house is a fake. It was only built a few years ago. We use it as a training device, to emphasize the danger of going in with preconceptions."

"So you mean . . . that was . . . a *placebo* house?"

Connie smiled.

"If you want to call it that, yes."

"Nothing ever happened there?"

He shot her a sideways glance. "You mad?"

"Mad? Connie, that's brilliant!" She felt a newfound respect for the institute. They might not be in the business of verification, but they were using a scientific framework. "Did you come up with that?"

"I wish I could take the credit, but no."

"Did you take the test when you joined the institute?"

"Yes. With another house, of course. They change places every few years to keep things fresh."

"How did you do? Did you pass?"

He ignored her question.

"You still haven't given me an answer. Do you want to be my student?"

"Do I have to be celibate? Because celibacy's a deal breaker for me."

"You only have to be celibate with people at the institute," he assured her.

She held out her hand.

This time, he took it.

"Deal."

Chapter Six

A wall of noise greeted Ellen at the door. The lecture hall was packed. She was glad Phil offered to go early and save them a place. It gave her the time she needed to recover. Now showered and changed, with a few hours' sleep, she felt human again.

As she threaded her way through the crowd, Ellen noticed that the traditional social divisions were being observed. The faculty occupied the front rows. The graduate students sat behind them. And the undergraduates—*the lowest of the low,* she thought bitterly—were in the very back.

There were some exceptions.

Her boyfriend was one of them.

He'd staked out a patch of floor in the faculty section.

Ellen smiled and crossed the invisible barrier, ignoring the stares of the people around her.

"Did you hear? They found another body," Phil said when he saw her.

"What?"

"They found another body. They think the serial killer struck again."

"Gee, it's nice to see you, too, Phil."

"Oh, I'm sorry," he replied and put on his best face. "Hey, sweetie. How was Jonestown? Drink any Kool-Aid?"

She pulled him into a tight hug. Even though he was joking, Ellen could hear his concern.

"They don't drink Kool-Aid anymore. Get with the times," she joked as she smoothed down his shirt. "Well, look at you. My little revolutionary."

"Not just us." He nodded at the spot across from them.

Martha Pickman also occupied the faculty section.

Ellen smiled at her friend. Martha was tall and pale, with hair so black, it looked blue. When she first met Martha, Ellen expected her to be a snob. She was, after all, a Pickman, a descendant of the famous painter. Her family was Lovecraftian royalty. But Martha didn't put on airs. She was kind. Humble. And she was the only friend Ellen had left from her freshman year. Some had died. Others fled, unable to handle Miskatonic's darkness.

"I'm so tired of sitting in the nosebleed seats," Phil complained as he guided her to their step. He plopped down on the floor behind her. "I mean, we're the ones who pay to come here."

Ellen looked around the overcrowded lecture hall.

"I'm surprised the fire marshal doesn't have something to say about this."

"If you're looking for safety, you're in the wrong place," a voice announced.

Ellen looked up, startled. Andrew Carter was in the aisle seat above her. Ellen recognized some of his graduate students sitting beside him. Their presence did not go over well with the other professors. There was much shifting and muttering. The occasional pointed look.

Carter ignored them.

Another revolutionary, she thought.

Ellen felt a rush of affection for him, as sudden as it was sweet.

"Hello, Dr. Carter."

He favored her with a quick glance. "Miss Logan."

A small, immaculately dressed man stepped up to the podium.

"Excuse me, ladies and gentlemen. Ladies and gentlemen, may I have your attention, please?"

"Well, well, it looks like the wizard has stepped out from behind the curtain," Carter muttered.

His students snickered as the little man fumbled with the microphone.

Phil leaned down and whispered in her ear.

"That's the president of the university."

Ellen gawked.

"*He's* the president?"

"My sentiments exactly, Miss Logan," Carter replied.

Her boyfriend stiffened. She could hear the question form in his head.

Why is Andrew Carter paying so much attention to her?

"Students, esteemed faculty of Miskatonic University, you all know me. You know where I stand, what I believe in. I do not indulge in fads. I do not pursue things just because they're hot. Miskatonic is better than that. Miskatonic *needs* to be better than that." The president paused to shoot a pointed gaze around the room. "But we cannot ignore the outside world. This man cannot be ignored. His online series *The Veil* has become a viral sensation. It has been viewed millions of times. For better or worse, he is the public face of what we do. And he has offered to talk to us. For free, I might add."

The president's attempt at a joke fell flat.

"You may not agree with him. You may not like what he does. All I ask is that you listen to him and make your own decisions. Ladies and gentlemen, allow me to introduce Mr. Solomon Reye."

A man dressed entirely in black walked across the stage. He wore a long coat and a top hat, and he carried a gold-tipped walking stick. The hide of an animal was draped over his shoulders. He kept his head down as he approached the podium. The crowd hummed with expectation. When he took off his hat, the noise turned to an angry buzz. His face was completely covered in white makeup.

Carter pressed his fingers to his eyes. "Oh, Jesus Christ."

"What?" Ellen demanded as the man on stage tapped his stick to restore order.

"He's dressed like Baron Samedi," Carter said in a quiet voice.

"The voodoo god of the dead?" she blurted, horrified. To dress as a powerful god was one thing. To be a white man dressed as an African god . . . "Is he *nuts*?"

Solomon Reye's eyes locked on Ellen.

A cold bolt of recognition shot through her.

She jerked to her feet.

"You," she hissed. "*You* were there last night. Standing in the shadows. Watching."

The man on stage opened his arms, offered her a deep, courtly bow. "*Oi chusoi Dios aei enpiptousi.*"

Out of the corner of her eye, Ellen saw Martha Pickman rise. A dreamy expression spread over her face. She knew what her friend was experiencing. A strong tug, an overwhelming desire to drift toward the man dressed as Death.

Ellen began to sway.

Carter grabbed her wrist.

"Don't," he warned her.

His face was expressionless, but she could feel emotions churning through his body.

Carter's fighting it, too, Ellen thought in disbelief.

"*Oi chusoi Dios aei enpiptousi,*" the man on stage said again.

The lecture hall faded: Ellen stood in front of an old house, at the cellar door. Behind the gray, rotting wood, people moaned.

Phil's voice pulled her back. "What's that guy saying?"

"It's Greek," Carter offered. "The dice of God are always loaded."

"What the hell is *that* supposed to mean?" Phil demanded.

Solomon Reye chuckled and shifted his attention to the unruly audience.

Ellen drifted back to the present.

"My children, my children, please, please. I bear you no ill will," Solomon Reye called out. "As a great man once said, 'If you kill a man like me, you will injure yourselves more than you will injure me.'"

"Great. Now he's quoting Socrates," Carter muttered.

A woman in the row in front of them glared at Carter.

"Andrew, would you please *shut up*," she hissed.

The people beside her murmured their approval.

Carter smiled, picking an imaginary piece of lint off his pants.

"You are entering a new age. After years and years of scratching, humans have finally made their mark on the world. You have carved into the earth, conquered the sky, invaded the oceans. And others have noticed. I have noticed. A price must be paid for such . . . curiosity. Exploration demands sacrifice. It demands submission."

Solomon swiped the air with his walking stick.

"You are knocking on the door between two worlds. I am here to let you in," he growled. "To make you see the way things really are. I am here to rip off the veil."

The lights dimmed, and an image popped up on the on-stage screen. Somewhere in the audience, a woman screamed. Ellen recognized the creature. Its sleek body. The long tail. Wings. It was the thing she saw on the roof.

This time, there was more than one. A half dozen of them danced inside a magic circle.

Solomon Reye stood in the center, naked, covered from head to toe in white make-up.

"They are fallen angels," he marveled. "Divine creatures. They can show you things. Take you to wonderful places. But you must first *submit* to them. You must surrender to them completely. It's the way you move forward. It's how you advance as a species."

Solomon Reye lifted his head. His eyes rolled back.

He shrieked words in a language she didn't understand.

Ellen felt a sudden burst of pressure in her head. Her vision blurred. The air around her thrummed. The creatures on the screen continued to circle Solomon Reye. Her head spun as she watched them dance.

One of creatures broke away from the pack. It spread its wings, casting a shadow on the screen.

Her mind repeated the message.

It . . . cast . . . a . . . shadow . . . on . . . the . . . screen.

She looked at Andrew Carter.

"Carter. It's real! It—"

Something hard hit her. It hauled Ellen to her feet and pulled her up the auditorium stairs. *That thing on the roof,* she thought dimly. *It's come back. It's come to finish the hunt.* But when she glanced at the stage, the creature was still there. It had only just begun to step away from the screen, to make its presence known. There was a momentary lull in the crowd. She knew she only had seconds before the audience saw the thing on the stage. Before screams filled the air.

If you don't do anything now, no one will hear you.

"Andrew, help!" she shrieked.

The thing smacked her in the head.

"Shut up, you manipulative little bitch," a man snarled in her ear. "Batting your eyes at me. 'Yes, sir. I understand, sir.'"

Words.

She looked down and saw an arm around her waist.

A human. Someone I can fight.

Ellen erupted in a fury. She kicked and thrashed. She did everything she could to knock her attacker off-balance. Her resistance slowed the man down a little, but he was dragging her closer and closer to the exit. To the point of no return. Ellen could almost see the white van waiting in the darkness. She could smell the stench of its previous passengers.

"Not me," Ellen snarled.

She sunk her teeth into his arm.

The man jerked, as if an electric current shot through him. He howled. At least, Ellen thought he did. The audience finally noticed the creature on the stage. If the man did cry out, the sound was lost in the roar of other voices. Ellen bit down harder, shook her head to tear the skin. She refused to let go, even as blood filled her mouth. She wasn't going to let go until *he* let go. Until he abandoned the lurid plans he had for her.

He threw her on the floor.

Ellen turned to face her attacker.

She blinked.

And blinked again.

Calvin Leonard stood over her, clutching his arm. Blood streamed between his fingers.

Calvin? Calvin, the Miskatonic bureaucrat?

Ellen remembered how angry he had been when she called him to deal with the landlord of the damaged house. But grabbing her in the middle of an assembly and dragging her up the stairs?

It made no sense.

"You fucking bitch!" he roared.

He lifted his leg to kick her, but he slipped on the stairs.

Someone grabbed her from behind.

Oh God, no, she thought dimly. *He's not alone. He has an accomplice.*

Andrew Carter shouted in her ear.

"Get up. Move!"

He yanked her to her feet and pushed her toward Calvin.

Ellen stumbled, almost colliding with her attacker.

"Andrew, what? What are you fucking doing?" she spluttered.

Calvin rose to his feet. He looked at a spot just above her shoulder.

His mouth split into a wide, wolfish smile.

"You have no idea what you're up against, do you?" he murmured in a dreamy voice.

A second pulse shot through her head. This time, it was much worse. Her body jittered. It vibrated, in tune with a strange frequency.

Ellen looked toward the stage. She couldn't see Solomon. Her view was blocked by people running up the stairs, their eyes hot with panic.

"We need to get out of here. Now!" Carter shouted again.

Ellen and Carter rode the first wave of hysteria out of the building. The swell deposited them in the courtyard. Other people followed, boiling out of the auditorium like confused ants. The air was thick with questions. "What happened?"; "Did you see?"; "It couldn't be real, could it?"

Ellen spun around, searching for Calvin Leonard.

He was gone.

"Fuck. Fuck, fuck, fuck!" Ellen chanted.

Carter looked at her and cringed.

"You're bleeding!"

She dabbed at her mouth.

"It's not my blood," she reassured him. "I bit him."

"You *bit* him?" Carter echoed.

He snatched a water bottle from a passing student.

"Wash your mouth out," he urged her. "Quickly."

Ellen's stomach dropped. She didn't think about the diseases she could get from biting a person. Now, her mind marched her through the grim list of possibilities. AIDS. Hepatitis. Herpes.

Herpes, if you're lucky, she thought.

She used the entire bottle to flush her mouth.

"Are you hurt anywhere else?" Carter asked when she was done.

"I don't know. I—"

"Ellen? Ellen!"

She looked up to see Phil running toward them. Ellen felt a stab of guilt. In the madness of the moment, she had forgotten all about him.

"Ellen, who *is* that?" Carter demanded.

"My boyfriend. Phil."

He gave her a flat look. "You're kidding, right?"

When he arrived, Phil wrapped her up in a tight hug.

"Oh my God, was that who I thought it was?" her boyfriend demanded.

"Who do you think it was?" she asked.

Phil frowned and pulled away. "You mean you don't know?" Carter snorted.

"I mean I want you to tell me because I can't quite believe it."

"That guy who grabbed you. He was the bureacrat, right? The guy who chewed us out when—" Phil stopped and gave Carter a cool look. "Oh, but we *never* talk about this, do we? Not in public."

Carter ignored him. He directed his questions to Ellen.

"The bureaucrat? Was he the one who gave you the paperwork you showed me?"

"His name's Calvin Leonard," she offered. "I called him when things got rough at the ghost hunt. When I . . ." Her voice dropped to a whisper. "What are they, Carter? Phil and I saw the thing Solomon called an angel. It landed on the roof of the house where we were ghost hunting."

"You should know what it is," he replied. "You've played *Call of Cthulhu*, right?"

She gestured at herself. "Do I look like I have the monster manual on me?"

Andrew Carter pulled out his cell phone and tapped at the screen. She thought he was accessing some online version of the game to show her the creature. She was confused when he held out a picture of a person.

"Is that Calvin Leonard?" He asked.

She stared at a balding, short man. Rumpled, yes. A smoker, no doubt. But . . .

"That's not Calvin Leonard."

"Are you sure?"

Phil moved in and peered at the screen.

"That's definitely not the guy we dealt with," he insisted.

Ellen's heart stuttered. "But . . . we called the emergency number Miskatonic gives students. He gave us paperwork. How could—"

"It looks like we have an intruder." Carter said, pursing his lips. "Do you still have the paperwork?"

"I do," Phil volunteered. He put down his backpack and began rummaging.

"Why do you have my paperwork?"

He looked up sheepishly.

"I thought I might give it a try. You know, being a business major and all."

Ellen made a soft cooing sound in her throat.

Carter snatched the paperwork from her boyfriend and flipped through the stack. A grim smile spread across his face.

"Just what I thought."

He held it up for them to see. The first few pages were dense with questions. Demands for details. Personal information. Then it went blank.

The rest was nothing but white paper.

"Wait a minute. I . . . I don't understand," Ellen spluttered.

"The paperwork is fake," Phil explained. "The guy who approached us was an imposter."

Carter said nothing for a long time. He watched the people still streaming out of the auditorium. Many of them looked dazed; some were crying. A few threw up in the bushes.

Andrew Carter rubbed his face.

"Well, I guess you'd better tell me what happened," he finally decided.

Phil stepped forward, like an actor responding to his cue.

"We can do better than that, Professor. We can show you."

Chapter Seven

The undergraduate offices were not part of Andrew Carter's world. He paused at the threshold and wrinkled his nose. Warren Hall had a distinct smell—a funky mix of stale pizza and burned coffee. There was also an underlying scent, a dampness that hinted at a water leak deep in the building. The students who worked there tried to make the best of a bad situation. They painted the walls, covered holes with old movie posters, threw rugs over the chipped concrete floor. But there was no hiding it. The place was a dump.

"This is awful," Carter complained when Ellen stopped to replace a burned-out light with the bulbs she kept in her bag. "The place should be condemned."

"Then where would we go?" Phil demanded. "They would knock down this place and put us in temporary trailers that would wind up being permanent."

"Phil, lay off—" Ellen warned.

"Actually, he's right," Carter admitted. "That's what *would* happen."

Phil paused mid-rant, shocked that Carter agreed with him.

Greg, one of their ghost-hunting teammates, popped his head out of an office.

"Hey, Lens. Is that you and your pain-in-the-ass boyfriend?" The moment he saw Andrew Carter, he did a double take. "Shit, Phil, I thought you were kidding when you said you were bringing the Big Man."

Carter shot Phil a look that sent him scurrying to the office. He turned to Ellen.

"The Big Man? What's that code for? Hide your stash?"

She folded her arms and leaned against a faded *Night of the Living Dead* poster.

"There are no drugs around here. I'm the mama bear of this den. That's why Greg calls me Lens. I keep everyone focused."

Carter grinned.

"Lens, huh? Maybe I should start calling you that," he said.

"And maybe I should start calling you Andy," Ellen replied.

"We're ready! Come on in!" Greg called out.

Greg and Jenny, one of the newest members of the team, lined up to meet Carter. *Like they're meeting royalty,* Ellen thought as she introduced them. Carter hated the attention. Jenny made things worse. She practically pushed Ellen aside in her eagerness to meet him. Ellen had witnessed that sort of behavior before, when she attended an all-girls school. Whenever they went to town and boys were around, her classmates acted differently. Sisterly solidarity went right out the window.

"Have a seat, everyone." Greg waved them to the couch in front of a large computer monitor.

Ellen steered Carter to the end of the sofa and sat beside him. Jenny refused to be deterred. She plopped on the floor in front of him and pressed against his legs like an eager cat.

"I really don't think you should sit there, Jenny," Ellen advised.

Jenny looked at her coolly. "Oh yeah? Why's that?"

"I think someone threw up there the other day." She turned to Phil for support. "Isn't that true?"

"Probably. Those beer-can pyramids don't build themselves, you know," he replied as he joined Ellen and Carter.

Jenny scooted away from the spot. "Oh, you guys are disgusting!"

Carter chuckled and crossed his legs.

"Well, this place may be a dump, but at least the university has given you good equipment," he observed.

"Actually, Greg bought all the stuff." She tipped her head back to look at her friend. "He's rich."

"Fuck you, Logan."

"You think this is impressive? You should see his car," her boyfriend added.

"Fuck you, Phil."

They quieted down when Greg started the footage. The clip was unpromising at first. It opened in a blur as Phil vaulted down the stairs. Ellen felt a stab of disappointment. *Rookie mistake,* she thought. Then Phil cleared the house. Once he reached the safety of the research van, he paused and took a deep breath. When he lifted the camera up, his hand was steady. Ellen watched as she scaled the Victorian roof. Heading toward the broken man.

"That's him," Ellen exclaimed, pointing to the blob on the screen. "That's the guy I was trying to reach."

She turned to ask Greg if he could enhance the image.

Greg stared grimly at the screen.

"Keep watching," he urged her.

They heard Phil scream for her to move as he panned the camera to the sky. The glare of the moon saturated the image. Then the camera adjusted. Phil zoomed in for a close-up.

A bat-like creature hovered over her.

Carter's hands tightened on his knees.

Ellen leaned forward, captivated.

"Jesus, what *is* that?" she said.

"It's a nightgaunt," Carter answered.

Nightgaunt.

Ellen didn't need a monster manual to know what a night-gaunt was. They were famous creatures from the Dreamlands. Monsters who carried humans between this world and the next. Whether the humans wanted them to or not.

A little nugget from H. P. Lovecraft popped into her mind.

"They never spoke or laughed, and never smiled at all because they had no faces to smile with," she recited from memory.

The creature on the video dove toward her. Its claws punched through the roof, missing her by inches. The impact made Ellen jump. *Too close,* she thought. *Way, way, too close.* She watched as she skidded down the steep roof, her fingers scrabbling at the slate shingles. She stopped her fall at the last minute, digging her feet into the rain gutter. Phil lifted the camera up, away from her, catching the creature as it flew away.

The video ended in a blur of feet as he and the others stormed the house.

The moment the footage ended, Carter jumped off the couch.

"You moron. You fucking moron!" he snarled.

At first, Ellen thought he was talking to her. But his eyes were fixed on her boyfriend. "You let Ellen go after that thing, and you didn't help her? You didn't back her up? You just ran down to the street and *filmed* it?"

The outburst shocked Phil. He expected to be praised for his camera work, for being calm in the face of chaos.

"I was only trying to—" he started.

Carter's eyes narrowed.

"Oh, I *know* what you were trying to do. You were trying to make your reputation. To get some sensational footage. Well, you came this close." Carter pinched his fingers together. "*This close* to killing her. You almost made a snuff film. But you would have liked that, wouldn't you?"

Phil launched himself at Carter.

In his eagerness to get to him, he kicked Jenny.

The woman yelped and dove under a nearby desk.

Ellen jumped between the two men. She moved quickly, without thought.

She stepped in front of Phil and kneed him in the groin.

Her boyfriend gasped. She gasped. They all gasped.

The air seemed to rush out of the room.

Greg vaulted over the couch and grabbed Phil before he could respond. Greg was a big man, a linebacker with the football team. It took all his strength to hold on to her boyfriend.

"You think I don't know? You don't think I *see* exactly what's going on?" Phil screamed, twisting and turning in Greg's arms.

His face was red, his neck a corded network of veins.

Ellen backed away. She had seen hints of her boyfriend's jealousy before, brief flashes. She chose to ignore them, but this, this . . .

If Greg loses his grip, just for a second . . .

"Ellen, you need to get out of here," Greg ordered.

"Yeah," she said shakily.

"Wait. Wait. Don't leave me," a voice pleaded.

Jenny scrambled out of her hiding place and grabbed Ellen's arm.

She held on until they were safely outside.

As soon as Ellen closed the office door, Jenny burst into tears.

"I'm sorry. I'm so sorry. I should have done something. But my father and my mother used to—"

She stopped midsentence.

Andrew Carter stood a few doors down, banging his fist against the wall.

Ellen put her hand on Jenny's shoulder.

"You go on. I'll take care of this," Ellen assured her.

"Are you sure?" she asked.

Ellen fought the urge to laugh.

If I said no, would you stay and help?

She watched Jenny run away.

Oh, baby bear, you shouldn't be here, she thought. *This place is going to eat you alive.*

"I'm not going to apologize to that maniac," Carter snapped when Ellen approached him.

"I'm not asking you to."

"Seriously, Ellen. *That* guy's your boyfriend?"

"Phil's my *ex*-boyfriend now," she corrected. There was no denying it. She and Phil were history.

"Yeah, well, I guess that's what happens when you knee a guy in the balls."

Ellen felt a strange tickle in her throat, an urge to laugh. Like everything else about this day, it felt wrong.

She swallowed hard.

"Not funny, Carter," she scolded as she slumped against the cold wall. "God, I can't believe it. He . . . he kicked Jenny in the head. He kicked her, and he didn't even notice."

Carter finally looked at her. "Is she all right?"

"I think so. I'll call her later. See how she's doing," Ellen said.

"Are *you* all right?"

"No," she replied. "But that doesn't matter right now."

She grabbed Carter's arm and tried to pull him down the hall. The last thing she wanted was for him to still be there when Phil came out of the office.

Carter resisted.

His forearm felt like steel.

"I'm staying," he insisted.

"Are you serious? What exactly do you plan to do?"

Carter said nothing.

"You know, you shouldn't get between two men like that. You'll get hurt," he warned.

She thought again of Carter, Connie Blake, and the mystery woman. A woman she had seen when she read Connie's mind. The woman he shared with Carter when they were young and crazy. Who was she? What happened to her?

You're getting obsessed, a voice whispered.

Her skin crawled with heat.

Ellen's cell phone rang before she had a chance to respond. She hesitated. This was the best time, maybe the only time, to ask Carter what happened.

When she saw the number on her phone, she let the opportunity slip away.

She listened for a moment, then switched to speakerphone.

"You need to hear this," she told Carter. "Tom, will you repeat what you just said?"

"I'm at the campus police station. After you left the lecture, Solomon Reye showed more video of that thing. Of a guy getting mauled by that . . ."

"Nightgaunt," Ellen offered.

"Yeah, nightgaunt." The name came out in a shaky whisper. "People freaked. The whole place erupted. Some of the audience stormed the stage and beat up the guy in that, um, nightgaunt costume."

"Nightgaunt costume?" Ellen mouthed at Carter.

He shook his head.

"The guy in the costume escaped, but they arrested Solomon Reye, along with twenty other students. Martha Pickman was one of them. She punched a cop."

"Oh, jeez." Ellen closed her eyes. "I'm on my way."

"So what now?" Carter demanded. He had regained some of his composure, but the anger was still there. She knew it was an ember that could be easily fanned.

"The way I see it, you have two choices. You can wait here, beat up the man who is now my ex-boyfriend, and jeopardize your career."

"Beating him up wouldn't jeopardize my career. I'm tenured, remember?"

Ellen ignored him. "Or you can come with me and help me figure out what the hell is going on. Either way, I'm out of here."

When he hesitated, she turned to leave.

"I'm coming! I'm coming!" he relented. "Anything to get away from this hellhole."

Chapter Eight

The crisis was over, but the police station still crackled with energy. Most of the people had been processed and released. Only two remained. Martha Pickman sat alone, handcuffed to a bench. Solomon Reye was in the opposite corner of the station, at one of the desks. The makeup on his face had melted. He looked more like Heath Ledger's Joker than an African god.

Despite his ragged appearance, he was still in control.

The officer interrogating him was spluttering, his face red with frustration. Solomon sat erect in his chair. He responded to the man calmly, his answers punctuated by mild shrugs. The only glimmer of interest he showed was when Ellen walked in with Andrew Carter. He looked up. His eyes widened, as if he were surprised to see them together. Then, like a predator sizing up his prey, his eyes settled on Ellen.

She ducked behind Carter to avoid his stare.

"What are you doing?" Carter hissed.

"That guy freaks me out," Ellen said in a low voice. "That guy really freaks me out."

"Him?" Carter scoffed. "He's a whack job. Just a guy who likes to play dress up."

"He's more than that. You know it. You *felt* it," Ellen reminded him.

Andrew Carter looked away.

She was relieved when she spotted Tom Sampson talking to a police officer. Tom was another member of the ghost-hunting team. While she was the mother bear of their unruly clan, he was the father. He looked the part. Tall, with brown hair and sweet, soft eyes, he was the young, hip dad everyone wished they had. That didn't mean he was a pushover. He came down on people when he needed to. Hard.

"Hey, Lens," Tom said as he sauntered over. "Heard you trashed a tourist trap that was about to open. Good for you."

"Who is this?" Carter demanded.

Ellen started to introduce him, but Tom stepped into the void.

"My name is Tom Sampson." He offered Carter his hand.

To her surprise, Carter shook it.

"You were there for the rest of Solomon Reye's lecture?" Carter asked.

"Front and center."

"What happened?"

"I wish I knew. Martha was fine during most of his presentation. A little tense, but she's always a little tense. Then that guy started showing . . ." He paused to look at Reye. A mixture of fury and fear crossed Tom's face. "What we saw was horrible. No doubt about it. Everybody flipped, but she . . . There was something personal about the way she went after Reye. And he just stood there. Waiting for her. With an amused little smile on his face."

"Do you think this has anything to do with her being a Pickman?" Ellen asked.

"What?" Carter shifted his attention to her friend, handcuffed in the corner.

Royalty, Ellen thought with a sigh. "That's Martha Pickman. She's part of—"

"Yes, I know who the Pickmans are," Carter snapped.

"I don't. Who are they?" Tom asked.

Ellen jumped in, grateful she had something to offer.

"Martha's related to Richard Pickman, a painter who specialized in, um, portraits of strange creatures. Mainly ghouls. The art world wrote him off as a madman, but there were rumors—that he used live models, that his art was based on reality. He disappeared in 1926, along with his paintings. No one knows what happened to him."

"Some people think he went native. That he joined forces with the things he painted," Carter offered.

This was a part of the story Ellen had never heard.

"Is that even possible?" she blurted.

"I don't know," Carter replied.

"I mean, how could—"

"I said, I don't know," he said, loud enough to make the police officers around them fall silent.

Ellen looked at Martha Pickman.

"Where's the recording? The one Solomon showed?" Carter asked.

"The chief of police has it," Tom replied. "They're trying to figure out what they can charge him with. The video showed a brutal attack, but the police think it was just another fraternity prank. Sure, they did a search—after all, there *is* a serial killer on the loose. But there's no body. No one's showed up at the hospital. No one's turned up in the morgue. They're not sure what to do with Reye."

Tom's expression darkened.

"And he certainly has an, um, interesting defense."

"Really? What is it?" Carter asked.

"He claims he's not human. That our laws don't apply to him."

The words from his lecture came back to her.

Humans have finally made their mark on the world. You have carved into the earth, conquered the sky, invaded the oceans. And others have noticed. I have noticed.

Ellen stiffened.

You, you, you. He talks about humans in the third person.

"It means nothing. A lot of people say they're not human," Carter informed her in a low voice.

Ellen jumped. She had forgotten he was psychic, that they could share a connection.

But only when he wants to, she reminded herself. *Only on his terms.*

Carter glared at her. "I'll talk to the police chief. See what's going on. Why don't you talk to Martha?"

"Well, isn't he the charmer?" Tom growled as Carter walked away.

"He's not usually this bad. He's just amped up," Ellen insisted, desperate to dismiss the thought that Solomon might be . . . "He got into a fight with Phil."

"Your boyfriend? A physical fight?"

"Greg had to hold Phil back."

"What were they fighting about?"

"Carter didn't like the way Phil treated me. He thought Phil put me in danger."

"How?"

"It's a long story," Ellen said, begging him off. "Look, I might as well tell you now. Phil and I are through."

"You broke up with him?"

"Not formally. But I'm going to. Soon."

As soon as this crazy day is over, she thought.

Tom nodded at Carter. "Is he the reason?"

Ellen took a moment to consider.

"In a way. Carter made me aware of certain qualities in Phil I didn't like. I mean, I'd seen them before, but I hoped . . ."

Ellen dropped her eyes to the floor and bit her lip.

"Oh, Tom."

He pulled her into his arms. At first, Ellen resisted. She was the strong one. She prided herself on her ability to handle any situation, to be brave in the face of anything.

She wrapped her arms around him.

"I'm stupid. I'm so fucking stupid," she murmured as she pressed her face into his crisp white shirt.

"You're not stupid. You made a mistake. Welcome to the real world," Tom replied. "Just be glad you didn't figure it out on your honeymoon. Or when you were living in a trailer park, saddled with a couple of kids."

Ellen laughed through her tears.

"My, what a glorious vision you have of my future."

"You're better off without him."

"You sound so sure."

"I grew up with three younger sisters. I'm good at spotting dead-end men."

She withdrew from the embrace. She didn't want to let go, but she felt like the entire precinct was watching them.

"He's staring at us, you know. Probably thinks we're talking about him," Tom muttered.

"Who?"

"Dr. Carter."

"I don't care what he thinks. This is none of his business," Ellen insisted, her voice razor sharp.

"Now *that* sounds more like the Ellen I know," Tom said brightly, even as he continued to watch Carter. "Do you want me to stay?"

"No. You go on. I'll check on Martha."

She was about to thank Tom for the pep talk when he swooped in and kissed her.

His mouth was soft. Inviting.

Ellen opened up to his warmth.

"There, that should give him something to think about," Tom said as he pulled away.

"Forget *him*. *You've* given me something to think about."

Tom blinked. "Yeah. That was pretty good, wasn't it?"

He looked at Ellen. Reconsidering her.

"You know, you and I should go out sometime," he suggested.

"I'd like that. A lot," she admitted. "Just give me a little time. I need to unwind a few things."

"Take all the time you want," he replied. "I'll see you later."

Ellen smiled. "Yes, you will."

This time, his kiss wasn't for show. Ellen wrapped her arms around him, yielding to the soft pressure of his tongue. When she pulled away, she felt as if she had been brought back to life.

The feeling didn't last long. The moment she joined Martha Pickman, the glow faded. Her friend looked terrible. Her makeup was smeared; her long black dress was rustled and torn. One of her Victorian boots had been taken off and sat beside her. Ellen soon saw why. Martha's ankle was angry and swollen. She assumed Martha had twisted it when she jumped on the stage to get to Solomon Reye.

"Excuse me, miss? You can't be here," a young cop informed her.

"She's my friend. Please let me stay. Just for a little while," Ellen pleaded.

The officer hesitated, looking to his boss for guidance.

The chief was deep in conversation with Carter.

"Could you get me some ice? I think she's sprained her ankle," Ellen asked sweetly.

"Okay, but you'll have to move when she's transferred."

"Transferred?"

"She's going to the Arkham Asylum for observation," he replied.

"Agares, Vassago, Gamigin, Marbas, Valefar, Amon, Barbatos, Paimon," her friend chanted, tracing strange shapes in the air with her finger.

"Martha?"

"Agares, Vassago, Gamigin, Marbas, Valefar, Amon, Barbatos, Paimon, Buer, Gusoin, Sitri, Beleth." Her body rocked as she spoke each name. "Who is he? Damn it, who is he? I should know. The answer is there. I just need to . . . Gusoin, Sitri, Beleth, Leraye, Eligor . . . Eligor, Eligor, Eligor, Eligor."

The officer handed Ellen a plastic bag and an Ace wrap.

"How long has she been like this?" she asked him.

"Since she was brought in," he said as he scurried away.

Keeping a safe distance, Ellen thought. *Even the university cops don't like to get too close to us.*

Martha locked eyes with her.

For a moment, her friend was back.

"You know, he is who he says he is. And he's going to get us," she whispered. "He'll take us all, but only one will be chosen."

"What are you talking about?" Ellen asked.

Martha nodded at Solomon Reye.

"'He discovereth hidden things and knoweth things to come and of warres and how the soulders will and shall meet.' That's him. That's him!" Her friend tilted her head, listening to a voice Ellen couldn't hear. "Only one will be chosen. King, queen. It doesn't matter to him. It's all about the connection."

Martha fell silent.

She reached into her sleeve and sighed.

She pulled out something bundled in a handkerchief. "Here, take this."

"What . . . ?"

"Take it! Take it before he sees!" Martha hissed as she urged it into Ellen's hands.

Ellen stuffed the object into her coat pocket.

A moment later, Carter appeared.

"Come with me."

"But I need to stay with—"

"Please, Ellen," Carter urged her. He looked pale. Stricken.

Ellen didn't want to leave; she wanted to be there for her friend, to see if she could figure out what she was saying. But Martha was rocking again, swaying and chanting those strange names. She had retreated into a dream world, a place where she was safe, at least for the moment. Carter, on the other hand . . .

Carter needed her.

She followed him past the desk where the officers were clustered around Solomon Reye. She assumed Reye had invoked his right to a lawyer. Both sides glared at each other, locked in a silent impasse. And Reye loved it. He had an infuriating smirk on his face.

When Ellen walked by, he shifted his attention to her. There was no movement of the head, no eye contact, and no outward display of interest. She just felt it.

Her body trembled in response.

What did they call it when a substance reacted to another substance by being near it?

A catalyst, she thought. *That's what Solomon Reye is. A catalyst.*

Her hand tightened on the package Martha Pickman gave her.

"You think she's going to protect you? You think a Pickman is going to stop me?" Reye murmured in a soft, surprisingly plain voice.

Ellen looked around, but no one else seemed to hear him. Not even the guard sitting next to him.

Solomon Reye smiled, showing big white teeth.

"Nothing's going to stop me if you're meant to be my queen."

She grabbed Carter's hand, clutching it between hers.

Carter flinched and tried to pull away.

"He won't be able to help you, my dear. He's a fraud. The sad, leftover remnants of a once-mighty family," Reye taunted.

"Dr. Carter, I don't have all night." The chief of police jolted her out of their trance. Ellen must have jumped because the policeman shot her a sympathetic look. "Miss?"

She dropped Carter's hand.

"Yes?"

"Dr. Carter's warned you about this, right?" the chief asked her.

Ellen was about to shake her head when she realized Carter *did* warn her.

His pale face said it all.

"Yes."

The policeman ushered them into his office. Ellen was glad he kept the blinds drawn on the window that looked out over the precinct. She didn't want Solomon Reye watching them. She had a feeling what she was about to see would be bad enough. She took a seat in the empty wooden chair in front of a small television. An image was frozen on the screen. She couldn't quite tell what it was. Carter took a spot beside her, leaning on the policeman's desk.

The police chief stepped in front of the television and picked up the remote.

"I'm going to keep the volume down because . . . well, you don't need to hear it."

Ellen watched the drama unfold. Actually, it wasn't much of a drama. A young man stood in front of the camera and adjusted his equipment. He paused every so often to talk to someone off-screen. Ellen felt an odd twinge, the kind she got whenever she saw a film with an actor she couldn't identify. She would sit in the dark theater, her mind looping on the same thought. *Who is he? What else has he been in?* She felt the same distraction now, the sense of nagging familiarity. She leaned forward in the chair, the hinges squealing as she shifted her weight. The man on-screen moved closer, almost in response. Ellen admired him.

He looks so healthy, she thought, *so healthy and eager and whole.*

Whole.

The word stuck in her brain.

A slow, creeping realization spread through her.

"Oh my God. That's *him.*"

The chief paused the video. "That's who?"

"That's the guy I saw on the roof. The one I was trying to get to."

"Fuck!" Carter exploded.

He was off the desk and out of the office before Ellen had a chance to react.

She turned to the chief.

"I don't understand. What just happened?"

The man only offered her a grim stare.

"I need you to give me a statement, Miss."

And for the second time that night, she relived the nightmare.

———— ·✦✦✦· ————

The university clock struck midnight when Ellen came out of the police station. The chief offered her a ride home, but she refused. She didn't want to spend any more time with the police. They let her down. No matter how much she talked, no matter how much painstaking detail she provided, they couldn't get past one simple fact. There was no body. No body, no crime.

She didn't see the man on the roof die. Sure, he was in bad shape. He probably took his last breath a few moments later. But there was no proof. *Corpus delicti*—that was the legal term for it. Solomon Reye's lawyer chanted the words like a spell. And it worked. The police were forced to let him go.

And now here I am, out in the world with him. Alone.

"Body of crime." She sighed as she pulled out the parcel Martha gave her.

She'd peeked at it while the detective took her statement. It was a ring made of a dark, burnished metal. In the center, a ruby was inlaid with a strange symbol. A snake-like arrow shooting through a square.

The stone burned in the dim glow of the streetlight, its rich ruby surface hinting at a depth she yearned to explore. Ellen had been tempted to put on the ring in the middle of the police station. What would have happened? Would she have disappeared, like Frodo in *Lord of the Rings*? She could only imagine what the poor detective would have done. The man tried to be cynical, but he was shaken by what he saw on the recording. They all were. But in the end, the police officers refused to believe. They retreated to the same worn-out explanation. The video was a hoax, a sick, elaborate hoax. The special effects were impressive, but anyone with a decent computer could create them. Solomon Reye? The man was a nutcase, an internet celebrity eager to capitalize on his momentary fame. The riot at the lecture hall? Nothing more than mass hysteria.

And what about her role in this? Why had the nightgaunt landed on the house where she was ghost hunting? The man she saw on the roof had been in the company of Solomon Reye and the nightgaunt only a few hours earlier. Was that a coincidence? Did the nightgaunt put the man on the roof to lure her outside?

And then there was Calvin Leonard . . .

Questions, she thought with a sigh. *Questions on questions on questions.*

A flash of motion jolted her out of her reflection.

Carter waited for her halfway down the precinct stairs.

"Hey," he called out.

Ellen stuffed the ring into her pocket.

More questions poured out of her. "What happened? Why did you storm off? Why did you just leave me?"

He winced.

"I'm sorry, but I . . . I couldn't stay."

"Why not?"

"That was my student, Ellen."

Ellen frowned. "Who? Solomon Reye?"

"No. That guy you saw on the roof. With that thing."

Her stomach dropped.

"Oh," she gasped. "Oh no."

"His name was Victor Ramsey. I was his advisor. He was six months away from graduation, but there was no sign of a thesis. No sign of anything but a strong case of senioritis. The last time we met, I came down hard on him. I told him if he didn't find a topic soon, he would have to consider a more traditional major. I don't think he liked that. I guess it made him reckless. More willing to take risks."

He stared up at the trees, his eyes scanning the bony branches. *Looking for a body,* she thought with a shudder.

"You were the last one to see him. Tell me. Do you think he's dead?" Carter asked her.

Ellen flashed on the man's broken body. The terrified face. And the fingers. The fingers torn off his hands.

"He's dead," she whispered.

"You're sure?"

"I saw something else. Something that wasn't on the recording." She took a deep breath and closed her eyes. "When I looked back up at the nightgaunt, after I stopped my fall, the thing was toying with him. Plucking at his—"

"Fuck!" Carter grabbed hold of the handrail and squeezed. Ellen half expected the metal to snap. "Did he say anything to you?"

"Yes—"

"What did he say?"

"Carter—"

"What did he say?!"

"That it was too late. That I needed to get away. That *it* was watching." She dropped her head. "I'm sorry, Carter. I'm so sorry. I tried to help him."

He whirled around, making the same pinching gesture he made with Phil. "This close, you came *this* close to getting killed. And you're doing it again. I told you not to, and you're doing it again."

"What are you talking about?"

"You're hiding something from me."

His eyes dropped to her coat pocket.

Ellen tried not to react, but her hand flexed over her pocket.

"Give it to me," he commanded.

"No."

"I said give it to me."

"And I said no!" she erupted, enraged by his tone, his arrogant demeanor. "She told me not to let you see it."

"Who did?"

"Fuck!" Ellen hissed.

"Who told you that?"

"Martha Pickman."

"Martha Pickman? Oh, you mean the lunatic? The one in the police station chanting the names of demons?"

Demons.

The world floated in front of Ellen like a ghost.

"Don't talk about Martha like that! She's my friend, goddamn it!"

Carter looked away.

The next time he spoke, his voice was softer.

"Give me what she gave you."

"No."

"Ellen."

"*No!*"

Carter lunged at her. They wrestled each other for the ring. Ellen was trained in martial arts, but it did her no good. Sure, Carter was strong. That wasn't the problem. What held her back was that she couldn't bring herself to hit him. Ellen remembered the visit to the nursing home where Carter's father lived. The moment his dad laid eyes on him, he punched Carter right in the face. The flat hatred that bloomed in Andrew Carter's eyes frightened her. It came from a deep, dark part of him, a place she wanted to avoid.

All she could do was push and shove and try to wiggle her way out of his grip.

Just as Ellen was about to twist free, everything stopped.

Carter was close, so close, she could feel his breath in her hair. His arms were locked around her waist, their bodies pressed tight together. At first, Ellen couldn't figure out what had happened. Then she realized she was dangling off the railing. At some point in the struggle, she'd hopped up on it to escape him.

And almost tumbled backward onto cold concrete.

He saved me, she thought. *He kept me from falling.*

Carter lowered her to the ground. Even though he was breathing hard, his face was still. A mask.

"Deep end. Always throwing yourself into the deep end," he muttered as he released her. "I can't do this. I can't do this anymore."

"Carter—"

He backed away, holding up his hands.

He reminded her of a magician. *No tricks. Nothing up my sleeve.*

"No. Enough. We're through," he announced.

Ellen soon saw the reason for his odd reaction.

A police officer watched them from the top of the stairs.

"Miss, is everything all right?"

It was the opening Carter needed.

He slipped into the night before she could answer.

Ellen sighed.

"I'm fine. But I think I need a ride home."

Chapter Nine

"Joshua, I need your help."

Her uncle kept flipping through his art catalog.

"That doesn't surprise me."

Ellen hated the way he treated her when she interrupted his work. For one thing, he only saw her by appointment. Then, he made her wait while she fidgeted like a nervous schoolgirl. *This is all I need,* she thought as she toyed with the ring in her pocket. *Another person to make me feel powerless.*

"It's about Carter," she added.

"That also doesn't surprise me."

Ellen fell silent and surveyed the room. No matter where they lived, Joshua's study was off-limits. When she was young, she made up all sorts of reasons. Joshua was a serial killer, a Bluebeard who stuffed women under the floorboards of his desk. Or he was a powerful alchemist who had to keep his secret formulas away from the powers that be. The reason wound up being simple. Joshua was an art dealer who bought and sold antiques. Some of them were used in magical rituals. And Ellen was psychic. He kept the study off-limits to protect her, to keep dark energy from bleeding into the house.

Her eyes wandered over the objects that filled the room. One caught her attention. It looked like a painting. Or a mirror. Whatever it was, it was draped by a cloth and tightly bound with cords.

Is it one of those magical mirrors? she wondered. *A mirror that traps souls? The kind where a ghost pops out if you chant "Bloody Mary" three times?*

Her uncle tossed his catalog on the desk. "You know, Carter came to see me the other day. When you were in class. Probably *because* you were in class."

She turned away from the mysterious object. "What did he want?"

"He was worried about you. Said you found something. Something that made you squirrely."

Ellen hesitated. Her first impulse was to keep the ring hidden, to show it to as few people as possible. She had no idea what it might do. But who better to examine it than her uncle, a man who specialized in all types of magic?

She placed Martha's lace handkerchief on the desk and unfolded it.

In the cold light of day, the ring looked ordinary. Unremarkable. As Joshua donned his linen gloves, she told him the story. The police station. Solomon Reye. Martha handing her the ring and urging her to hide it.

Her uncle tried not to react, but Ellen saw him struggle with something. It wasn't small. It loomed between them like an iceberg.

He pulled out a jeweler's loupe to take a closer look. "Let me ask you a question . . ."

"Of course."

"Why did you assume she was talking about Andrew?"

"Excuse me?"

"When your friend told you not to let *him* see. There were two people she could have been talking about. Why did you assume it was Andrew?"

At first, Ellen didn't understand.

Then it clicked.

"Oh my God, Reye! Martha wasn't talking about Carter. She was talking about Solomon Reye!"

"That would be my bet." Her uncle focused on the stone in the center of the ring. "What does your gut say?"

"My gut?"

"The world you're in requires split-second decisions. Decisions the head and heart can't make. So I'm going to ask you this, and you answer quickly. Do you trust Andrew?"

One image flashed through her head. Andrew Carter catching her as she fell. How he stopped everything when he realized she was in danger.

"Yes," she responded without hesitation.

A ghost of a smile drifted across Joshua's face.

"Jesus, you two," he said.

"Not that it matters." Ellen sighed. "Carter said he's through."

"With you?"

"I assume so. He was backing away from me when he said it."

She shook her head. *I blew it. I really, really blew it.*

"Carter's not done with you. He doesn't have a choice. The ring Martha gave you is his."

"His?"

"His family's, at least." He motioned for her to move closer. "You see that symbol in the stone? The squiggly arrow shooting through the square? That's the Carter family emblem. There's a saying that goes with it. God, what was it?" Tapping his fingers on the desktop, he hesitated. "The only . . . the only way—"

"The only way out is through." Ellen felt a strange chill. She had heard those words before. When she traveled to the Dreamlands for the first time and met a man who guided her through the twilight world.

Her uncle gave her the same still look Carter did when he lowered her to the ground.

Always throwing yourself into the deep end, she thought.

"Listen, old man, I need to ask you a question. And no bullshit."

"Okay," Joshua agreed.

"Is Andrew Carter my father?"

Joshua blanched. "Andrew, your fa—Jesus, girl! No!"

"Is he my uncle?"

"No."

"Is he my brother? My nephew? My grandson?" She rattled off every possible connection, no matter how absurd.

"There's no biological connection between you."

"There *is* a connection, though, isn't there?" she pressed.

He pursed his lips and pushed the ring across the desk.

"You can't keep that. You need to give it to him."

Ellen bundled it up in the handkerchief. "I don't think he'll give me a chance."

"Why not?"

"Because I betrayed him."

Joshua raised his eyebrow.

"That's a little strong, don't you think?" her uncle replied. "Ellen, you protected him. You had no idea who your friend was talking about. And the ring might have hurt him. There could have been some very powerful magic in it."

"He's not going to see it that way."

"He already sees it that way. That's why he came to see me," he explained.

Her uncle glanced at his art catalog. Anxious to return to his work. To something less complicated than relationships.

"Let me give you a quick crash course on Andrew Carter," he announced as he sat back at his desk. "Here are a few rules. One. Never meet him in his office if you want him to listen to you. He's on high guard there, especially if you're a woman. I know that's sexist, but that's just the way it is. Two, when you talk to him, he'll try to distract you. Don't let him do it. Just ignore him and keep going. You'll feel like you're trying to swim upstream, but trust me, it works. And three, when all else fails, look at his fingers."

"His fingers?" she echoed, convinced she misheard him.

"He bites his nails. He bites his nails bloody."

"Why?"

"Have you ever heard of imposter syndrome?" Joshua replied. "He may come off as an arrogant asshole, but under that thick layer of bluster and bravado, he's an insecure man. A shy, deeply insecure man."

Insecure? Andrew Carter?

Ellen found it hard to believe.

"And now that I'm done being Dear Abby, we need to talk about something else."

He tossed the morning paper across the desk.

"Riot Erupts at Miskatonic Lecture."

Ellen smirked as she scanned the headline.

"You don't think *I* started it, do you?"

"You and I had an agreement when we moved to Arkham. Do you remember?"

Her smile disappeared. *Agreement.* A word Ellen had grown to hate.

"We agreed to move here for three years, and if you didn't get into the advanced program by then, we would move on," he reminded her. "And you would finish your education somewhere else."

"But I still have a few months."

He tapped the newspaper.

"This place is dangerous. And it's getting worse. I don't know what's happening, but . . . I'm not sure this is a good place for you."

"It doesn't matter. Miskatonic is where I want to be," she insisted.

"Honey, you know Andrew Carter. Personally. If you were going to get into the program, it would have already happened."

"Give me more time."

"Ellen."

"Just give me more time. Please."

He glanced at the wrapped-up object she'd spotted earlier.

"All right. I'll give you more time. I need a few months to close a deal anyway. But once I'm done—"

"Understood."

As Ellen left her uncle's study, she realized she was in the same position as Andrew Carter's student. Desperate. Running out of time.

There is one difference, she reminded herself. *You're not dead. At least you're not dead.*

✦✦✦✦✦

"Henry Fuseli was probably best known for his works for John Boydell's Shakespeare Gallery and his paintings of well-known scenes from Greek mythology. But his mind churned with darker themes. The most famous of these is *The Nightmare.* One of the only paintings that depict hypnagogic hallucination."

Ellen watched from the darkness as Carter lectured about the grim side of Romantic art. Only a week ago, she had been here with Phil. So much had changed since then. Phil was history. The end came in a brutal text that suggested she fuck Carter and "live out her fantasy." Then, and only then, would he consider taking her back.

Consider taking me back.

The words rankled.

Ellen wanted to shoot him an equally snarky reply. Something along the lines of, *What makes you think I'll come back after I've had* him? There was no point. She had Tom now. They hadn't slept with each other yet. They were only in the early stage of their relationship, but . . . the potential was there. Tom was kind, smart, and handsome—with none of Phil's emotional baggage.

She needed a man like Tom in her life.

Ellen was still thinking about him when she joined the students waiting to speak to Carter. To kill time, she pulled out her phone and checked her messages.

One of the students tapped her on the shoulder.

She looked up to find Carter pointing her to the other side of the stage. To the spot where he isolated the problem students.

Ellen crossed the lecture hall, trying her best to look casual. She could hear the other students buzzing . . . wondering what she'd done to deserve such "special" treatment. Their thoughts echoed in her head. *Cheating? Plagiarism? Trying to sit on his lap?*

God, I wish she'd sit on my lap. I wish she'd just smile at me.

The last thought came from a chubby, sweet-faced man at the end of the line. Ellen shot him her warmest smile. He dropped his gaze and blushed into the carpet. *Insecure. Painfully shy.* She expected Carter to be mean to him. But when the student approached the podium, Carter treated him kindly. Almost as if he knew he could destroy him. Almost as if . . .

Shy? Insecure? Andrew Carter?

"Am I going to have to get a restraining order on you? Because I'm about to slap one on your boyfriend."

Carter's words blasted her out of her reflection. The shy student was gone.

She was alone with Carter.

"Tom? Are you talking about Tom?"

"Oh, it's Tom now? Terrific. Is he going to threaten me, too?"

"What are you talking about?" she demanded.

"You *really* don't know?"

"Not a clue."

Carter whipped out his cell phone. After stabbing at the screen, he showed it to her.

> Stay away from my princess. She will be my
> queen, and if you get in the way, you . . .
> will be hurt.

> You are trying to protect her. I admire you
> for that, but you can't protect her. There is
> nothing you can do.

> I know what you want. You can't have it.

For a moment, Ellen couldn't breathe.

She pulled out her own cell phone and compared numbers.

A sick feeling washed over her.

"That's not Phil. The phone number is different." She gasped. "Oh my God, it's Reye. It's Solomon Reye."

Andrew Carter grabbed her phone before she could stop him.

She could only watch as he read Phil's final message about living out her fantasy with Carter.

"Your boyfriend's quite the charmer, isn't he?" he announced after an awkward silence.

"*Ex*-boyfriend, in case you didn't notice. And no, he doesn't have another number. He barely knows how to use his phone."

"You like men with brains, huh?"

She ignored him as she took her phone back.

"Look, I came here for a reason. I wanted to give you this."

She offered him the ring.

He gave her a long, sideways look.

His mouth twitched with a smile.

"Are you proposing to me, Miss Logan?"

"A maniac is stalking me, and you're making fucking jokes?"

She closed her eyes and took a deep breath.

Joshua's advice came back to her.

He'll try to distract you. Don't let him do it.

"Look, I made a mistake. When Martha gave me this and told me not to let 'him' see it, I thought she meant you. But she meant Solomon. Solomon Reye." She nodded at Carter's phone. *She will be my queen.* Did that mean he had already made his choice? "I showed it to Joshua, and he said it belonged to your family. That the Carter family crest was engraved in the stone."

"That doesn't mean anything. There are plenty of fakes floating around."

"Still, you should have it. Just in case," Ellen insisted.

She tried to press the ring into his hand.

He refused.

She dropped it into his bag instead.

"I'm sorry, Carter. I screwed up. I kept something from you I shouldn't have."

"It seems to be a habit with you."

"Excuse me?"

"Keeping stuff from me. As insurance. To make sure I stay interested."

"Keeping stuff from you? To make sure you stay interested?" Ellen echoed. "Jesus Christ, Carter. I'm trying to protect you!"

"No. You're using me. You're just trying to keep me interested. Don't get me wrong, you're better at it than most, but . . ."

His accusation ended with a shrug.

For a moment, all Ellen could do was stare.

A single word bubbled out of her throat.

"Unbelievable."

"Do you deny it?" he challenged.

"God, your arrogance. It's . . . it's just," she spluttered, searching for the right word. "Unbelievable."

"You already said that. Don't you have anything else?"

"Why are you being like this?"

"Like what?" he shouted, his voice echoing in the hall. "Just because I don't roll over like all the other men in your life. Just because you can't manipulate me—"

A man cleared his throat. The teacher for the next class hovered at the foot of the stairs. Some of his students had arrived as well.

They watched Ellen and Carter from the seats.

The only thing they need is popcorn, Ellen thought.

Andrew Carter snatched up his things and pushed by her.

"Fuck you, Logan," he snarled.

"Oh my," the professor said as Carter slammed the door. "What was that all about?"

"I'm dead," Ellen murmured. "And getting deader by the moment."

Chapter Ten

The sword of Damocles.

The last question on the final for Carter's class was, "What myth speaks to you and why?" In the weeks that followed her strange encounter with Solomon Reye, Ellen felt like Damocles, the mythical king. A sword hung over her head, ready to drop at any moment. She found it ironic that she identified with a story about the perils of power. She didn't feel like a king. Not even a bishop.

Ellen felt like a pawn.

She tried her best to forget. She went to class, took care of her uncle, continued her relationship with Tom. She managed to carve out a few fleeting moments of happiness. But whenever Ellen started to relax, she remembered the sword. And the texts on Andrew Carter's phone. *She will be my queen. There is nothing you can do.*

Every weekend, Ellen took the bus to visit Martha Pickman at the asylum to see if she had anything more to offer. Her friend couldn't help her. Martha was gone, trapped in a deep web of drugs and delusion. All she did was chant names.

Agares, Vassago, Gamigin, Marbas, Valefar, Barbatos, Paimon, Buer, Gusoin, Sitri, Beleth.

Ellen wrote them all down, desperate to crack the code.

Botis, Purson, Asmoday, Forus, Naberius, Ipo, Bune. Leraje, Ronove, Morax, Glasya-Labloas, Zapar. Eligor, Eligor, Eligor.

The pieces of a jigsaw puzzle were there, but there was no picture on the box. Ellen had no idea how they fit.

She had just returned from her latest visit when her uncle called out to her. "Honey, we're in here!"

Ellen groaned as she hung up her coat.

Her uncle's greeting meant only one thing. They had company. Company that required dinner and entertaining. She slumped against the closet door. Her visit to Arkham Asylum drained her. She had nothing left to give.

"Ellen?"

She glanced at the front door and considered escaping.

There was no point. Joshua knew she was here, and if she ran off . . .

Ellen checked her appearance in the mirror and padded into the study.

Like a faithful little servant, she thought, not for the first time.

The moment she walked in, Andrew Carter leaped out of his chair. He looked as startled as she was. The ring she'd given him sat on Joshua's desk. The flames from the fireplace danced on the red stone.

"What perfect timing," Joshua announced from behind his desk. "Andrew and I were just talking about you."

Carter's eyes darted around the room. He studied the floor. The books. He looked at everything but her.

Ellen was still mad at him. What Andrew Carter had said cut her deeply. But what Joshua was doing infuriated her. To see him toying with Carter, to realize he set them up, like a scientist conducting an experiment . . .

"I didn't know about this, Carter. I'm sorry."

"It's okay," he muttered.

"No. It's not." She shot Joshua a pointed look. "I don't have time for this, old man. I need to study."

She marched upstairs before Joshua had a chance to respond. Since her uncle was confined to a wheelchair, the second floor was Ellen's domain, her safe space. She loved the freedom it gave her. She could wander from bedroom to bedroom, occupying each, depending on her mood. This time, she chose the snug little room that, judging from the wallpaper, once belonged to a child.

As Ellen unpacked her things, she could hear Carter and Joshua arguing. They fought with an intensity that shocked her. She couldn't imagine yelling at her uncle like that. *That's because you're a lap dog. An obedient little lap dog.*

Ellen sat on the bed and pulled out her notebook.

She couldn't concentrate.

It had gone quiet downstairs.

Ellen waited for the front door to slam.

"Can I come in?"

Carter's presence startled her. She was used to this part of the house being her territory. The thought that anyone could just walk up here seemed . . . strange.

She patted a spot beside her on the bed.

When he hesitated, she pointed to a child-size chair in the corner of the room. "Would you rather sit there instead?"

"What's with this stuff?" Carter said as he worked his way around the furniture.

"I think it came with the house," she replied. "Either that or Joshua's developed a sudden interest in 1970s suburban crap."

"Maybe 1970s *haunted* suburban crap."

"Is there such a thing as a haunted beanbag?" she wondered aloud as he joined her on the bed.

"If there is, I'd pay serious money for it."

"You know you shouldn't say that too loudly around here."

"Joshua doesn't give discounts to family friends?"

She snorted. "Not a chance."

And just like that, the mood between them lightened. They weren't back to where they were, but they were a step closer.

Carter stared at the floor.

"You know, I came to Joshua for a reason. And it wasn't the ring," he admitted. "I needed his advice. On the best way to apologize to you."

Ellen snorted. "I asked him the same thing a few days ago."

"You did?" Carter looked up, a grin twisting his face. "Well, that worked out well for both of us, didn't it?"

His eyes dropped to the floor.

"I'm sorry, Ellen," he whispered. "I didn't mean a word of what I said to you."

She stared at him through a blur of tears. "Neither did I."

His leg started to bounce.

"Can I tell you something?" he asked.

"Sure."

"I hate the way Joshua treats you. I really hate it. You know what he asked me after you left?"

"If we were sleeping together?"

"No, that was his *second* question. He asked how long he should wait before he asked you to make dinner. I threw some money at him and told him to order a fucking pizza."

Ellen smiled.

"*What?*" Carter tensed, unsure how to react.

She leaned over and nudged him.

"You're a feminist, Andrew Carter. I would never have suspected it. Not in a million years."

He shot her another lopsided grin.

"Yeah, I know, huh?"

All Ellen wanted to do was kiss him. He looked so sweet, so vulnerable. A shy boy on the verge of discovering girls.

"Have they found your student yet?" she blurted, searching for his name. "Victor?"

"Actually, that's the other reason I'm here."

Ellen held her breath.

"Solomon Reye disappeared. He was supposed to stay in town, but as soon as they let him go, he vanished. His lawyer is pissed. Apparently, his client skipped out on him as well. The cell-phone number Solomon gave him? They tracked the phone and found it abandoned in a graveyard."

"That seems appropriate."

"What do you mean?"

"He dressed up as Baron Samedi, remember? The spirit of the dead."

"I'd forgotten that." He looked out the window. "Man, there is a lot of crazy shit going on around here."

Speaking of which . . .

"I need your help with something, Carter."

"Sure."

"I've been visiting Martha Pickman in the asylum . . ."

He winced. "God, I'd forgotten all about her. How is she?"

"She's getting worse," Ellen said, plucking at the bedspread. "All she does is chant names. Every time I visit her, it's a different set. And she says them over and over—like they're part of some sort of spell. I've done research. I know where the names come from, but I have no idea what it all means."

"Tell me what you've got," he said.

Ellen retrieved her notebook.

"The names she chants are from *The Lesser Key of Solomon.* You know, Solomon, the great judge who recommended splitting a baby in half?" Ellen shuddered. "I don't care how wise Solomon was supposed to be. The baby-splitting story always freaks me out. Anyway, he allegedly had great mystical powers. Some say he was an exorcist who controlled evil spirits. He even commanded them to build his temple. *The Lesser Key of Solomon* is supposedly his book, a catalog of seventy-two different spirits and how to summon them."

"You say supposedly. He didn't write it?"

"Not unless Solomon managed to live until the fourteenth century." She leafed through her printout. "Actually, no one can agree when it was written. Some scholars say it was written as late as the seventeenth century. Others say it was taken from *Pseudomonarchia Daemonum,* which was compiled in the sixteenth century. All that is beside the point. When Martha babbles, she chants the names of the demons in the book."

"Does any one name stand out?"

Ellen consulted her notebook. "Eligor. She circles around that name a lot. She goes through a few and then returns to that name. Like it's a chorus. 'Eligor, Eli—"

Carter clamped his hand over her mouth.

Ellen thought he was kidding.

Don't say things three times. It was such a joke, a horror cliché.

Carter held her mouth closed, his face as grim as death.

"Jesus," she gasped once he let her go. "I can't even say . . . That actually works?"

"A lot of things work that shouldn't." He grabbed the printout of *The Lesser Key of Solomon* and scanned through it. "You don't have any illustrations."

"Illustrations?"

He nodded at the computer on the desk. "Mind if I use this?"

"Go ahead."

"Is there anything I shouldn't see?"

"You mean porn?"

"Yes, I mean porn."

"No. I'm more of a traditionalist when it comes to that."

"What? You prefer brass etchings?"

Ellen laughed.

"What's going on up there?" her uncle bellowed from downstairs.

"Leave us alone, old man. We're having make-up sex," Carter shouted as he sat down in front of the computer.

All Ellen could do was stare. She couldn't believe what he'd just said.

Andrew Carter smiled at her wolfishly.

"That's the way you need to talk to him."

"Are you kidding? I couldn't possibly," she spluttered.

"You're sarcastic with me all the time."

"But I don't have to live with you."

"And you don't have to live with him."

Before she could say anything, an image popped up on the computer screen. A supernatural knight rode a horse. The horse had enormous, bat-like wings.

"Oh my God," she whispered.

She could almost hear the leathery rasp of the creature's wings, the crack as its talons splintered the wood beside her.

Carter vacated the desk chair and guided her into it.

He stood behind Ellen, his hands anchored on the armrests. Almost as if he were protecting her from the creature.

"That's a nightgaunt," she whispered.

Carter pointed at the knight. "And that's Eligor." He sounded like he was making a personal introduction. "Eligor is the great duke of hell. He controls sixty legions of demons."

"I can see why you didn't want me to say his name." She studied the figure astride the nightgaunt. He wore a plague mask and waved a nasty-looking lance over his head.

"Eligor is one of the less powerful demons. He sometimes communicates with humans. Gives us secret knowledge, warns us of bad things to come."

"Martha said that. When we were at the police station." Ellen turned in the chair and looked at him. "Right before she gave me the ring, Martha looked at Solomon Reye and said one thing: *he is who he says he is.*"

Andrew Carter swayed slightly.

"Uh-huh."

"Is that even possible?"

"Ellen!" Joshua bellowed from downstairs.

They both jumped.

"Ellen, get down here!"

Carter's face darkened.

"I've about had it with that old man," he muttered as he stormed out of the room.

Ellen waited for the yelling to start again. The two men kept their voices low, which she found much more disturbing. When Carter returned a few minutes later, she could tell she had lost him.

"I have to go," he announced. He sounded formal. Distant. Like a waiter asking whether she was ready for the check.

"Two more questions."

"Maybe."

"What did Joshua just say to you?"

"It's none of your business."

Ellen shook her head.

"Oh, it is. I'm certain it is."

"What's your other question?"

"There's no point. You're not going to tell me anything." She felt sadness spread through her like a bruise. She liked Andrew Carter. She enjoyed his company. And her uncle seemed to be intent on sabotaging their connection. "There's something else I need to tell you. About the ring."

He tried to act aloof, but she could tell she had his interest.

"Every time I visit Martha, I ask her about it. Usually, she stonewalls me or chants those horrible names. But today, she told me something."

"What?" he demanded when she hesitated.

"She said the ring fell from the sky. That it was a gift from someone on the other side."

"The other side?"

"The Dreamlands. Martha said it was a gift from your grandfather, Randolph Carter."

Chapter Eleven

The Arkham Institute for Behavioral Rehabilitation. No one called it that. The name only appeared on health insurance forms. It was Arkham Asylum. It would always be Arkham Asylum. Ellen thought it was a shame that the hospital tried to hide behind a new name. The institute formerly known as Arkham Asylum achieved what most people thought was impossible. It emerged from its dark past, from its history of patient abuse, mysterious deaths, and medical experimentation. It was now considered the best psychiatric hospital in the state.

Ellen paused in front of the main building. Tucked into the side of a hill that overlooked a narrow river valley, Arkham Asylum looked like a resort, a country retreat where the elite entertained themselves. It only revealed its true face when Ellen got closer. Metal bars on the second- and third-floor windows. A high-security fence that separated the building from the forest. Floodlights tucked into the landscape.

Despite all the security, the place was inviting—soothing, even.

Better-looking than the million-dollar mansions down the hill, she thought with a stab of glee.

"Hello, Miriam," Ellen greeted the woman at the desk, handing her a thermos of coffee.

Good coffee went a long way in places like this.

"Hello, Ellen," the nurse replied without looking up. "Your friend's quite popular today."

Ellen glanced at the sign-in sheet, trying to sneak a peek at the name before hers. All she saw was an illegible scrawl.

"Is it all right if I go in?" she asked after she signed the book.

"The more people who see her, the better," Miriam said, voicing the hope many of the staff had. That confronting the patient with enough friends and family would jolt them out of their delusions.

Of course, if your family is the Pickmans, it might have the opposite effect, Ellen thought as she headed to the visiting room.

Snow fell outside like a lace curtain. The weather usually didn't bother her, but as Ellen walked down the corridor, her skin prickled. *So many places to hide out there,* she thought. She glanced out the window, half expecting to see Solomon Reye. *It's nothing—nerves, just nerves,* she told herself. Even though she acted casual in front of the nurse, Ellen worried about her friend. A mysterious visitor was not a good thing. She shivered as she remembered what Martha had said at the police station. *He's going to get us. He'll take us all.*

When she walked into the visiting room and saw Andrew Carter with Martha, she sighed in relief.

They were huddled on the couch, talking intently. He had a ring in his hand. *The* ring.

A wave of jealousy engulfed her, hot and irrational.

He's mine. You can't have him . . . He's mine!

Martha turned pale when she saw Ellen.

She jumped to her feet, her eyes darting around the room.

"Oh no. Oh no, no, no," she gasped. "We shouldn't be together. No. No, no, no. Not in the same place."

The lights flickered. Arkham Asylum plunged into darkness. The emergency generator spluttered to life a few seconds later, bathing the visiting room in a bloody twilight.

Ellen expected the inmates to erupt, to fill the air with noise.

They were silent.

Ellen moved to one of the windows.

A pair of nightgaunts stood outside the asylum. Their tails flicked, catlike, in the snow.

Solomon Reye stood between them.

"Oh my God," Ellen whimpered.

Solomon Reye marched toward the asylum with the same strutting confidence she'd seen on the stage at Miskatonic. As he got closer, he pushed back the hood of his long robe. She had never seen him without his makeup. She expected Solomon Reye to be dark and threatening, but he was pale, with blondish-brown hair. He had high cheekbones and full lips, a face that practically screamed European royalty. Solomon reminded her of her first boyfriend, Mikhail.

Your dead boyfriend.

The moment Ellen remembered Mikhail was killed in a car accident, Solomon transformed into Phil. Then Tom. *He's trying on faces,* she thought. *He wants to distract me by taking on a familiar form. Or making himself more appealing. Changing into someone I might . . .*

Ellen's stomach churned.

Carter and Martha joined her at the window. They watched Solomon and his creatures approach the asylum, melting through the fence like ghosts.

"*Oi chusoi Dios aei enpiptousi, mon,*" Martha murmured.

Ellen looked at her friend. She wondered what form Solomon took for her. Human? Ghoul?

"The dice of God are always loaded," Ellen whispered. She turned to Carter. He stared at the creatures with wide, blank eyes. She waved her hands in front of his face, then grabbed his shoulder and shook him. "Carter? Carter!"

The nightgaunts crashed through the window, blasting them with pebbles of tempered glass. Ellen pushed Carter away and turned, letting her back absorb the impact. Martha took the full force of the blow. Her friend crashed to the floor with a sickening thud.

The world erupted around Ellen. The asylum alarm wailed. Inmates howled in terror and delight. But the worst thing? The angry buzz that filled her head. The sound was so intense, she crumpled on the floor beside Martha. Something hot streamed from her nose. Ellen watched as crimson drops pattered on the floor. *Blood,* she thought dimly.

She tried to get to her feet but couldn't move. The pressure was too intense.

She felt like she was on the bottom of the ocean floor.

"My, my, aren't you fierce?" Solomon Reye taunted. "I can almost forgive my assistant for losing you."

"Assistant?" She gasped.

"The man you bit, remember?"

Calvin Leonard.

The name shot through her like fire.

"He's very mad at you," Solomon scolded.

Ellen kept her eyes fixed on the floor. The only thing she could see was the bottom of his robe as he paced in front of her.

"Oh, how I'd love to take you, too, but I can only take one candidate at a time. There's a way these things must be done."

"What things?"

"Why, choosing my consort, of course. Didn't you get my messages? I sent them to that, um, 'friend' of yours—just another thing Andrew Carter pretends to be."

Rage rose inside Ellen like bile.

"Fuck you, you deranged bastard. I don't care what you *think* you are. Fuck . . . you."

"Oh my, I'm almost certain you're the one," Solomon drawled, his words thick with longing. He turned to one of his companions. "Take the ghoul bitch . . . just to be sure. Don't harm this one. Give her a little taste."

The nightgaunt plunged its stinger into Ellen.

Martha Pickman's limp body twitched.

"No! Martha! *Martha!*" Ellen screamed.

She tried to crawl away on her stomach to escape the nightmare.

Questions bloomed in her head.

What is happening? Why isn't anyone helping? Did everyone run away when the nightgaunt crashed through the window?

When Ellen finally managed to raise her head, she saw she was not alone. All the orderlies, visitors, and patients were still there. Carter lay on the floor a few feet away, surrounded by broken glass. He blinked and breathed, but he didn't move. No one did. No one *could*. They were catatonic, frozen by some kind of spell.

He's stopped time, she thought in disbelief. *This crazy bastard can stop time.*

"Now. Now do you see? Do you see what you're up against?" Solomon crowed. She heard a soft raspy sound. She looked up and saw Martha Pickman's body being dragged away.

Ellen moaned.

"Why don't you just give up? It would make things *so* much easier."

"Andrew!" she screamed, her eyes blurring with tears. He was close. So close. She reached out for him, desperate to make contact. Only one thought filled her head. *Pull me back. Andrew, please pull me back from the edge again.*

"He can't help you, you know. He's never even been to the Dreamlands," Solomon taunted.

Ellen stretched her arm as far as she could.

The moment their fingers brushed, Carter jerked. He grabbed her wrist and yanked her toward him.

The room unfroze, exploding in a burst of noise and motion. Solomon and the nightgaunt were gone. And she was in excruciating pain. The flesh on her leg crawled. It crawled and itched and burned with a white-hot fury.

It hit me, she thought as she rolled on the floor. *It hit me, and I don't even remember.*

"What the hell?" Carter scrambled off the floor. She could feel his anger rising. But when he saw her, bloodstained and writhing on the floor, he stopped. "Ellen . . ."

"Solomon. Solomon took Martha," she gasped. "Gaunt hit me. In the leg. Gaunt hit me in the leg."

Her teeth started to chatter. She could feel the night-gaunt poison spreading, seeping deep inside her. She knew she should stay still, but she kicked and squirmed. Ellen couldn't stop moving.

Her body no longer belonged to her.

Andrew Carter dropped to his knees.

She saw something she had never seen in his eyes before. Panic. Blind, mindless panic.

"Ellen. Oh, Ellen. My dear, sweet girl."

Carter lifted her off the glass-strewn floor. Ellen felt light in his arms. Insubstantial.

She wrapped her arms around his neck and held on.

"Andrew, I'm scared," she whispered.

"You'll be all right. Do you hear me? Just stay with me. Stay with me."

She smiled and buried her face in his chest.

"You know, you're a terrible liar."

As she slipped away, Ellen took comfort in her last thought. *At least I'm not dying alone.*

Chapter Twelve

The pain was gone. Ellen's head throbbed with every heartbeat, but the nightgaunt poison no longer coursed through her. Still, something didn't quite feel right. As she emerged from her haze, she realized she was moving, even though her feet dangled in the air. All around her were the sounds of daytime: birds chirping, animals chattering, the distant growl of a chainsaw.

When she opened her eyes, all she saw was darkness.

Ellen tried to sit up.

Her body bent the wrong way.

A man chuckled and tightened his grip on her legs.

"Now, now, my dear," a man scolded her. "It's a little too late for that."

Solomon Reye.

Her heart hitched. It froze for so long, Ellen thought it would never start again.

Upside down. That's the reason my head is pounding. I'm being carried upside down. Solomon Reye didn't just catch Martha.

He caught me.

Ellen squirmed, trying to move her hands and legs, but they were tied up. Solomon had trussed her like an animal.

"What are you doing?" she rasped. Her voice sounded different. Huskier.

"I knew you weren't the one. You come from a rather . . . dubious family. To be honest, my dear, it's a bit of a relief. I absolutely *hate* ghouls."

Ghouls . . . dubious family . . .

"You think I'm Martha Pickman."

"Think? I *think* you're Martha Pickman?"

Solomon deposited her on the ground and plucked off the hood that covered her face. Ellen squinted against the sudden daylight. Two figures loomed over her. Solomon and Calvin Leonard. *The fake bureaucrat,* she thought with a shiver. She looked at his arm. He had a bandage where she bit him.

"I'm not Martha Pickman," Ellen insisted.

"People will say anything to save themselves, won't they, boss?" The fake Leonard joked.

Ellen expected Solomon to agree, to share a laugh at her expense.

He stared coldly at his companion.

"You would break, too, if you were in her place," he replied. "In fact, I think you would break sooner. I think you would shit yourself the moment you laid eyes on me."

Calvin Leonard growled. For a moment, it looked like they were about to fight.

The man turned his anger on Ellen. He pulled her roughly to her feet and slapped her. He paused. Then he slapped her again.

I'm dreaming, she thought as she brought her hand to her face.

An idea bloomed in Ellen's head.

She spat in Calvin Leonard's face.

"Third time's the charm," she chirped.

Solomon cackled in delight. His outburst made Leonard even more furious. Ellen watched him wind up for the punch. She closed her eyes, hearing the man grunt as he swung. Then, just as his knuckles slammed into her cheek, as a ripple of pain spread through her . . .

Her eyes flew open. Ellen lay on her back on a layer of cold, stiff grass. Branches poked her body. She wasn't sure how long she had been knocked out. Her hands scurried to her face. She felt for blood, broken bones, missing teeth. Nothing. No signs of trauma.

"You can't fix everything with a hammer, you know," Solomon Reye scolded.

Ellen sat up. She was on the edge of a forest, behind the thick remains of a bush. Solomon and Leonard were in an open field about fifty feet away, standing in front of a house Ellen couldn't see in the glare of the sun. As her eyes drifted across the structure, her stomach dropped. It was the same place she saw when Solomon Reye strutted on stage. A two-story structure, its windows jagged with broken glass. An old house, the wood rotting and gray.

A breeze picked up.

A thick, cloying stench filled her nostrils. Ellen gagged. The sweetness masked something dark and disturbing. It reminded her of a woman she cared for when she volunteered at a hospital. The poor woman tried to mask her disease by bathing herself in perfume. No amount of Chanel No. 5 could hide the spread of her cancer.

Diseased, Ellen decided. *That house is diseased.*

"Be careful with this one. She may be the last of her kind," Solomon ordered.

His companion grunted and lifted the body off the ground. Ellen studied the woman as he carried her to the cellar door.

Dark hair.

White porcelain skin.

Ellen's flesh crawled.

"Martha. Martha Pickman," she gasped.

I was her. I was Martha Pickman. I was on the ground in front of that rotting house only a split second ago.

Her rational mind rushed to her defense.

No. Impossible. That's impossible. What you're thinking doesn't make sense.

She shook her head.

Suppose it is true. Who are you now? the voice demanded.

She grabbed a fistful of hair and held it in front of her. Blonde. She looked at her hands and found the finger she'd cut when chopping vegetables.

"Ellen Logan," she reassured herself. "I'm Ellen Logan."

Solomon Reye looked up. He sniffed the air.

Ellen scrambled to her feet. The branches thrashed around her. She knew what she was doing was stupid, that the best thing to do was hide behind the bush. She couldn't stay where she was. She couldn't watch as her friend was carried away.

Then do something, a voice urged her. *She's your friend. Stop them!*

Ellen tried to move forward, but the fear was too strong.

I can't get trapped in her body again. I can't, I can't, her mind babbled.

"I'm sorry, Martha," she whimpered as she backed away.

Solomon Reye's eyes locked onto her. He practically purred with pleasure.

"There you are. Clever girl. You're *learning.*"

Ellen turned and plunged deeper into the woods. She didn't care where she went. The only direction that mattered was away. Ellen didn't fancy her chances. Solomon was an experienced outdoorsman, and she was his bewildered prey, a kidnap victim who only just had a hood ripped off her head. She had no idea where she was. She had no compass, no map. She didn't even have a winter coat. Ellen refused to give up. The thought of Solomon Reye catching her, of being tied up like an animal again . . .

Ellen managed a fresh burst of speed.

Cold air scorched her lungs.

The old house popped up in front of her. She had no time to stop. Ellen crashed through the ground floor and down a set of stairs. *The cellar,* she thought as she tumbled in the darkness. *All this running, and I still wound up in the cellar.* It didn't seem fair. Even the fall took forever. As if Solomon Reye was stretching out her torment. When Ellen finally landed, she hit the ground in a twisted heap. She played dead. She hoped it would give her a few moments of peace. And let her figure out how badly injured she was.

A pair of boots walked up to her.

"Quite the entrance," a man announced.

"Oh, for Christ's sake. Can't you leave me alone for just one *fucking* minute?" She groaned as she rolled onto her back.

The man who stared down at her wasn't Solomon Reye. And he wasn't Andrew Carter. He looked like Andrew Carter. The resemblance was uncanny. But there were differences. This man had a beard—a trim, dark beard. And his eyes held no warmth, no compassion. She remembered a picture she had seen in the *Call of Cthulhu* role-playing guide she had flipped through in the Miskatonic library.

Ellen stumbled to her feet, ignoring her body's protests.

"You . . . You're Randolph Carter."

The man said nothing.

"You're Randolph Carter, aren't you? Andrew's grandfather," she spluttered.

He scowled, which made his face look even more severe.

"Who are you? And why are you dressed like a man?"

Ellen glanced at her torn-up jeans and flannel shirt.

"My name is Ellen Logan. I'm a student of your grandson, Andrew. He's a professor at Miskatonic."

"You? A student?"

"Yes."

"At Miskatonic?"

Ellen held her tongue. *If he's who I think he is, the last time he was in the waking world was 1928.* Women voted, but they weren't liberated. Blacks were still treated as second-class citizens. And fascism . . . well, fascism was respectable, even fashionable among the upper classes.

He's from a different world, she reminded herself.

"What do you want?" he demanded.

"I'm not sure where I am. I could use a little help."

He waved his hands. The fog cleared from her head. *Or was it the landscape that responded?* Ellen stood at the top of a cliff, peering into a dark ravine. A set of stairs jutted out of the rock like crooked, rotten teeth. The path led down to what she assumed was a river.

"Where am I?" she asked, astonished.

"You don't know?"

"I think I'm in the Dreamlands."

Randolph Carter nodded.

Ellen shivered. The Dreamlands. The parallel world featured in the "fiction" of H.P. Lovecraft. She had been here once before, but she had been heavily drugged.

She didn't think being sober would make a difference.

"What do I do?" she asked.

A snarky smile spread across her companion's face.

"Isn't it obvious? You go down the stairs," he replied. "I'd recommend walking this time."

Ellen stared into the deep valley. She didn't want to show fear. Not in front of this man. She thought she knew who he was, but she wasn't sure. If he turned into Solomon Reye, she wouldn't be the least bit surprised.

"Yeah, well, thanks for all the help, Virgil," she snapped as she turned to leave.

The man grabbed her wrist. The physical contact startled Ellen. There were two ways to enter the Dreamlands—in spirit form or in the flesh. Being here physically was much more dangerous.

"What did you just call me?" he demanded.

"Virgil. You know. Dante? Virgil? *The Inferno*?"

He looked at her like she'd sprouted two heads.

Ellen jerked free from his grip and walked to the edge of the landing. The next set of stairs didn't look bad. She wouldn't have to ride down them on her butt. Or crawl. Ellen was thankful for that. She could still feel the man watching her. His eyes bored into her back.

She studied the winding stairs.

"The journey of a thousand steps," she whispered as she worked up the courage to move.

Randolph Carter pressed his hand into the small of her back.

"I'll take you as far as the Gateway," he announced.

Ellen kept her eyes on the ground. She didn't want to show too much curiosity. Still, she couldn't help sneaking glances at the man beside her.

This is Randolph Carter, she kept telling herself. *The Randolph Carter.*

"Am I really that famous?" he demanded.

Ellen pursed her lips.

Psychic, too. Should have known.

"You *are* him, aren't you?"

The man winced. "Yes."

"You're a legend at Miskatonic. Your picture hangs in the president's office. They've named buildings after you. Streets. There's even a statue of you in the main courtyard."

Randolph Carter shook his head in disgust.

They fell silent as he led her down the endless flight of stairs. Ellen counted the steps. Just as she was about to reach sixty, he spoke again.

"Why are you here?" he asked.

"I don't know."

"You don't know?"

"I didn't exactly come here of my own free will."

He paused on the stairs.

"I was stung by a nightgaunt, and when I woke up, I was here," she offered.

"A nightgaunt? In the waking world?"

"They attacked the Arkham Asylum and kidnapped one of my friends. Martha Pickman."

A strange look passed over Randolph's face. "That crazy bastard. He's done it again. He's pushed through," he muttered softly to himself.

"Pushed through?"

"There you are," a voice bellowed.

The world around her quivered. Randolph's face blurred, then snapped back into sharp focus.

He shot her a sad smile.

"This is as far as you go, I'm afraid."

"Wait a minute! Where are you going? You're just going to leave me here?"

"I'm not the one who's leaving," he insisted.

Ellen felt a strange stretching sensation. It reminded her of the Roadrunner cartoons when Wile E. Coyote ran off a cliff and suddenly realized he was treading thin air.

"The thing you call Solomon left you something," Randolph announced as he headed back up the stairs. "A clue. He left it in your secret hiding place."

The thing you call Solomon.

Ellen shivered. She'd never mentioned Solomon Reye.

"No, wait," she called out. "Wait!"

"You just relax, ma'am. We'll get you back to the hospital safe and sound."

Ellen woke up facedown, her arms pinned behind her back. A policeman stood over her. She felt cold steel bite into her wrists, heard the unmistakable snick of handcuffs. *A patient,* she thought as he hauled her to her feet. *He thinks I'm an escaped mental patient.* She opened her mouth to protest but couldn't speak. She felt woozy. Like someone coming out of surgery.

Ellen watched the officer rummage through her pockets. He frowned when he came across her wallet. He glanced at the contents, then at her, then at the contents, then at her, until Ellen wanted to scream. *I'm not a patient! Patients don't have wallets. Patients don't wear street clothes!*

He called dispatch and fed them her information. After a few minutes, a disembodied voice returned its judgment. *No record. Not in the system.* The man made no move to free her. Her eyes drifted across his uniform. She tried to focus, to get a name or a badge number, but the letters kept shifting.

"What is going on?" she murmured.

The man moved closer. She could smell his breath. It carried the odor of open graves, of places of desolation and despair.

The police officer changed in front of her eyes.

The face disappeared.

A pair of wings popped out of its shirt.

"You come here without permission," the nightgaunt snarled. "You come here to upset the balance."

"I don't know what you're talking about," she stammered, powerless to look away.

She shut her eyes and chanted a mantra from her childhood.

"If I can't see it, it's not there. If I can't see it—"

A cloud descended on her, turning the world a flat featureless gray. Ellen didn't mind. Anything was better than the nightgaunt. Shadows drifted across her eyelids. Occasionally, she felt a warm hand press against her forehead. People shouted in the distance. She heard the sounds of struggle, but the heated exchange was blurry and indistinct.

She continued to drift through the cloud. Ellen enjoyed the weightlessness, the liberation of mind from body. She felt calm. Centered.

I'm safe, she thought as she swayed gently with the current. *The storm can't reach me here.*

The placid feeling didn't last for long.

She suddenly found herself at the bottom of the ocean. Water pressed down on her with all its might, crushing her flat. Forcing her eyes open. A sunken city loomed before her, a tangle of shapes and angles. Underwater grass clung to the buildings in a sordid embrace.

Ellen's vision blurred. She almost passed out.

R'lyeh.

Her mind rattled off the ancient city's titles. The kingdom beneath the sea. The home of Cthulhu, the alien invader.

The destroyer of worlds.

Her body started to rise. Ellen tried to grab hold of something. She knew if she surfaced too fast, she would die. But if she stayed here . . . Her head felt like it was in a vise, her skull split in two. She was incapable of thought. Only fear guided her. Ellen kicked her legs, waved her arms. She thrashed in the space between two agonizing deaths. She tried to drift with the current, to stay in the safe zone.

The ocean wouldn't let her.

Something snaked around her legs. Seaweed? Or was it . . .

Tentacles.

A scream erupted from her lungs, boiling in the warm, salty water.

She scrunched her body into a tight ball and straightened, moving toward the dim sunlight.

When she reached the surface, Ellen hit something hard.

A rock, she thought.

She scrambled onto it, trying to get as much of her body out of the water as she could.

The rock shifted beneath her.

"Get off me!" it snapped.

"Ellen, wake up. Wake up!" another voice commanded.

She opened her eyes, gasping.

Her arms were wrapped around Andrew Carter. Not just her arms. She had climbed halfway up him. Her fingers were tight in his hair, his face lodged between her breasts.

Ellen let go, falling back on the . . .

Bed?

Her eyes swept the room.

Ellen waited for it to dissolve, to turn into another part of her nightmare.

Nothing changed.

She was in a bed, in a strange room.

In pajamas she didn't recognize.

Andrew Carter sat beside her.

He glared at her as he straightened his clothes.

"Where am I?" she croaked.

A woman appeared at the foot of the bed.

Connie Blake stood next to her.

"You're at the Eibon Institute," Miss Cummings replied.

Eibon Institute . . . Arkham Institute . . . Arkham Asylum . . .

Reality came rushing back so quickly, Ellen felt like she was drowning all over again.

"Carter . . . it was Solomon. Solomon Reye. He took Martha. He broke into the asylum and kidnapped her."

"They know, Ellen," Carter assured her. "The police have a vehicle description and a license plate number. They're looking for Martha now."

"Solomon Reye? Did you just say Solomon Reye?" Ms. Cummings muttered.

The woman pursed her mouth so tightly, her lips disappeared.

"You've heard of him?" Ellen asked.

"Not by that name, but we've seen him," Miss Cummings offered. "People here have been having nightmares for weeks. Some of them have . . ."

Her voice trailed off.

A sudden jolt jarred Ellen.

Miss Cummings saw it, she thought. *She saw everything that happened to me.*

"You need to leave," the woman insisted.

Carter looked at her, startled. His eyes were bleary and rimmed in red. It had obviously been a long night.

"Leave? What are you—" he spluttered as he rose to his feet. "She's not ready yet! She's only just woken up, and you're going to toss her out on the street?"

"We've done all we can do for her. I must protect my people."

"Ms. Cummings?" Ellen called out before Carter had a chance to respond.

"Yes?"

"He's for real, isn't he?"

Her mouth tightened even more. "What do *you* think?"

Ellen pulled off the covers. "I have to leave."

Her legs were tangled in the bedsheets.

Tentacles, she thought as she unraveled herself.

"Are you serious, Fran?" Carter snarled at Miss Cummings. "I know six-year-olds who are braver than you!"

"Carter, don't." Ellen sighed. She didn't want him to say or do anything he would regret. Besides, she was tired. She wanted to go home. To burrow into safety of her own bed. "Where are my clothes?"

"We had to get rid of them. They were . . . well, let's just say they were ruined." Ms. Cummings winced. "Andrew brought you a fresh change of clothes. I'll help you get dressed. Would you gentlemen excuse us?"

Carter wanted to stay. She could see it in his eyes. He wanted her to resist. When Ellen didn't join the battle, he hissed and stormed out of the room. Connie Blake pursued him. The outburst confused her. Why was Carter so angry? *She* should be the one who was mad. Yet she bore the institute no ill will. They took her in when she needed help. They tended to her wounds. Ellen looked down at her leg as Miss Cummings helped her out of the bed. She expected to see a horrible gash. There was nothing.

"Nightgaunts don't leave marks. The wounds are up here." Ms. Cummings tapped her head.

"God, it felt so real," she whispered.

"It was real. It just wasn't physical. That's why Andrew brought you here. You needed a different type of treatment."

The older woman fixed Ellen with a strange look. "He's very possessive of you. Almost territorial."

"I don't know why."

"You two have a connection. A powerful connection. I could feel it from across the room. He feels it, too," Ms. Cummings said as she helped Ellen into her new clothes.

Ellen wondered if he could see her naked by peering into Ms. Cummings's mind. Ms. Cummings smiled. "He can, but I won't let him. If he wants to see you naked, he'll have to do that on his own. The old-fashioned way."

"It's never going to happen."

"Aren't you interested?"

"No."

"Not the slightest bit curious?"

Ellen slowly got to her feet, favoring her injured leg.

"Do you have any crutches?"

"You don't need crutches. It's all in your head," Ms. Cummings reminded her.

At first, Ellen was cautious. The pain in her leg felt real. Like a muscle about to cramp.

The moment her foot touched the ground, the discomfort vanished.

She thought about Martha. Wondering. Hoping. "Does this mean . . . ?"

The director of the Eibon Institute shook her head. "If what I saw in your head was accurate, the nightgaunt didn't hold back with her. You—"

"Only got a taste." Ellen shivered as she remembered Solomon's words. "Do you think Martha—"

"I don't know, Ellen. I can only see so much." Ms. Cummings threaded her arm through Ellen's and donned a brave face. "Let's see what the boys are up to, shall we?"

They emerged to find Carter and Connie at the end of a long hall, locked in a deep argument. Ellen was too far away to make out words, but she could see the fury in their gestures. Miss Cummings didn't seem concerned. She watched the exchange the way a sports fan watched a fight.

"You've created quite a stir."

"That? That's not about me. Not really." Ellen thought about the other woman. The woman Carter and Connie shared.

Ms. Cummings glanced at her, surprised.

"Oh, so you know?"

Ellen jerked to attention.

"Who was she? Was she someone at the institute?"

"The story's not mine to tell, my dear."

The older woman led Ellen right between the two men.

Connie and Carter stopped fighting and backed away.

This woman has balls, Ellen thought. *I want to be like her when I grow up.*

"I'm sorry we couldn't be more hospitable," Ms. Cummings continued. "Under normal circumstances, I would insist you stay until you were fully recovered."

"I understand." Ellen felt sad and lost. She thought about the asylum, how she was alone even in a room full of people. How she crawled helplessly on the floor while Solomon Reye taunted her. "No one can help me now."

"That's bullshit, Ellen. That's total bullshit," Carter snapped.

"Oh. Are you done with your posturing, Andrew?" Miss Cummings said as she inspected a rack of coats near the front door.

Carter muttered something under his breath.

"I'm afraid your coat got lost somewhere in the mayhem," the woman informed Ellen. She pulled out a navy blue over-coat and slid it off its hanger. "But this might work."

Ms. Cummings helped Ellen into the coat. She smoothed it down and did up the buttons.

Ellen's eyes filled with tears.

She couldn't remember the last time anyone took care of her.

Ms. Cummings pulled Ellen's hair out of her coat and looked deeply into her eyes.

"You know, you really are a lovely girl."

She kissed Ellen. On the mouth. Right in front of Carter and Connie. There was no tongue, but it wasn't a motherly kiss. The embrace was steamy. Ellen closed her eyes, letting the warmth seep into her body. *For a moment,* she promised herself. *I'll give in for a moment.* Then one moment became another. And another. Finally, Carter pulled her away. Ms. Cummings smiled. Her voice echoed in Ellen's head. *Territorial. He's very territorial.*

"You never change, do you, Fran?" Carter snarled as he steered Ellen toward the door.

"My dear boy, why should I?" Ms. Cummings called out, taking one last parting shot before they returned to the outside world.

"There's no way. There's no way in hell that woman is celibate," Ellen said once they were a safe distance away.

She pressed her hand to her mouth.

Her lips were full. Throbbing.

"People at the institute aren't celibate. Where did you get that idea?"

"That's what Connie said."

His mouth twisted into a bitter smile.

"Of course he did."

"What's that supposed to mean?" she demanded.

Carter gave her a long, murky look. Ellen suddenly wanted him to kiss her. To pull her back to the world she understood.

"So how did it feel exploring your other side?" he asked.

"There is no other side. I'm straight."

"Not from where I stood." He moved closer. The next words were a warm grumble in her ear. "You almost slipped her some tongue, didn't you?"

Ellen backed away. "Please, don't. Don't make fun of me. Not now."

Carter moved toward her.

"Hey. What's wrong? What's wrong, swee—"

Sweetheart. The word almost spilled from his lips.

Carter grabbed her elbow and steered her to a nearby bench, all that remained of an old bus route. "I'm not kissing you," he announced as they sat down.

"I don't want you to kiss me. Not really. I just thought—"

"What?"

"Never mind."

"What?"

"I thought I'd wake up if you kissed me."

"You'll have to wake up on your own. I'm not some fairy-tale prince," he snapped.

"Really, Carter? Never would have guessed."

"Andrew."

"Excuse me?"

"I think we've moved beyond Carter. Call me Andrew," he insisted as he leaned back and rubbed his eyes. "I don't want to have a panic attack every time you call me by my first name."

"Do I call you Andrew when I'm in trouble?"

"Every time."

"But I should still call you Dr. Carter when we're in public?"

"No. You call me Andrew all the time."

"Do you think that's wise? There are rumors about us, you know. Being lovers. Joshua's heard them, so I assume they're public knowledge."

"There are *always* rumors about me. You're just one of many." Carter tried to act casual, but his leg started to bounce. "And I really don't care, do you?"

"No."

He shrugged. "Then nothing's changed between us."

"I wouldn't say that. You saved my life." She looked over at him as the truth sunk in. "God, Andrew. If you hadn't been there—"

"It's best not to dwell on the what-ifs, Miss Logan."

"Don't call me Miss Logan. I'm Ellen, remember?"

The silence stretched between them.

"I traveled to the Dreamlands," she announced.

"Did you really?" He stifled a yawn.

"I met Randolph Carter."

Carter tilted his head back and laughed. The sound was hard. Sharp enough to cut glass.

Ellen wondered how many students claimed to meet his grandfather on one of their "mystical" voyages.

She hugged the borrowed coat closer to her body.

"Does Joshua know about what happened? At the asylum?" Ellen asked, desperate to change the subject.

"No," Carter replied. "And I'd prefer to keep it that way. He already thinks I'm a bad influence on you."

"You're not, you know. I'd be doing this even if you weren't with me."

"I told him that, but he refuses to listen."

"He made you promise to look after me, didn't he?"

"He wants me to take care of you, *and* he says I'm a bad influence. Kind of ironic, isn't it?"

"More like schizophrenic." Ellen exhaled. Her breath came out in a white puff. "Joshua has no right to ask you to protect me. You won't be able to stop what's coming."

"Don't talk like that."

"It's the truth."

"People who talk like that die."

"We all die."

"Oh, please. Spare me." Carter tried to be sarcastic.

It didn't last long.

The moment their eyes met, he looked away.

"It was bad, wasn't it?" she murmured.

"It was awful. Watching you struggle, trying to wake up—" He stared at the facade of the institute. "Trust me. I wouldn't have brought you here if there was any other way."

"You were a member of the Eibon Institute, weren't you?"

"I'm not talking about it."

"And the woman that you and Connie—"

"I said I'm *not* talking about it, Ellen." He shot her a warning look. One that made it clear they were crossing the boundaries of . . .

Ellen didn't know how to finish the thought. What? What exactly *were* they to each other?

"I should go." She moved off the bench. She was eager to get away from him, to move forward.

A clue, Ellen reminded herself. *That's what Randolph Carter said. Solomon Reye left me a clue about Martha's whereabouts in my room.*

"You're not going anywhere," Carter said.

"Why not?"

He reached into his pocket and dangled a key. A key to the room she kept when she wanted to get away from Joshua. "Because I have your stuff. I went back to the asylum and got it."

Seeing Andrew Carter with the key to her secret room made her feel odd. Turned on in a strange sort of way.

"You're not letting me out of your sight, are you?"

He put the key back in his coat.

"It's like you said. I made a promise to Joshua. And I intend to keep my word. So what's our next step, Nancy Drew?"

"Okay, this is where it gets kind of strange."

Chapter Thirteen

"Ellen. Ellen, is that you?"

Steven Boyd popped out of his room the second she walked through the front door.

Boyd considered himself the unofficial manager of the old Victorian home where Ellen rented a room. Every time the front door opened, he stepped out to investigate. Investigate and, if need be, interrogate. He was well suited for his role as neighborhood watch. As far as she knew, Boyd never left the building. And he didn't seem to sleep. Most of the residents avoided him. Ellen didn't. She liked him. Beneath his jittery exterior was a man who cared about people.

"Hey, Steve," Ellen said.

When he stepped out of the shadows, she saw he was injured. He had a black eye and scratches on his face.

Ellen moved closer to examine his wounds.

"Oh my God, what happened?"

Boyd's eyes filled with tears. "I tried. I tried not to let him in. But he was strong. So powerful. He pushed his way past me and went up to your room."

The hair rose on the back of her neck.

"When did this happen?" Ellen asked, trying to say calm.

"A couple of hours ago."

"What did the man look like?" Carter asked.

Boyd blinked, noticing Carter for the first time.

"Dr. Carter?"

"Yes. And you're Boyd. Steven Boyd, right?"

Ellen looked at Carter, shocked. She knew Andrew Carter had a photographic memory, but she assumed he reserved it for more important things. Ancient texts. Incantations. Not the names of his former students.

"You took my class a couple of semesters ago."

"Yes, sir. I did, sir. And I am. Steven Boyd, sir," he stammered, grateful to be recognized.

"What did the intruder look like?" Carter asked.

"I know this is going to sound kind of strange. And I know I'm not the most reliable witness." Boyd flashed them a self-conscious glance. "But he looked like my grandfather. My favorite grandfather. He died a long time ago."

"He reminded *me* of a boyfriend I had when I was in Russia," Ellen offered. Her stomach churned as she remembered how Solomon shifted identities. *Searching for the right one to lure me.* "He's dead, too. Car crash."

"That's weird." Boyd inched toward the safety of his room. She heard the squawk of his police scanner. The sound of other people's tragedies spilled into the hall. Domestic violence. A home in flames. A residential burglary.

"Have they found Martha yet?" Ellen asked.

Boyd shook his head. "No, but they're looking for a vehicle that sped away from the scene."

She turned to Carter. "Not your car, I hope."

Carter stared at Boyd. He didn't seem to hear her.

"Andrew?"

"No. They've already interviewed me," Carter finally replied. "That reminds me. They want to talk to you, Ellen. Once you've 'woken up,' of course."

"Terrific. One more thing to look forward to." She peered at Boyd. "Do you think the guy is still up there?"

"I don't know. It's been quiet, but I haven't gone up to investigate." Boyd gave them another self-conscious look. "Sorry."

"Nothing to be sorry about, Steven," she reassured him. "Could I borrow one of your baseball bats?"

Boyd nodded, eager to do something to help.

"Aluminum or wood?" he asked.

"Oh, aluminum. Definitely aluminum. I love the sound it makes when you hit someone."

Boyd snickered as he retreated. Even though they guarded the door, he closed it, engaging an impressive array of locks.

"That guy's a serious tweaker," Carter muttered.

"Meth! Of course." She snapped her fingers. The lack of sleep, the jittery behavior, the almost constant surveillance of the house . . . it all made sense.

"He also has a massive crush on you," Carter informed her.

Ellen felt him staring at her. As if he were trying to figure out *that* mystery as well.

"Tell me, is there any man you can't charm?" he asked her.

"You."

"I'm here, aren't I?"

"Only because Joshua made you."

"Joshua doesn't *make* me do anything," he said.

"Jeez, Andrew. What an attitude." She rolled her eyes at him. "You must have been a real pain-in-the-ass teenager."

He gave her a crooked smile.

"I told you before. I'm not talking without my lawyer."

Boyd emerged from his fortress and handed her a silver bat. Ellen weighed it in her hand, looking down it like she was inspecting the barrel of a gun.

"You're lending me Minnie? Steven, I'm touched."

"Minnie?" Carter echoed.

Ellen held up the bat so that he could see the sticker on the thickest part. Minnie Mouse in a dress and heels, looking irresistibly coy. "He names all his weapons after things he hates."

"Minnie Mouse?" Carter snorted at Boyd. "What the hell do you have against Minnie Mouse?"

"With all due respect, Dr. Carter, that's between Minnie and me."

Boyd gave a polite nod to the cartoon character. Ellen almost expected him to tip an invisible cowboy hat and say "ma'am" as he closed the door. Carter just stood there, staring at the door. Then he laughed. The sound was rich, full bodied. It reminded her of coffee.

"I think it's a sex thing." She twirled the bat in her hand, watching Minnie spin like a kaleidoscope. Ellen was happy to delay going to her room. "I mean, to be fair, Minnie *is* a bit of a tease. Don't you think?"

"I don't think about cartoon characters that way."

"Hey, we all have cartoon characters on bats." She shrugged. Before she could say anything else, a loud creak came from upstairs.

Ellen closed her eyes. "Oh, no."

"I'm really getting tired of this." Carter reached for his gun and marched toward the stairs.

Ellen grabbed his arm.

"Don't!"

"Why not?"

"Well, for one thing, you don't even know where my room is," she pointed out. "I don't want you shooting my housemates."

Carter glared at her. Then he stepped aside. "Lead the way."

They heard a snuffling sound as they climbed the stairs. Someone was crying. She knew it wasn't Solomon Reye. She didn't think Solomon Reye was capable of crying. Still, she was surprised when she saw Charles Montgomery, the resident ghost. Her more-than-friendly ghost. He sat outside her door, as if he had been locked out. Ellen had never seen Charlie before. His presence was always indirect—a ruffled bedsheet here, a playful pinch there. She knew from her ghost hunting that full-body apparitions were rare. The energy required for spirits to manifest was too great, the gap too wide for most ghosts to cross. But here he was, his figure so sharp, Ellen could see individual buttons on his coat. *Not just a coat,* Ellen thought, struggling for something to help her focus. *A great coat.* The kind a nineteenth-century gentleman would wear. Despite his dapper appearance, Charlie didn't look like the well-mannered man she saw in the old photographs. He looked wild. Unstable.

The ghost flew toward her.

"Ellen," Carter called out.

She could tell by the tightness in his voice that he saw Charlie as well.

Carter grabbed her by the shoulder to pull her away from the ghost.

The moment he touched her, he hissed. "Ow! Son of a bitch!"

Thin red welts rose on Carter's arm.

Ellen recognized the injury.

She had suffered her fair share of cat scratches before she made peace with Charlie.

"Charlie, knock it off! He's a friend!" Ellen scolded.

"Charlie?" Carter echoed.

"His name is Charles Montgomery. He's the original owner of the house," she explained as she reached out and touched the apparition.

Her fingers brushed against the scratchy wool of his coat.

He's real, as real as he was the night we made love.

Ellen looked away, biting her lip.

"I tried to stop the man who came into your room. To defend you," the ghost rasped. "Just like that boy downstairs. I couldn't protect you. I couldn't even protect myself." The ghost's features wavered. Ellen gasped as he changed form. She always assumed Charlie had killed himself neatly. A clean shot with a derringer. But he chose a shotgun. He went out in a blaze of bone-blasting glory.

"Oh God. Did Solomon—"

"It tried to take over. To assume my form. And when I resisted, it stripped me. It stripped me down to what I was when I . . ." A tear flooded the eye that had somehow escaped the blast.

"I can't stay," the ghost whispered.

"Charlie, please." She shivered as she said his name. "It doesn't matter. The way you look."

"I'm sorry. It's too much. Staying here. It's too much."

Ellen closed her eyes. She didn't want to watch him fade away. She had a terrible feeling she would never see him again. That the damage Solomon Reye inflicted on him was too great.

"Ellen . . ." Carter said after a long silence.

"Is he gone?"

"Yes."

Ellen opened her eyes.

"You saw him?"

"What was left of him," Carter replied. "Did he, um . . ."

"Right here." She motioned vaguely to the space around them. "After he lost all his money."

"He blew his brains out."

"With a shotgun." She glanced down at the Minnie Mouse on her bat. She suddenly felt childish. Out of her element. "That's the first time I've ever seen him like that."

"Like what?"

"Unmasked. Unable to hide what he'd done to himself." Ellen remembered what Martha had told her at the police station. "Reye discovers all your secrets. There's no hiding from him. That's what Martha said. Even ghosts aren't safe."

"Ellen."

"What?" She looked at him eagerly, hoping he could offer her something, some tiny crumb that would keep her from starving.

He looked as uncertain as she felt.

"You should get out of here. Now. Grab that new boyfriend of yours and run to Mexico."

She shook her head. "I can't. Martha is out there. Cold. Alone. I can't just leave her. I won't."

"Look, I appreciate your loyalty to your friend—"

"You don't understand. She's all I have left. All my friends from my freshman year. They're dead. And Martha . . ."

Ellen almost choked on her friend's name.

"Martha helped me through a very dark time in my life." She bowed her head. "I don't know if I'd be here without her."

Carter tensed.

"What do you mean?"

"Not now," she replied as she pushed away the memory. "Maybe later, but not now."

Ellen nodded at the door to her room.

Not with a demon listening on the other side.

Carter said nothing.

"I can't give up. Not if there's a chance she's still alive," she insisted.

"You know, you're loyal to a fault," he told her.

"I know."

"It's going to get you killed."

"I know that, too."

There was nothing left to say.

She took out her key and turned the lock.

They burst into the silence of her room. Ellen felt like she was invading her own space, bringing chaos and darkness with her. The room was empty. It looked like it always did. A small angular space tucked tightly into the roof. Its wood floors and lemon-colored walls glowed in the sunlight. There were only three pieces of furniture in the room—a bed, a desk, and a chair. They filled the space. So did Carter. She wasn't aware of how small the room was until she saw Andrew Carter standing in it. He had to hunch to avoid banging his head on the beams.

"Look around. Is anything out of place?" he asked her.

"Just you. Why don't you sit on the—"

The words died in her throat.

A piece of paper lay on the mattress, neatly folded into the shape of an origami bird.

"Andrew."

Carter reached into his pocket for a pair of gloves. "I see it."

He sat down on the bed. Ellen joined him, watching as he carefully picked up and unfolded the paper.

An oddly serene image filled the page. It was a reproduction of a painting. A man drove an ox down a road that overlooked the sea. On the water below him, a tall ship sailed toward a distant port. All around them were quiet pastoral scenes—a man tending a flock of sheep, a fisherman on the shore casting his net into the ocean. Ellen stared at the scene. And the words scrawled beneath it.

Come find me. In the place where a man fell from the sky.

"Interesting," Carter observed. "It's Pieter Bruegel. *The Fall of Icarus.*"

"Icarus?"

"The Greek myth about the guy who made wings of feather and wax," Carter said as she studied the strange scene. "He flew too close to the sun, and the wax melted."

"And he fell to his death and drowned. But where is he?" Ellen asked.

Carter pointed to a pair of legs kicking in the water, just below the ship.

"But he's barely visible."

"That's the point. Huge, epic events go on, but they're irrelevant to most people. Part of the background. Something they don't see."

Something they don't see.

Ellen suddenly felt weak.

"Just like the asylum," she whispered.

"What are you talking about?"

Ellen couldn't speak. Her body felt cold—as if the night-gaunt poison still coursed through her system.

"Ellen?"

Tears spilled down her face.

"That bastard. He's taunting me."

She tried to pull herself out of a dangerous spiral. Ellen knew that if she went into a tailspin, she might never recover.

"Ellen, talk to me."

"It's what you just said. The entire point of the painting," she said. "Huge events go on, but they're part of the background. Something most people don't see." She looked at Carter. "That's what happened at the asylum. You were there. Martha was there. The orderlies, the other patients, the visitors. But none of you saw him. You didn't see what happened."

"I don't understand."

"All of you were vacant. Spaced out." She waved her hand in front of her eyes. "Every single person in the room. You looked like you walked in and forgot why you were there. Martha was unconscious. I was on the floor, crawling, trying to reach her. And Solomon was walking beside me. Taunting me. Stalking me."

"Jesus."

"You didn't see any of this?"

"No."

Ellen heard the quiet rage in his voice. Being ignorant made him angry. Which made her next question even more difficult.

"I need to ask you something. It's going to piss you off, but I really need to know."

"What?"

"Have you ever been to the Dreamlands?" she asked.

She expected Carter to resist. For them to engage in a familiar give-and-take. And he *did* think about it. Then he let out a deep sigh and looked at the floor.

"She beat it out of me," he said.

Ellen thought she'd misheard him. "She beat it out of you? Who?"

"My mother." The words came out soft, full of pain.

"I don't understand."

"People develop their ability to go to the Dreamlands at a very young age," he explained. "My grandfather started traveling when he was five, six years old. Apparently, I had the same ability. My mother knew what to expect when she married a Carter. We're famous for our mystical abilities. And she thought she was okay with it."

"Until she had a child," Ellen said.

Carter stiffened beside her. "You know about conditioned responses, don't you?" he asked.

"Vaguely."

His face darkened. "She trained me like one of Pavlov's dogs. Except she didn't reward me. Every time it looked like I was drifting off, she hit me. Even if I was just daydreaming or thinking about a girl. This went on for years. By the time I escaped to Miskatonic, the damage was done. So, no, I can't go to the Dreamlands. I can't even meditate, thanks to her."

"Did your father know about this?"

"He didn't stop it, if that's what you're asking."

"Oh, Andrew—"

He silenced her with a lethal glare. "Don't you dare. Don't you *dare* feel sorry for me."

A thick, pea-soup silence filled the room.

"So now you know. I'm crippled. Useless." Andrew shrugged.

"You're not crippled, and you're not useless. Don't be so fucking ridiculous!" she said. "That's like saying you're blind because you need glasses."

"Some people *are* blind without their glasses," he pointed out.

Blind. Glasses.

The words connected.

"The ring!" Ellen blurted.

"What?"

"The ring. The ring Martha gave me. What if the ring is like a pair of glasses? A way of correcting your vision? Of helping you get past obstacles?"

"What are you saying? That the ring is some magical shortcut? Some way for a mentally deficient person like me to get into the Dreamlands?"

"That's not what I'm saying, and you know it," she scolded.

It was too late.

Carter was too wound up to hear her.

"So what *are* you suggesting? That if something happens to you, I should put on the ring and see what it does? Throw myself into the darkness? Well, you can forget it. I'm not your fucking Prince Charming."

"I know you're not Prince Charming. You drop *way* too many f-bombs to be Prince Charming."

"Then what do you want? What do you want from me?" he demanded.

Ellen drifted to the open window over the desk.

The curtain flapped in the wind.

Solomon's escape route, she thought as she closed the window and latched it shut.

"I don't know. I guess. . ." She leaned against the desk for support. Tears bloomed in her eyes, blurring the street below. "If you wake up in a pool of glass, like you did in the asylum, and you're not sure what happened, Reye was there. And if I'm gone, he's taken me. I want you to find someone. Find someone who might be able to help. Because I'd rather have a slim chance than no chance at all."

"Ellen—" Carter started.

"Ellen!" a man shouted, pounding his fists on the door.

Ellen lunged for the bat.

Carter intercepted her.

"Relax. It's Boyd."

He crossed the room and opened the door. She expected him to lash out, but Carter's voice was gentle. "What is it?"

"State police found the car. The one they think Martha was kidnapped in."

Ellen sighed, feeling a mixture of dread and relief.

At last, she thought, *something's happened. The loaded dice have been thrown.*

Boyd glanced at Carter suspiciously.

"What's wrong, Ellen?" he demanded.

"Nothing. I'm just worried about Martha," she assured him. "Where did they find the car?"

"It was abandoned in rural New Jersey. In a place called the Barrens."

Chapter Fourteen

"Let me get this straight."

Ellen waited for her boyfriend to go through the plan one more time.

Andrew Carter stood a few feet away, waiting by his car. They had a long drive ahead of them. Ellen didn't care. She needed to say goodbye to Tom properly.

Just in case, her mind whispered.

"You're going to the Pine Barrens?" Tom asked.

"Yes."

"To the middle of nowhere?"

"Yes."

"To find Martha?"

"I hope so."

"Even though the police are already searching the area?"

"Yes."

"And you're going with Mr. Sunshine over there?"

"Andrew's all right."

Tom tensed. "Andrew? You're on a first-name basis with him?"

"Is there a problem?" Ellen blurted, her words a little too sharp. Ever since she'd broken up with Phil, she'd been sensitive to any signs of jealousy.

"Of course not." Tom dug his hands into his jacket. He presented her with a small square object and a pair of earbuds. "Here. You might need this."

"What is it?"

"An iPod. I put some tunes on it—just in case Dr. Carter is a less-than-ideal travel partner."

Ellen's eyes filled with tears.

She grabbed Tom and pulled him into a tight hug.

"Hey, hey, hey, girl. Calm down. You're only going to New Jersey," Tom said.

"I know." She pressed her face into his neck, into the spot where his hairline ended. He smelled clean, a mixture of sweet oranges and spring air. "And when I get back, I'm coming after you."

He smiled as he pulled back to look at her. "Oh yeah?"

The moment their eyes met, the mood between them changed. They kissed each other. Hard. All the familiar feelings came rushing back. Ellen groaned in relief. She'd told Carter she wasn't attracted to women, but Miss Cummings made her wonder. For one heart-stopping moment, she wasn't sure which side she was on. Or whether there were any sides.

"Wow. I needed that," Ellen croaked.

He reached out and touched her cheek. "Me, too."

Please, God, let me get back, she thought. *I may have finally found the right man. Let me get back.*

"Jesus. You took long enough. We're only going to New Jersey," Carter sniped when she approached him.

"Tom said the same thing." Ellen watched him disappear around the corner. Tom didn't look back. She wasn't sure why, but she liked that about him.

"He's better than your last one—I'll give you that."

Ellen shot Carter a sideways look.

"Are you going to comment on all my boyfriends?"

"Probably," he said as he helped her with her things. "You brought Minnie?"

"On loan from the Steven Boyd collection." She spun the bat until Minnie Mouse was faceup. "I also brought this. Just in case." She dropped a fire axe on top of her bag.

"Joshua didn't lend you a gun?"

Ellen made a sour face. "Joshua tried to stop me from running off with you. I guess he thought that if he didn't give me a gun, I'd stay at home. So, I improvised."

"*Running off with me?*"

"His exact words." She didn't tell Carter the rest of the story. That Joshua threatened to kick her out if she got involved in another so-called adventure. "I don't know what his problem is. I really don't."

"You're growing up. That's Joshua's problem. And he needs you more than you need him."

"That's not . . ." She fell silent as she thought about it. She had a steady job. A place to stay. Living alone might require belt tightening, but she could do it. She could easily do it. "God, Andrew, you're right."

"Don't sound so surprised. I do have my moments."

"Did Joshua do the same thing to you?"

He slammed the door shut and moved to the other side of the car.

"We should get going. A friend of mine owns a B&B in Medford. We'll spend the night there and head into the Barrens first thing in the morning. Maybe by then, we'll figure out where we're going."

"I think I know."

"What?"

"I think I know where we're going."

✦✦✦✦

The modern world slipped away. One minute, they were on the freeway, racing toward the clogged arteries of New York and Philadelphia. The next, they were on a quiet two-lane blacktop surrounded by a dense, primordial forest.

Carter tried to prepare her for the Pine Barrens. He'd rattled off the statistics, but the numbers didn't register until now. One million acres of forest. The largest unsettled area between Boston and Richmond, Virginia. One of the lowest population densities on the East Coast. The last fact bothered Ellen the most. The sheer isolation of the place. She gazed out the window, hungry for a glimpse of civilization. Occasionally, she spotted a gas station, a weather-beaten tavern, a converted house renting kayaks and canoes. During the summer, they were busy social hubs, places where adventurers traded stories and recommended hiking trails.

In January, the buildings were closed, their windows barricaded against the winter.

Is the winter all they're worried about? Ellen wondered. *Or are they trying to keep something else out?*

Ellen shifted in the passenger seat. She wasn't a fan of consumer culture. But at that moment, she would have given anything to spot an Applebee's. Or a Hard Rock Cafe. Anything to lift the gloom.

"Tell me the story again," Carter asked after endless miles of silence. "About our destination."

"Tabernacle Township, New Jersey. That's where the memorial to Emilio Carranza is."

"Who?"

"He was a famous pilot. The Mexican Charles Lindbergh." Ellen glanced down at the pages she'd photocopied. "He set all kinds of records, flying nonstop from San Diego to Mexico City. He made a similar flight from Mexico City to New York City. In fact, he'd just completed the trip and was in New York when he got a telegram."

"And?"

"It was from the Mexican war minister. It said, 'return or the quality of your manhood will be in doubt.' No one knows why the war minister sent such a strongly worded message." Ellen stared out at the growing darkness. "Can you imagine? A macho man like Carranza receiving that kind of message? I can almost picture it. Carranza in a restaurant, celebrating his victory with friends. Eating a steak so rare, it bled onto the plate. And then . . . boom! A gauntlet thrown down. Right in his face."

Carter glanced in the rearview mirror. "He was set up."

"Charles Lindbergh urged him not to go. Said the weather was too unpredictable. But even Carranza's hero couldn't persuade him to wait. He left New York and flew straight into a thunderstorm. And his plane . . . his plane just blew apart. Disintegrated over the Barrens. They found his body the next day."

"Come find me. In the place where a man fell from the sky," Carter said.

"His memorial says as much. It doesn't say he crashed. It says he fell to his death." Ellen huddled deeper in her coat. Even though the car's heater was on full blast, she shivered.

"And how did you learn all this?"

"From a book I found at Mote It Be." She braced herself for a blast of sarcasm. Carter was not a fan of the New Age bookstore where she worked. "It was part of a series on strange tales in the United States. Kind of an *Encyclopedia Britannica* of the supernatural. I found Carranza in *Weird New Jersey*. He was in the section about the Barrens. Right next to the Jersey Devil."

"The Jersey Devil. God, I'd forgotten about that. We're right in the middle of Jersey Devil territory."

Carter fell silent.

Ellen could practically hear the gears turning in his mind.

"Jersey Devil? Do you think Carranza and the Jersey Devil are—?"

Her question was cut off by the sudden squeal of brakes. Carter threw out his arm to protect her as the Range Rover fishtailed across the slippery road. Ellen saw a dark form dart across the road. *A deer,* she thought. *We're going into a ditch because of a deer.* But they didn't crash. Somehow, Carter regained control of the car and brought it to a stop. The car straddled both lanes, but they were still in one piece.

"Are you okay?" Carter gasped.

He stared wide-eyed at the road, his arm still locked in front of her.

"Yeah. You?"

When he didn't respond, she reached out and touched his arm.

"Andrew?" she called out.

"I'm all right."

"What did you see? A deer?"

"A deer." He seemed to be trying the idea on for size. It must have been a good fit because he broke out of his haze. "Goddamn thing. Nearly killed us."

"You know, you're a terrible liar," she started, then fell silent. There was no point pushing him. And she didn't *really* want to know what they just saw.

Carter sat back and rubbed at the spot where the seat belt bit into his neck.

"It's getting dark. How much farther is it?" she asked.

He consulted the GPS.

"Not far. Another mile or so."

Assuming we don't run into another deer.

Her thought did not amuse her.

She kept her eyes on the road for the rest of the trip.

Chapter Fifteen

ngie's Oasis. The name alone was a lie. Perched in a meadow surrounded by trees, the converted farmhouse sparkled like a jewel in the twilight. Ellen soon saw the reason. The owner had placed floodlights around the house. At first, she'd assumed the lights were to attract visitors, to make the house visible from the road. Then she saw the strange symbols—the sigils painted above the doorways and windows. Statues of gnomes and fairies flanked the house.

An army to keep the darkness at bay, she thought as they pulled into the gravel driveway.

They were barely out of the car when a woman burst out the front door. She was about Carter's age, an attractive blonde in a velvet dress and a long wool coat. Ellen recognized the look. She wore the same outfits at Mote It Be. It looked better on Carter's friend. Her body was fuller, more voluptuous. She was a more convincing earth goddess.

The woman threw her arms around Carter and kissed him. For a moment, Ellen thought he would push her away.

He didn't.

Carter melted into the kiss.

Former flame. Or current one, by the looks of it.

Ellen stared at a nearby garden troll, waiting for their reunion to end.

"It is *so* good to see you, Drew," the woman gushed. When Ellen looked back, Carter was still in her arms. He looked stunned. And a little disturbed.

After a moment, he recovered enough to withdraw from the embrace.

"It's nice to see you, too, Angie," he replied, a polite grimace frozen on his face.

Angie frowned and searched for the source of his distress.

Her eyes settled on Ellen.

"Who's she?" Angie demanded.

Carter pushed Ellen at her like she was a human shield. "I'd like you to meet my niece, Ellen Logan. Ellen, this is Angela MacGruder."

Ellen held out her hand and hoped for the best.

"It's a pleasure to meet you."

Angie smiled, an expression that didn't quite reach her eyes. "I should have known you two were related. She has your eyes, Drew."

"Does she?" Carter replied with little interest. He was too busy inspecting the faded symbols above the door to notice the "family" resemblance.

Angela moved closer. Ellen caught a whiff of French perfume. Not what she expected from an earth goddess.

"I see he's still monster hunting," she whispered.

"He never stops."

"And he lured you into the family business, I suppose."

"Not exactly. I was the one who approached him," she admitted. Ellen didn't know why, but she felt the need to protect Carter. "My parents wanted me to be a lawyer, but I had other plans. Andrew helped me realize them."

"You mean Uncle Andrew?"

Ellen leaned forward. "He doesn't like me to call him that. It makes him feel old."

"Enough," Carter called out.

Angie beamed at Ellen.

"I take it you're a student at Miskatonic?"

"I'm in my junior year."

"I'm surprised they let you work with your uncle. Isn't that against university policy?"

"I never follow the rules. You know that," Carter replied. "So tell me, Angie. How are you?"

"Why don't I tell you over dinner and a nice bottle of wine?"

⁙

"Oh, and did you hear that Susan Ramsey and Gabriel Keats are an item? Can you believe it? They couldn't *stand* each other. Remember when he accused her of being a witch? Almost drowned her in the Miskatonic River?"

Ellen felt like she was at a class reunion. The moment they sat down for dinner, Angie began updating Carter on all their college friends. Who was dating. Who was married. Who was alive. Who was dead. The names swirled around her, a social calculus with far too many unknowns. Only one name was familiar. Connie Blake. Angela mentioned him in passing, almost as if she were afraid to put too much weight on the memory. Carter seemed equally reluctant to talk about his friend.

As Ellen sat there, full of pasta and wine, half listening to the conversation, a new equation popped into her head. Connie, Carter, and Angie. Was it possible? Was she the woman who had been with Carter and Connie? The one she saw in Connie Blake's memories?

Ellen tried to imagine what she looked like twenty years ago. She couldn't picture Angie as a younger woman; she was too firmly settled into middle age. *Not like Carter,* she thought, sneaking a glance at her "uncle." She found it hard to believe Andrew Carter was old enough to be her father.

Well, old enough to be my teenage father.

She couldn't imagine him being a teenager, either.

"Ellen?" Carter broke into her thoughts.

She looked up from her pasta.

"Huh?"

"Angie asked you a question."

"Oh? Oh! I'm sorry." Ellen forced herself back to reality. "It was a long drive from Arkham. I'm fried."

"And I'm sure our trip down memory lane isn't helping." The woman flashed Ellen an apologetic smile. "I was asking how your advanced studies were going. What do you think of Dr. Cochoran? He was a real beast in my time."

A blush spread across Ellen's cheeks.

"I, um . . . I'm not part of the advanced program yet."

"What?"

"I'm not part of the program yet," Ellen repeated.

Angie was no longer paying attention to her.

"Wait a minute. You're taking her on one of your expeditions, and she's not part of the program? Why isn't she part of the program?"

Carter scowled. "That's between Ellen and me."

She turned to Ellen.

"Don't you want to be part of it?"

Ellen's blush deepened. "More than anything in the world," she mumbled into her wineglass.

"Then what's the problem? Drew could easily arrange—"

"Lay off, Angie. Just lay off."

"I'm not smart enough," Ellen blurted.

Carter and Angie stopped midargument.

Her voice trembled. "I try hard. I try so hard, but I don't think I have what it takes."

"That's bullshit, Ellen. That's total bullshit," Carter snapped.

Ellen continued to talk to Angie.

"I'm doing what I can. I'm trying to work my way around it. Find alternatives," she offered.

Angie frowned. "Alternatives? Like what?"

"There's this place. The Eibon Institute. They asked me to join them."

"Excuse me?" Carter blurted.

The two words were far from polite.

Angie turned to him. "The Eibon Institute? Didn't you belong to that, Drew?"

He crossed his arms, radiating hostility.

"Tell me, Ellen, when did they extend this invitation? Was this before or *after* they kicked us out?"

Ellen's stomach dropped. It never occurred to her that she was no longer welcome at the Eibon Institute. Now, thinking about that night, she remembered how pale Miss Cummings looked when she'd mentioned Solomon Reye. How she couldn't wait to get rid of them.

She practically pushed us out the door.

"Fuck," Ellen hissed under her breath.

"Forget about the Eibon Institute," Carter insisted. "They're a waste of time."

Angie jumped into the conversation.

"Wait, wait. Let me get this straight. You're giving her career advice, *and* you're holding her back?"

He bristled. "I am not holding her back."

"You are, Drew. One snap of your fingers and—"

"Look, all I'm saying is she shouldn't get involved in something that's a dead end. That would be a monumental waste of her time. And her intelligence."

Ellen perked up.

"Intelligence? You think I'm smart?"

Carter scowled at her.

"Oh, please, Ellen. Don't fish."

Ellen looked away, stung.

She reached for the safety of her wineglass.

"You know, when you talk like that, you sound exactly like your father," Angie said softly.

Ellen spluttered, almost choking on her wine.

Carter looked at Angie like she'd chucked a dead body on the table.

He threw down his napkin and stormed out of the room.

"He deserved that," Angie insisted when the back door slammed.

"He did," Ellen agreed.

She sighed. "I take it he still has issues with Robert."

"Robert?"

"His father."

"I don't know. He doesn't share much with me."

Angie rose and retrieved her coat. "I better go talk to him." She paused in the doorway.

"You know, you're not like his other partners."

"I'm his niece."

"No, you're not," Angie said with a knowing smile. "Andrew forgot that he tried to pass me off as his sister when we went on *our* adventures."

"You were his partner?"

Angie cocked her head.

"What, did you think you were his first Nancy Drew?"

Nancy Drew.

Ellen's face flared.

"To be honest, I never really thought about it."

"It's probably for the best. Andrew . . . well . . . It's a cliché, but Andrew's complicated."

As if my life isn't complicated enough, she thought.

"Is there anything I can do while you're gone?" Ellen offered, eager to change the subject.

Angie looked surprised by the offer.

"You can clear the table. Put things in the dishwasher. I'll run it later."

Ellen found it ironic she turned to chores for comfort. One thing she and Joshua argued about before she left was how much housework he expected her to do. That wasn't her only concern. She worried about how isolated Joshua was becoming. He used to spend only a few hours each day in his office. Now he barricaded himself in his study day and night. Ellen couldn't remember the last time they had dinner together. Or how long it had been since her uncle expressed any interest in what she was doing.

Except what I'm doing with Carter.

Ellen leaned against the kitchen counter and looked out the window.

The wind had picked up since they'd arrived. It had already knocked down some of Angie's figures. Ellen's eyes caught on a statue that seemed out of place. A black gargoyle towered over the army of gnomes. She knew people put gnomes in their gardens because they worked at night. In fact, their original name, Kuba-Walda, meant "home administrator."

So what does the gargoyle do? Ellen wondered. *Maybe he's their supervisor,* she thought with a smile.

The air grew thick. Heavy.

Ellen's smile evaporated.

Gargoyle. You thought it was a gargoyle the last time.

The nightgaunt rose from a crouch, its dark wings reaching for the sky.

She backed away from the window. "Oh, no. No, no, no!"

The creature whipped its faceless head in her direction.

Ellen dropped to the floor, writhing. Her feet stabbed the air. Something spilled inside her, spreading like ink. The wetness stung. It tickled. She could feel the nightgaunt trying to possess her. To disorient her so it could snatch her and take her to the Dreamlands. To Solomon Reye. She tried to resist, but the stinging, the tickling, the oily slickness . . . She rolled on the floor, clawing at her head. Her frantic scrabbling only increased the creature's power.

Ellen's mind grew fuzzy, her thoughts lost behind a buzzing wall of white noise.

Don't have much time. Not long before . . . before . . . before.

She blinked, looking up in disbelief.

Martha Pickman stood over her, her face tight with disgust.

What are you doing? her friend barked. *You know better than this!*

"Mar-Mar-Mar-tha," Ellen babbled.

You know what to do. Do it now!

Ellen wasn't sure she could.

She'd only tried a few times.

She closed her eyes and forced herself to go slack.

Suddenly, she was outside. Enveloped in darkness and deep, deep silence. The only thing she could feel was the winter air biting into her skin.

Not your skin.

Ellen jerked.

She opened her mouth to scream.

She had no mouth.

No ears, no eyes, no mouth.

The buzzing started again. It was loud. All around her. This time, it sounded different. Not a confident, hypnotic drone, but short staccato bursts.

The sound of a fly caught in a spiderweb.

The nightgaunt straightened. It was aware of her. She felt its shock. Its fear. Or what passed for fear.

A psychic cord stretched between them. She saw it in her mind, snaking from its talons to the body—*my body?*—sprawled in the kitchen.

Ellen reached down and yanked on it.

She woke up gasping, twitching on the cold linoleum floor. "No, no, no. No way. No fucking way," she said, panting.

A scream pierced the night—high and crystal clear.

Ellen scrambled to her feet. At first, she thought it was the nightgaunt.

No mouth, she reminded herself.

Ellen. Carter's voice vibrated in her head.

Is it really Carter? she wondered. *Or is the nightgaunt playing tricks on me?*

Get your ass out here!

Ellen smiled. "Andrew."

She ran to the front door. Thankfully, they hadn't been shown to their rooms yet. Their bags were still piled in the hall. Ellen grabbed her bat. She considered searching Carter's bag for weapons, but there was no time.

She looked at Minnie Mouse. "Don't let me down, sweetheart."

She slid out the front door and snuck around the house. In the dead of winter, Angela's Garden was nothing but skeletal remains. Ellen crouched behind a dense thicket of rosebushes.

As she got closer, the buzzing in her brain got louder.

She thought she heard a chuckle.

A large, ornate fountain stood in the center of the back garden. It was ugly, stacked like a wedding cake—the kind of heavy-handed art the Victorians liked. Ellen liked it for a different reason. She could hide behind it and watch what was happening. The nightgaunt was only ten feet away, its back facing her. Carter stood in front of it, trying to protect Angie. The creature was much larger than the other nightgaunts.

It swished its tail like a cat.

The small, confident gesture pissed her off.

Andrew, I'm here, she called out to him psychically as she crept around the fountain.

The creature lifted its featureless head.

Listen, I will come in on your left. Do you understand?

Yes.

To your left, to your left, to your left.

"Enough!" he snarled.

The nightgaunt reacted the way she hoped it would.

It turned to Carter's left.

She popped out on the other side and whacked the creature in the back of the legs.

Ellen had never hit anything so hard in her life. She thought of the cartoons she used to watch. How a shock wave rippled through poor Daffy Duck when he ran into a wall. The same terrible sensation ripped through her. *Hold it together, girl,* she coached herself as the nightgaunt fell to its knees. *This is your only chance. Line up your shot.* Ellen reversed direction, swinging at the creature's head. There was a loud crack. Another sickening impact rode up her arms.

The creature crashed to the ground.

Angie screamed again, splitting the air with a pure, agonizing sound.

Carter stared at Ellen in disbelief.

The nightgaunt twitched. She struck it again with the bat.

"Run," Ellen barked in a choked voice. "Run! Run! *Run!*"

Ellen didn't wait for them to react. She turned and made a beeline toward the kitchen door. She crashed through the rosebushes. Thorns tore at her coat and dug into her jeans. Her body burned, but she knew she couldn't slow down. The pain was nothing compared to what the nightgaunt would do if—

Her foot caught on a gnome.

Ellen fell hard, slamming into the ground.

She saw stars.

"*Ellen!*" Carter bellowed.

I never got to sleep with Tom, she thought as she lay dazed on the frozen earth.

It made her angry.

Her anger gave her the energy she needed.

Andrew? she called out.

Yeah? he replied.

I'm going to move to my right, okay?

Okay.

My right. I will move to my right, my right, my right, she chanted. When she heard the nightgaunt leap, she rolled to her right. The creature veered left. It smashed headfirst into the house, with enough force to make the ground shake.

It's learning; it's learning very quickly.

Ellen looked up just in time to see the kitchen door slam shut.

He left me, she thought as she stared at the stunned nightgaunt. *I can't believe it. Carter's left me out here to die.*

"You bastard." Ellen raised her bat. She was determined to do damage before the nightgaunt killed her.

Front door.

She paused midswing.

Front door. Get to the front door. Now!

Ellen turned and ran.

She could hear the nightgaunt behind her, full of white-hot rage.

Carter waited for her at the door. Legs spread, shotgun leveled at her head. Ellen dove onto the porch. She covered her ears as a deafening roar filled the air.

An inhuman shriek sliced through Ellen's mind.

The nightgaunt twisted in agony.

Its body blazed with phosphorescent light.

Carter reracked his gun.

"The basement. Get to the basement," he commanded. "Angie's there. You'll be safe."

"I'm not leaving you."

"Ellen!"

"I'm your eyes. You're my firepower. We won't make it without each other."

She grabbed the back of his shirt and guided him down the hall.

Carter kept his shotgun trained on the nightgaunt.

Finding the basement wasn't hard. It was the only door on the ground floor made of reinforced metal.

And Angie was there.

She watched them from behind a half-open door, her eyes glazed with shock.

Ellen felt sorry for her.

This isn't her world anymore, she thought. *She's out of her element.*

The woman moved, almost in response to the thought.

"No!" Ellen screamed, leaping at Angie as she backed away. She wedged her bat in the doorway before the woman slammed the door.

Angie kicked at the weapon, trying to knock it loose.

"What's going on?" Carter demanded.

"She's shutting the door. She's trying to lock us out."

"You listen to me, Angela," he snarled as he pumped another round into the creature. "We don't have to stay here. Ellen and I can take our chances and run for the car. We can leave you to fight this thing on your own. Or you can be reasonable and *open the fucking door!*"

There was a snuffled croak. A moment later, the door flew open. Ellen and Carter tumbled inside. The nightgaunt hurled itself against the door just as Ellen threw the dead bolt. She tensed, waiting for the monster to break through. For her to be crushed by its weight.

The steel door held.

A buzzing rose in her head, so fierce and frantic it made thought impossible.

Then . . . silence.

Ellen staggered down the stairs, collapsing on the bottom step.

She could hear Carter and Angie shouting at each other. Smell the musty dampness of the concrete floor. Her eyes latched on to ordinary things. The washer and dryer. The home office tucked into a corner. The gardening tools stacked on a table, waiting for spring to arrive.

Ellen felt a stab of sadness.

I won't survive the winter.

She slumped against the wall and closed her eyes. She imagined warm grass pressing into her back. Tom tickling her with a flower.

Cold hands touched her face.

Ellen screamed.

"Hey, hey. Calm down."

When she opened her eyes, Andrew Carter was kneeling in front of her. His shotgun rested on the floor beside him.

"Are you hurt?" he asked.

"I don't know."

"Why don't you let go of Minnie so I can take a look at you."

"Minnie?"

Somehow, through all the chaos, she'd managed to hold onto the bat. Her fingers gripped it so tightly, her skin was white. She tried to loosen her grip, but her hands felt like stone.

"I don't think I can," she admitted.

Carter said nothing. He reached down and pried her hands off the bat. His touch was gentle, gentle and so unexpected, Ellen's eyes filled with tears.

Upstairs, the nightgaunt thrashed.

She moved closer, pressed her forehead against his.

Carter backed away like a spooked horse.

"I got inside it," she whispered.

"What?" The word came out soft. Shaky.

"I got inside it. Martha showed me how. Martha Pickman."

"Andrew, are you done?"

Ellen looked up to see Angie glaring at them.

"Are you quite done flirting with your niece?" Angie said, air-quoting the last word.

Carter dropped Ellen's hands.

"I'm not flirting with her," he insisted, a little too loudly.

His eyes swept the basement, searching for somewhere, anywhere to land.

They settled on a duffel bag.

He stiffened.

"What's that?"

"You're changing the subject," Angie protested.

"What . . . is . . . that?"

Ellen stood, disturbed by the tension she heard in Carter's voice.

"Oh, that! That's just another person from Miskatonic screwing me over!"

"What's wrong, Andrew?" Ellen asked.

"That looks like Victor Ramsey's bag."

"Your missing student?"

"Missing?" Angie echoed.

Carter whipped out his cell phone. After a few quick swipes, he pointed it at Angie.

Her face fell.

"Yeah. He was here."

"What happened?"

Angie shrugged. "There's not much to tell. The guy arrived a few weeks ago. I knew he was a Miskatonic student right away. He was amped, bouncing off the walls. He kept babbling about some important discovery. Something that would knock his advisor off his feet."

Carter winced.

"He only stayed a day. I had a hard time even convincing him to have breakfast before he took off. He said he'd be back late that night, but that was the last time I saw him. I just assumed he skipped out on the bill."

"Someone from Miskatonic disappeared, and you thought he skipped out on you?" Carter echoed.

"A person from Miskatonic flakes? Not exactly news, Andrew." Angie paused, realizing how heartless she sounded. "Look, I *was* concerned. I did everything I could to find him. I called the police. I told everyone around here about the disappearance. I even posted what happened online. Nothing."

"Did he have a car?" Ellen asked.

Angie thought for a long time.

"You know what? I don't think he did. That's strange."

"Someone must have dropped him off," Carter offered. "There's no easy way of getting here except by car. Let's face it, this place is in the middle of fucking nowhere."

Angie's mouth tightened.

"Have you searched the bag?" Ellen asked.

Angie snorted. "I'm not touching it."

Ellen looked at it.

A shiver skittered up her spine.

"I'll take a look," Carter volunteered.

She snagged his arm before he could walk away.

"Gloves," she reminded him. "Don't forget to wear gloves."

He blinked at her, as if he didn't understand.

For the first time, Ellen saw how exhausted he was.

"Yeah, of course, yeah," he mumbled.

He rummaged in his pockets and came up empty-handed.

Ellen picked up some gloves from the gardening table.

"Let me," she offered.

"I'll do it," Carter growled.

"In these?" Ellen dangled the women's gloves in front of him. "You have as much of a chance as fitting into my prom gown."

He raised his eyebrow. "I can't imagine you in a prom gown."

"Thank God. I looked ridiculous."

Angie chuckled. "We all did," she said.

Ellen knelt by the bag and unzipped it. She felt like she was part of a bomb squad. She sifted carefully through the belongings Carter's student had left behind. Most of it was ordinary—clothes, toothbrush, the latest Jack Reacher novel. Then her fingers caught on the cardboard at the bottom bag.

It wiggled.

"False bottom," Ellen announced as she lifted it.

A pungent smell filled the room.

Ellen coughed and turned away. She wished she hadn't eaten so much pasta.

She carefully excavated the contents of the secret compartment. Feathers. Sticks. The mummified remains of a lizard. Glass vials filled with mystery oils. At some point, one of them had spilled in the bag. It was the source of the stench.

"A ritual kit," Carter announced. "Police find stuff like this when they arrest serial killers. They have a kit with everything they need for their, um, craft. Garbage bags, handcuffs, an axe, some bleach. This is obviously a kit for performing magic."

"Good or bad?"

Carter gave her a long look.

"I think you know the answer to that question."

Ellen forced back the bile in her throat. She continued to search the bag, hoping there would be no more messy surprises.

Her hands closed on a small rectangular shape.

She pulled out a leather notebook.

Two words were scrawled across the cover.

"*Espacio angosto*," Carter read over her shoulder.

"Thin place," she translated.

"You speak Spanish?"

"A little." She flipped through page after page of spidery handwriting.

"Do you think you can translate it?"

"I'm not sure."

"Will you try?" he asked.

Ellen looked across the basement to Angie, who sat forlornly on the stairs.

"Why not?" She shrugged. "I've got nothing else to do."

Chapter Sixteen

llen rose from the office chair and stretched her aching muscles. She glanced at her watch. Three thirty. She moved to the grubby sink in the corner. Turned on the faucet. Dipped her head to take a drink.

It had been a couple of strange hours.

As soon as Ellen started working on the journal, Carter had steered Angie into the pantry. She'd heard angry words, crying. Then the sounds changed. There was urgent whispering. Low moans that rose in intensity. Ellen blushed and reached for her headphones before she remembered—the iPod Tom gave her was upstairs.

Hope the nightgaunt likes Tom's playlist, she'd thought.

She'd tried to focus on the journal.

It was difficult.

The sounds that came from the pantry made her miss Tom.

Now, Ellen stood in front of an inflatable bed, watching Angie and Carter sleep. There was no reason to disturb him. The journal didn't offer much. Still, Ellen wanted to talk. She *needed* to talk. Being alone while the people around her slept, while the nightgaunt thrashed above her head . . .

It reminded her of what had happened at Arkham Asylum.

She knelt next to the bed and shook Carter's shoulder.

Carter blinked. For a moment, he looked confused by his surroundings. Then he looked at Angie and groaned.

"God, we're still here?"

"I'm afraid so." A sudden crash upstairs made Ellen jump. "Jesus!" Ellen glanced at the ceiling. "What do you think it's doing up there?"

"I don't know. Why don't you go up and look? I'll wait here." He yawned as he turned onto his side. Even though he sounded casual, Ellen noticed he was fully clothed. He was even wearing his hiking boots.

She smacked one of his shoes.

"Wake up, lover boy."

He flipped to face her. "Lover boy?"

"I could hear the two of you. Kind of hard to ignore."

Carter turned bright red. Ellen had never made him blush before. She took great pleasure in embarrassing him.

It didn't last long.

"Are you jealous, Ellen?"

"No," she replied. "But I really miss Tom right now."

He nodded at the half-open door. "I'll take you into the pantry if you want."

"And do it on a stack of old, rusty cans? I'll pass," she scoffed.

"The cans aren't rusty," he insisted.

"Still a no go."

Carter shrugged as he sat up and rubbed his face. "Probably a good call. I don't think Angie would like to see an uncle and niece going at each other."

"She knows I'm not your niece."

He gave her a sharp look.

"Did you tell her?"

"No. Apparently, when you two were partners, you passed her off as your sister," Ellen informed him. Once again, Carter turned red. "You know, you should change your cover story more often. Once a decade seems like a good idea."

"All right. All right, smart ass."

She sat on the floor next to the bed and opened the notebook.

The playful mood in the room evaporated.

"What did you find?" he asked.

"Not much. Just scraps."

"Then why did you wake me up?"

Ellen sighed. "Because I'm scared, and I needed someone to talk to."

Carter shook his head.

"I'm sorry. It's not you. Being back here with her . . ." His voice trailed off as he looked at Angie. "What do you have?"

"Like I said, it's not much."

"Do you remember what I said on the first day of class?"

"You said a lot of things."

His mouth curled into a grin.

"I said that most of what we know about the world must be hidden. Sometimes we can only communicate in fragments."

Ellen nodded and took the plunge.

"The journal is from an anthropologist named Benicio Alvarez. He studied native tribes in Northern Mexico in the 1920s. It's an all-too-familiar story. He wanted to document groups before their cultures were destroyed. One group fascinated him. The Yaqui."

"Yaqui?"

"They're an old tribe, one that resisted Spanish colonization well into the twentieth century. And they had a belief uniquely their own."

"Let me guess. *Espacio angosto*," Carter offered.

"That's what Alvarez called it. The Yaqui never named it, but they did talk about overlapping worlds. And their ability to travel between them. They viewed themselves as the guardians of all the worlds they occupied. It was their responsibility to keep things in balance. And to eliminate the harm that's been done to them. In fact, Alvarez was there when they performed the ritual to do just that."

Carter gawked at her. "They opened a thin place while he was there? Did he describe it?"

"He must have. There were pages torn out of the journal. My guess is your student took them."

Carter groaned. "Goddamn it."

"Like I told you. Scraps." Ellen thumbed through the worn pages. "But look at the date the ritual took place."

"July 12, 1928," Carter read.

"The same day Emilio Carranza's plane crashed."

"So?"

"Before he became the Mexican Lindbergh, Carranza was in the Mexican Air Force. One of the things he did was put down a rebellion in Sonora. A *Yaqui* rebellion."

It took Carter a moment to digest the information.

"What are you saying? That this tribe opened a thin place and brought Carranza's plane down?"

"I'm not sure what I'm saying," Ellen admitted. "Is there such a thing? Thin places? I mean, you read about portals to another world all the time. *The Chronicles of Narnia. The Wizard of Oz.* Are they real?"

Carter's face tightened. "I can't tell you."

"Because I'm not part of the program?"

He nodded.

She looked away, pursing her lips.

"Listen to me, Ellen. It's not because you're not smart enough. And it's not because you're a woman, if that's your next thought."

"Is it Joshua?"

He looked annoyed by the question.

"It's because you're my *friend.* And bringing a friend into the program is a conflict of interest. Even if I got someone else to sponsor you, it would have my fingerprints all over it. You'd never make it past the review board."

Friend. That was the only thing Ellen heard. Her first impulse was to reject the thought. *Someone like him . . . friends with me?* But the more she thought about it, the more it made sense. The way he sought out her company, the way he defended her against an abusive boyfriend. Not to mention the fact that he saved her life countless times when it would have been easier to let her go . . .

He shot her a sideways look. "Are you mad at me?"

"Mad at you? How could I possibly be mad? You just told me you're my friend!"

"For all the good it does you."

"Friendship isn't about what you can *get* out of a person," she insisted. "Even if you could get me into the program, it wouldn't matter. There's no way I could afford it."

"Josh—" Carter started.

"Joshua has made it clear he's not going to support me. In fact, he's given me a deadline. If nothing happens by the end of the school year, he's leaving."

"And you?"

She sighed. "I don't know."

A crash came from upstairs.

"Maybe we should focus on something else. Like how the hell we're going to get out of here," Ellen suggested.

"All we have to do is wait until the morning," he informed her. "Nightgaunts are creatures of the Dreamlands. They can only take physical form when the world they're in dreams. Once people wake up, their hold on this world is severed."

"So we have to wait until New Jersey wakes up?"

Carter chuckled. "Pretty much."

"And until then?"

"Until then, we should get some sleep."

"They won't get us in our dreams?"

"Even if they could, I think the one upstairs would avoid you. You rang its bell. Hard." His eyes lingered on her. "You know, that was the bravest thing I've ever seen. You coming at that thing with a bat? That was seriously badass."

"You weren't so bad yourself. Standing in the doorway with a shotgun. You looked like a big-game hunter."

They smiled at each other.

Ellen felt a lightness she hadn't felt in a very long time.

She rose off the floor and headed toward a battered couch in the corner.

"What are you doing?" he asked.

"Like you said, we need to crash."

He nodded at the bed where he sat, and Angie still slept. "What's wrong with this?"

"I don't think your girlfriend would appreciate waking up and finding me in bed with you."

"She's not my girlfriend. And I don't care what Angie thinks. Get in the bed," he ordered her.

Ellen tried hard not to laugh.

"How many schoolgirls would sell their souls to hear you say that?"

"I'm serious, Ellen."

"Only if you get between us," she insisted.

When Carter hesitated, she pushed him in front of her. He gave her a strange look but obeyed. Ellen crawled onto the bed, turning away from him and curling into a tight ball.

She didn't think she could rest. Every time she closed her eyes, she saw Emilio Carranza's plane tumbling out of the sky. Then, slowly, the images lost their hold. They faded into darkness, and Ellen fell into a deep, exhausted sleep.

Chapter Seventeen

"**L**ook at this place, Andrew! You're the reason this happened! You brought darkness into my house!"

Angie was no longer the peaceful earth goddess. When they finally emerged from the basement and she saw the damage to her B&B, she transformed. Her eyes blazed as she lit into Carter. And he took the abuse. Carter reminded Ellen of Calvin Leonard, the fake bureaucrat, who visited the site of her ill-fated ghost-hunting expedition.

Along with his master, Solomon Reye, Ellen thought with a shiver.

This time, the damage went far beyond a roof. Angie's house was trashed. The nightgaunt had destroyed almost everything. The coffee tables, the china cabinet, the couches . . . all toppled and gouged by huge claws. Even the bags they left in the hall were shredded, her iPod smashed. Ellen gathered what was left of their belongings and carried them to the car. She knew they were useless, but she wasn't comfortable leaving their personal belongings behind.

Just in case Angie knows witchcraft.

When she passed Carter, he followed her outside.

Angie ran after them.

"I thought you were different, but nothing's changed," she ranted. "You're still a Jonah. You know that. Have you told her, huh? Have you told her what you are?"

Carter whirled around to face her.

"Jesus, Angie, what do you want me to do? I phoned it in. Miskatonic will pay for all the damages."

Ellen groaned. *Phoned it in. That's the last thing she wants to hear,* she thought as she put their things in the car.

"You know what, Andrew? Fuck you, fuck Miskatonic, and fuck that little girl wonder of yours," she snarled. Her next words were directed at Ellen. "You're doomed. You know that, don't you? If you stay with him, you're doomed."

Ellen slammed the back door shut. She moved to the driver's side of the car and peered over the roof at Angie. "I'm sorry for what happened here. I hope you can reopen soon."

"Finally, a proper apology."

"For God's sake. Don't be such a fucking martyr," Carter snapped. "You'll get a lot of money from Miskatonic. More than enough to fix up the place. And this place *does* need some work. Everything looks a little long in the tooth."

Angie's lips curled into a snarl, and she slapped him. The sound was crisp in the cold morning air. Like the crack of a whip.

Carter absorbed the blow without complaint.

He cocked his head and smirked, staring at his ex-girlfriend with flat hatred.

Ellen had never seen such a dark, disturbing look.

You do not want this man to be your enemy, she thought.

She could tell Angie was reaching the same conclusion.

"Get away from me. You get away from me, you son of a bitch," she said, her voice rising as Carter moved toward her.

"Andrew?" Ellen called out.

"What?" he responded without taking his eyes off Angie.

She gestured for his car keys. "We need to go."

He hesitated, glaring at his ex-girlfriend.

He tossed the keys to Ellen.

"I see you've made your choice," Angie announced.

"No. *You* made *your* choice," he growled. "You've reduced everything we learned to a joke. As something to . . . *amuse* people."

"Andrew?" Ellen called out again.

He snapped out of a haze. "What?"

"Let's go."

"Yes, Andrew. Do what your little girl wonder says. *Get out!*" Angie roared.

Ellen didn't bother to adjust the car seat. She wanted to leave before things got worse. As they drove off, she glanced in the rearview mirror. She half expected to see Angie chasing them. Wielding a knife. Or an axe. Or one of her gnome statues. But the woman just stood there, surveying her shattered kingdom.

"Why did she do that?" Carter's words were thick with hurt. "I mean, we've fought before, but she's never hit me."

Ellen glanced at him.

"Are you serious? You *really* don't know?"

"No, I don't. Enlighten me."

"You said she was old. Long in the tooth."

"I said her *place* was long in the tooth."

"She didn't hear it that way."

He fell silent and looked out the window.

When they reached the main road, she pulled over.

She dug into her pocket for her cell phone.

"What are you doing?" he demanded.

"I have to enter in our destination."

Carter got out of the car and slammed the door. It took her a few minutes to find the address. Once she entered it, she followed him outside.

The winter sun felt good on her face. After spending the night in a dank basement, Ellen was eager to get outside, to take a moment before they faced what was next. She walked down the empty road, enjoying the clear morning. The gravel crunched under her feet. The pine trees swayed, their bare limbs creaking in the wind.

She sat beside him on the hood.

"It's beautiful, isn't it?" she said.

"All strange places are," Carter replied, sounding distant.

"I'm sorry. For the way things ended between you and Angie."

He shrugged.

"Were you serious?"

Carter frowned. "Serious about what?"

"Each other."

"I thought about marrying her if that's what you mean."

"That's pretty serious." She held down her hair, which whipped wildly in the wind.

He shot her a sideways look.

"Aren't you going to ask me what she meant when she called me a Jonah?"

"A Jonah?" she echoed, confused. Then she remembered. Angie called him that when they were fighting. "People throw around a lot of names when they break up. They don't mean anything."

"A Jonah is someone who brings bad luck to a ship. Who dooms his fellow travelers to almost certain death."

"You're not a Jonah."

"That's rich, coming from someone who bitches and moans about being doomed."

"I told you before. What happens to me is not your fault."

"Are you sure? Are you absolutely sure I have nothing to do with it?" he demanded. Ellen noticed a strange glow in his eyes. "How much do you actually know about me?"

"What do you mean?"

"We're here. Out in the middle of nowhere. You seem to trust me. But what do you *really* know about me?"

"I—"

"Do you know how many people have died on me?"

"It doesn't matter. It's my job to stay alive, not yours."

"Twenty," he blurted, ignoring her response. "I have a higher body count than most serial killers."

Ellen was appalled, but not by the number.

"Jesus, Andrew, what's with the psycho act? You sound like you're proud."

"Maybe I am. Maybe I'm the one you should be afraid of."

"Why are you doing this?"

"Doing what?"

"Why are you trying to make me doubt you?"

His expression turned flat.

He looked at her the way he looked at Angie.

"Because you should wake up," he snarled. "You think I don't see?"

"What are you talking about?"

He leaned closer and murmured in her ear. "You're smart. And you're brave. But deep down, you're nothing but a school-girl with a crush."

The words pierced her like a spear, but Ellen held his gaze.

"Wow. You're burning a lot of bridges today, aren't you?" She breathed.

A crack appeared in the sky. At first, Ellen thought she was seeing things. The timing was too perfect. She and Carter breaking up the exact moment the world around them split . . .

Carter's eyes locked on the same spot.

He frowned as the fracture spiderwebbed, spreading like broken glass.

"What the hell?"

"*Espacio angosto*," Ellen whispered.

"Thin place," Carter replied.

The world swirled around them, shifting like a sand dune. One moment, it was a bright winter morning. The next, they were in the middle of a fierce summer storm.

Off in the distance, Ellen heard the cough of an engine.

A plane popped out of the bruised sky.

She read the words painted on the side.

Mexico-Excelsior M-SCOM.

"No. No. It can't be," she stammered. "This isn't possible."

"What?"

"That's his plane. That's Emilio Carranza's plane."

Electricity grew thick in the air. The atmosphere around her suddenly felt heavy. As if the world were trying to crush her.

A thought hit her with the force of a lightning strike.

The storm wasn't what brought him down.

She leaped off the hood of the car and ran toward the approaching plane.

"Don't look at the trees!" she screamed in Spanish. "Look up! Look up! The danger's above you!"

The plane roared over her head. She could see Emilio Carranza peering down from the cockpit. He was close, so close that she could see the grim expression on his face. He was shining a flashlight on the road, searching for a place to land.

"Look up! The danger is above you! In the sky! In the sky!"

The tragedy played itself out a long time ago. What happened couldn't be changed. Ellen knew that. She still ran after the doomed plane. Carter yelled at her, trying to pull her back, to bring her to the present.

Ellen ignored him.

A flash of lightning illuminated the sky.

That's when she saw it.

A nightgaunt dropped out of the clouds, its claws outstretched like a hawk closing on its prey. The monster latched onto the tail of the plane and pushed down. Carranza struggled to maintain control. The creature responded by lifting the plane's tail and letting go. The plane flipped. Its wings sheared off with a sickening crack. Carranza tumbled into the trees, blazing a grim trail through the forest. A moment later, a fireball flared in the distance.

Ellen chased the orange glare, vaulting over rocks and fallen trees.

The crumpled plane was empty when she reached it. The forest around the site was on fire, but the rain came down so hard, the flames could only splutter.

"Señor Carranza! Señor Carranza! *Dondé estás?*" she shouted. *Where are you?*

Carter crashed through the trees.

He surveyed the wreckage. He looked stunned. Dazed.

"Help me. Please, help me," a voice called out over the pouring rain.

Carter stiffened. "Wait. He's not dead? He wasn't killed instantly?"

A chill ran up her spine. Even in the pounding rain, she could see drag marks in the mud.

"I thought he was," she murmured.

Ellen glanced down at her cell phone: 39°46'38.6" N 74°37'56.6" W. This was the place. These were the coordinates she found on a state forest website. The exact spot where Emilio Carranza's plane crashed. Where he died on impact. Yet she could see him crawling away from the crash, his legs trailing behind him. He clutched a metal flashlight. The light bounced off the trees.

Carter grabbed her arm before she could head into the clearing.

He pointed at the ground.

At first, she saw nothing. Then she spotted a small stone object stamped into the earth. A few feet away, there was another stone. And another. They surrounded the dying man and his plane.

Carter shook his head.

"It's a trap. We walked right into a ritual circle."

"What do we do?"

His eyes met hers. She saw no animosity, no sign of the storm that had just torn them apart. "I don't know. Just keep an eye out."

For what? she almost said.

Ellen swallowed the words.

She didn't want to know.

Andrew Carter led her across the muddy field. Everywhere she looked, there were magical stones.

One step. One wrong step, and . . .

Ellen looked back at the spot where she and Carter entered.

The stones of the circle narrowed and shot out in parallel lines. They winked as they trailed off into the darkness.

Dread climbed up her back.

This isn't a ritual circle.

It's a ritual runway.

"The Yaqui," Ellen gasped.

When she looked back, the circle had closed.

The way out was gone.

"My dear, my dear. Are you there?" Emilio Carranza called out in Spanish.

A few feet away, a figure squirmed in the mud.

Ellen sighed.

There's nothing left for you to do. Just help him.

She knelt in the mud and took his hand.

"I'm here," she whispered.

Andrew Carter joined them, shifting nervously behind her.

Carranza looked up at them. His face was mangled. Shredded. He looked like something out of a nightmare. But when Ellen gazed into his eyes, she saw only softness. Softness and fear.

"Close. I came so close to getting out," he said, gasping. "He trapped me. He trapped me, and he won't let me out."

"Who trapped you?" Ellen asked.

"I did," a voice growled behind her.

A cold hand gripped her heart.

She leaped to her feet. "No. No, no, no, no," she chanted.

Andrew Carter was gone.

Solomon Reye stood in his place.

He favored her with a low, courtly bow. Ellen felt the same pulse of attraction as when he crossed the stage—when he sauntered so casually into her world.

She started to move toward him and stopped.

What is wrong with you? a voice screamed at her. *He killed Carter's student, he kidnapped Martha, and now . . .*

Ellen spun around wildly.

"Where's Carter?" she demanded.

More questions filled her head.

How long? How long has Carter been gone? How long has Solomon been with me?

"Which Carter are you talking about?" Solomon Reye drawled. "You seem to have the attention of both men."

"My Carter. Andrew Carter."

His lips curled into a twisted smile.

"Such loyalty. Especially toward a man who won't remember you," he teased. "Don't worry. My nightgaunt is keeping him company."

"You're lying."

"I assure you, I'm not."

"Let him go."

"You're not in a position to bargain."

"Yes, I am. I'm your queen. You know that now. I think you knew all along. Why else would you pursue me with such . . . vigor?"

Ellen took a deep, steadying breath.

"Here's what's going to happen. You're going to let Andrew Carter go. If you don't, I'm going to run. And you'll have to peek down every rabbit hole to find me."

Solomon Reye smiled at her.

"How? How did I not know you're the one? Such spirit. Such resistance," he marveled. "Well, at least I won't waste my time on your Carter."

"Carter? You mean Andrew Carter was—"

"What I seek has nothing to do with gender."

A voice boomed in Ellen's head—the loudest psychic broadcast she'd ever heard. *This. This is the key. This is the key.* She looked at Emilio Carranza just in time to see him throw his metal flashlight at the magical barrier. The circle shattered. Ellen didn't know whether that ended Solomon's hold on her. She didn't care. She ran for the stone border. Out of the corner of her eye, she saw Emilio Carranza. His arms were stretched out. His hands shaking. Imploring.

Don't leave me here.

She reached out to him, letting his ghost melt into her body.

When she jumped over the stones, the world changed. It was a cold winter day again.

Solomon Reye howled. His white-hot rage bounced off the treetops.

Well, I must be doing something right, she thought as she raced toward the road.

She stumbled into the clearing where the plane had crashed.

A large granite monolith towered over them. Numbers were etched into the stone:

39°46'38.6" N 74°37'56.6"W.

His memorial, she thought.

She jerked as Emilio Carranza left her body.

He stood in front of the monument in full flight gear. He looked young. Young and incredibly dashing.

He bowed as she ran past him.

Ellen wanted to stop, to say goodbye. She suspected he would be the last friendly face she would see for a while. But she knew if she did, she would lose whatever advantage Carranza gave her.

"Hurry," he urged her. "Fly, fly."

Andrew Carter still stood by the car. He looked bored, like someone waiting for a tow truck. He didn't see the nightgaunt hovering over him. Ellen screamed as she hit the road. He didn't see her. He didn't even respond when she ran up to him.

"Andrew!"

She grabbed him and pushed him against the car. She shook him. Tugged his hair. Andrew Carter was cold, unresponsive. *A corpse,* she thought as she gazed into his blank eyes. *Or maybe it's me. Maybe I'm already dead.* "Andrew, please. Please, please, please—"

"He can't hear you," Solomon informed her.

Ellen spotted a gun inside Carter's coat.

She grabbed it.

"I told you. He can't cross over," Solomon said as he walked up to them. "He's only here because I want him here. The man's useless."

"No, he's not."

"Watch." He grabbed Carter and yanked his head back. Solomon pressed a knife to his throat, hard enough to make a dent in his skin. Carter didn't react. "You see? The poor bastard doesn't even know he's about to die."

"Stop it."

When Solomon showed no signs of letting him go, Ellen cocked the gun and put it to her head. "I said stop."

He snorted. "You wouldn't dare."

"I will!"

"Andrew Carter means that much to you?"

"He does," she said, her voice breaking.

He does, she thought in silent wonder. *Dear God, when did that happen?*

"If he dies, I'm going with him," she insisted.

"You don't mean it."

"I do! I'm serious! Dead serious!"

"Dead serious," he repeated with a chuckle.

"Let Andrew go. Don't hurt him. If you do that, I'll come with you."

"No more scurrying down rabbit holes?"

"No more scurrying down rabbit holes," Ellen agreed.

Solomon lowered the knife from Andrew Carter's throat.

"Fair enough," he said after a few moments. He shoved Carter into the invisible border between the two worlds. Ellen tensed, expecting the wall to shatter like it did with Carranza. The barrier bent. Carter popped out on the other side.

He squinted into the morning sunlight, looking confused.

"Give me the gun," Solomon commanded. When she hesitated, he sighed. "I told you, I'm not going to hurt him."

"Or your nightgaunt. I don't want your nightgaunt to hurt him."

"Nothing will hurt your precious Carter," he assured her.

Ellen was far from convinced. She had seen enough movies to know the dangers of making deals with the devil.

She opened the gun and emptied the bullets on the road. Solomon Reye chuckled when she handed him the weapon.

"My, aren't you the smart one."

"I have my moments."

"Too bad this isn't one of them."

He tossed the gun at Carter. It skittered across the road, landing at Carter's feet and snapping him out of his trance. His eyes widened when he saw her. Ellen looked down and saw that she was wearing a black gown. A gown made of crow's feathers. *My wedding dress,* she thought as Carter struggled to make sense of what he was seeing.

"I'm giving him a glimpse. Something he will forget," Solomon said softly in her ear. "Well, almost forget. I'm going to leave him with a little piece of you. Just enough to give him nightmares."

She closed her eyes and reached out psychically to Carter.

Andrew, listen to me. I'm alive. I'm on the other side. Find me.

Ellen wanted to move closer, to pull him into her arms and tell him not to forget. She resisted the urge. She didn't want to give Solomon any reason to hurt him.

Find me. Do you hear me? Find me, Andrew!

"It's time, my dear." Solomon's words oozed into her brain like a drug.

The nightgaunt landed in front of her and spread its wings.

Ellen surrendered to the darkness.

Chapter Eighteen

The entire world swayed beneath her. Ellen's eyelids fluttered, but she didn't open them. She let the world reach her through her other senses. She took in the mingled smell of salt air and damp wood. Heard the muffled thump of feet over her head. The clanging of a bell.

A ship, she thought, *I'm on a ship.*

It was a strange choice. The Barrens had its fair share of lakes and rivers, but why was she on a ship? If she was injured and needed medical care, why not choose a faster form of transportation? An ambulance or a helicopter? Finally, curiosity forced her to open her eyes. She lay in a narrow bed. All around her were crates, ropes, and barrels. Candles flickered in smoky glass lanterns, throwing off murky light.

Three images flashed through her head.

Solomon Reye. Andrew. The nightgaunt.

Ellen sat up.

She banged her head on the bed above her.

"Ow. Shit!"

A figure stirred in the shadows.

"You're awake. It's about time."

A man stepped forward. He had dark hair, cold blue eyes, and a beard. He was dressed like someone's romantic idea of a pirate.

Despite his outfit, Ellen recognized him immediately.

"You're Randolph Carter."

The man stiffened.

"Where am I?" she asked.

"You're on a ship in the Cerenarian Sea."

"The Cerenarian Sea?" Ellen frowned. She knew the Pacific, the Atlantic, and the Mediterranean. Her knowledge of seas and oceans ended there. "Where's that? Between Japan and Russia?"

He gave her a withering look.

"You're in the Dreamlands."

"How did I get here?"

"You fell out of the sky. Just like Icarus."

Ellen shivered. She thought of the picture Solomon Reye left in her room. The boy falling into the water. The ship sailing past him, the crew unaware of the drama being played out.

"We were on our way to Celephais when we saw you," he informed her. "You made quite a splash. You must have fallen a long way."

"Only from New Jersey."

"New Jersey? New Jersey as in America?"

She heard the eagerness in his voice. Somehow, it made him less intimidating. "New Jersey as in America. The Pine Barrens, to be more exact."

"What were you doing there?"

The words came out in a torrent. Andrew Carter. Emilio Carranza. Solomon Reye summoning a gateway to the Dreamlands. Randolph sat and listened. Ellen thought she saw him cringe when she mentioned Solomon, but she couldn't be sure. She was still getting used to the Dreamlands. Everything seemed blurry—as if the world had yet to define itself. When she finished her strange tale, Randolph got up and moved closer, shining a lamp in her face.

Ellen shied away from the light.

"I thought I recognized you," he said. "You're that girl I took to the Gateway."

"My name is Ellen. Ellen Logan."

She offered him her hand.

He stared at it.

"You can't expect me to remember your name. A lot of people drift in and out of here. Most of them looking for me."

Ellen opened her mouth to say something sarcastic. Then she remembered what her Carter, the other Carter, once told her about the weight of his reputation.

"The Carter Curse," she murmured.

"What?"

"Your grandson calls it the Carter Curse. That people expect him to do amazing things because of who he is." She stared at Randolph, trying to think back, to remember what she knew about him.

All she had were stories.

Legends.

He shifted under the weight of her stare. "What are you doing?"

"I'm trying to remember what I read about you." She paused, waiting for Lovecraft 101 to kick in. "You were born in Boston in 1894. When you were nine, you traveled to the Dreamlands for the very first time. You made a few more trips, but World War I robbed you of your ability to travel there freely. You spent your life trying to find another way in. On October 7, 1928, you finally found a physical passage in a cave near your family homestead in, um . . ."

"Elm Mountain," he whispered.

"You disappeared. They discovered your car nearby, covered in strange markings. The police suspected foul play, but they never found your body. Eventually, the case went cold."

"I'm glad they're teaching you something at Miskatonic."

"You came back in 1932, disguised as an Indian mystic. To settle your estate—"

His face contorted into a mask of pain. "I don't want to talk about that."

They were interrupted by the thunder of approaching footsteps.

A nightgaunt appeared in the doorway. Ellen scrambled out of bed, clutching a sheet to her body. Since she tumbled into the sea, she assumed she was naked. She was relieved to discover she was wearing a pair of wool pants and a white shirt. The clothes of a cabin boy.

At least you're not wearing a feathered gown, she thought as she cowered in the corner.

The creature seemed just as disturbed by her presence.

It turned to Randolph.

A frantic buzzing filled her head.

Wait a minute. It sounds like the one I . . .

"Mr. Poe says you attacked him," Carter blurted.

"Mr. Poe?"

He nodded to the creature beside him.

Ellen gawked. "They have names?"

"Of course they have names! What did you think?" Randolph spluttered. "He says you attacked him. In a garden. While the gnomes watched."

"Gnomes?" Ellen looked at the nightgaunt. "Wait. That was you?"

"He said you hurt him."

"I had no choice. He attacked Andrew."

"Andrew?"

"Your grandson, goddamn it!" she exploded.

"All right, that's it," Randolph snapped. "You come falling out of the sky with an outrageous tale. You tried to kill one of my crewmates. I'm throwing you back into the sea. Let someone else deal with you."

Randolph yanked her out of her safe space.

Ellen fought him as he dragged her out of the room. He was stunned by the strength of her resistance. Randolph Carter was used to women being submissive. Delicate. But no matter how hard she struggled, she couldn't break free. Like the other Carter—*her Carter,* she thought—he was strong. Once they reached the deck and she saw the rest of his nightgaunt crew, Ellen wilted. There were too many of them for her to fight.

He hauled her to the railing of the ship.

I'm going into the ocean, she thought as her feet dangled in space. *Just like the painting.*

A loud voice boomed over their heads: "Bring her to me."

Randolph was so startled he almost dropped her. "What?"

"Bring her to me. And treat her well, or there will be consequences."

"You're kidding me. You've got to be kidding me," he snarled, but he pulled her back from the edge.

"Who is that? Are you Solomon Reye?" she called out.

"No."

"Good. Because I've had enough of that fucking moron," she yelled at the empty sky.

Randolph hissed in disapproval.

The invisible presence chuckled.

"I look forward to meeting you, my dear."

"Who was that?" Ellen asked once the voice went away. Randolph said nothing. He dropped her on the deck and pulled aside a nightgaunt. "I don't understand. Why won't you help me? Why won't you tell me anything?"

He turned to her.

"Because I'm not your guide," he seethed. Now that the invisible voice made it clear Randolph was responsible for Ellen, he was furious. "God, I'm sick and tired of people wandering in here, begging for help. You know, when I first came here, I didn't expect help."

"You still got it."

"What?"

"A lot of people and things helped in your journey through the Dreamlands," she offered. "H. P. Lovecraft wrote all about your adventures."

He scowled. "H. P. Lovecraft? You mean Howard? The strange recluse who lived with his aunt on Angell Street?"

Ellen tried hard to contain her excitement. "You knew him?"

"He was a sad man. A sad, deluded man."

"You know, they say the same thing about you."

"Do they?"

She gazed out at the flat, slate-gray water.

She wondered what sort of things lurked beneath its murky surface.

A chill crawled up her spine.

You almost found out.

Ellen glanced at Randolph.

"Do you have any books or maps I can look at?" she asked.

He nodded at the hold. "There's a library below decks. You can stay out of my way there."

Ellen bit her tongue. She longed to put this arrogant man in his place. But what was the point? Once they reached their destination, she and Randolph would go their separate ways.

She retreated to the silence of the library, where she could hide.

And figure out what to do next.

Chapter Nineteen

Ellen flipped through every book in Randolph Carter's library. It did her no good. She was fluent in Spanish and English, knew a smattering of Russian.

All his books were in Latin.

She sat back and let out a long sigh.

Uncle Joshua had urged her to learn Latin. He argued it was the key to the ancient world, a vital part of any education. Ellen resisted his appeals. To her, Latin was a dead branch on the linguistic tree. Now she regretted it. Ellen pushed the thick books aside. *If I get home, I'll take a crash course,* she promised herself.

Not if, when. When. When.

It was too late. The poisonous thought was free.

Ellen put her head on the table. Her time in the Barrens already seemed impossibly distant. Angie's Oasis was a dream—and this, the reality. She wasn't even sure where the waking world was. Backward, forward, up, down?

"You're too ambitious. You dive into the water without knowing how to swim," Randolph said from the doorway.

Ellen jumped. "Andrew said almost the same thing," she told him once she recovered. "He said I'm always throwing myself into the deep end."

"He sounds like a wise man." He fixed her with a sideways look. "Are the two of you lovers?"

She shook her head.

"Hmm. Interesting." He rummaged through the warren of cubbyholes above his desk, picked up a scroll, and sat down beside her.

He spread a map out on the table.

"Let's start with the basics. This is the Dreamlands."

Ellen leaned in to get a closer look.

The map was magnificent, a detailed, handcrafted work straight out of the Middle Ages. It showed a vast inland sea. The stretch of water reminded Ellen of the Mediterranean. Almost all the cities hugged the coast. As the world spread out to the far corners, things got hazier. *Here be monsters,* Ellen thought as she stared at the fanciful creatures that lurked on the edges. A distant universe hovered above the strange world. She recognized some landmarks. The moon. Saturn. Mars. Polaris.

Carter punched a town on the northern coast.

"My crew and I started from here."

"In-ga-nok." She sounded out the name.

"You know it?"

"No. The only places I'm familiar with are Leng and Kadath." She looked at the tall mountain labeled *Kadath.* It reminded her of Mount Doom in *Lord of the Rings.* "Lovecraft said you went there on one of your dream quests."

"*Leng? Kadath?* The man's an absolute lunatic. Why on earth would I go there?" The coldness seeped back into him. "God, is Lovecraft what passes for Flatland history?"

"Flatland history? What's Flatland?" A fierce blush rushed to her cheeks. "Oh. I get it. It's an insult. Like calling someone trailer trash or a redneck."

"A red-*what?*"

Ellen sighed. "Some things never change, do they?"

"Did you really expect them to?"

"No, I guess not." She bit down on her lip. There was no point arguing with this man. "So where are we headed? You mentioned somewhere named Cellophane?"

"Celephais." He pointed at a city on the southern shore. "We're going here. King Kuranes wants to meet you. Which is convenient since we were headed there anyway."

"King Kuranes?"

"The voice in the sky. The man who kept me from throwing you overboard, remember? Celephais is his city."

"Is he really a king?" she asked.

Randolph carefully weighed his response. "He thinks he's a king, but he's not. Not really. He's more like Emperor Norton."

"Who's Emperor Norton?"

"For God's sake! Is there anything you *do* know?"

Ellen looked at the pile of books and the secrets they contained. *So much to learn,* she thought. Her eyes filled with tears. She wanted nothing more than to escape this world, with its strange maps and strange creatures.

She hit herself in the leg.

Wake up, she pleaded. *Wake up. Wake up.*

Randolph grabbed her wrist.

The next time he spoke, his voice was quieter. Gentler.

"Emperor Norton was a man in San Francisco who decided he was the king of America," he explained. "He demanded the US government be dissolved. He printed his own currency. Appointed officials. He even tried to pass and enforce his own laws. You would think that someone like that would get arrested. Thrown into jail."

"Or an insane asylum," Ellen offered.

Randolph looked at her.

For the first time, he seemed interested in her world.

"Are there still insane asylums?" he asked.

"They're called mental institutions."

"Mental—" he started but pulled back before he could get distracted. "Anyway, the people in San Francisco didn't arrest him or commit him. They treated Emperor Norton with respect. They even honored his currency. When he died, thirty thousand people attended his funeral. He was hailed as a visionary. A great dreamer."

"And King Kuranes is like that?"

"When Kuranes arrived in the Dreamlands, he was poor. Destitute. But here . . ." Randolph paused. Ellen could hear respect in his voice. "Humans didn't have a foothold in the Dreamlands until he came along. He created a place for us, a haven where people could arrive from the Flatlands. He made it into the magnificent city that it is. And it is incredible."

"I can't wait to see it," Ellen said.

A long silence settled between them.

"What's my grandson like?" Randolph blurted.

Ellen wondered how much she should tell him about the other side. Was she betraying *her* Carter's trust by telling Randolph his secrets?

"Andrew's very intelligent." She paused. "But he's also deeply insecure. Troubled."

"Why?"

"Because he can't get here."

Randolph frowned. "On my ship?"

"To the Dreamlands. He can't cross over."

Something shifted inside her.

Ellen closed her eyes.

She had a brief vision, a flash of people walking in a line, deep in the forest. *A search party,* she thought. Ellen watched them advance, scanning the ground for any trace, any clue to her whereabouts. She wondered whether they would find anything. Was her body still in the Barrens? Was she freezing to death in a ditch somewhere?

"No. You crossed over completely. There's nothing for them to find."

When she opened her eyes again, Randolph had moved closer.

He pressed his face into her hair and took a long, deep breath.

Ellen fought hard not to shiver.

"You seem so real," she said.

"I *am* real. I'm also married," he mumbled, more to himself than her.

Ellen tried to hide her amazement.

"You? Married?"

He cocked his head. "I even had children. Where do you think Andrew came from?"

"Yes. Of course. It's just . . . Lovecraft never said anything about you having a family."

"Lovecraft wouldn't. That's not the part of my life he was interested in."

"What's your wife's name?"

His eyes locked on a spot just above Ellen's shoulder. "Olivia."

Ellen turned and saw a small photograph on the wall. "That's her?"

"It was the only thing I was able to carry into this world."

She walked over to the picture. The woman in the photograph surprised her. She was not the prim matron Ellen expected, her bookish features frozen in a Puritan grimace. Olivia was a vision, an early-twentieth-century rebel. Her dark hair was short, shaped into a bob. She wore a thin gown draped with pearls. *A flapper,* Ellen thought as she gazed into the woman's dark eyes. Her head was tossed back, and she beamed with delight. Looking at such an exotic creature made Ellen feel bland. Washed out.

"She's beautiful." Ellen turned back to Randolph. "Is she nice?"

"When she wants to be."

Ellen knew what that meant.

She could see the hunger in Randolph's eyes. Raw, sexual hunger.

"When was the last time you saw her?" she asked.

"It's been a long time. A very long time." He moved closer.

Randolph Carter crossed over physically, too. We could—

"Yes, we could," he agreed.

Ellen backed away. She felt like a mouse caught in a trap. "My loyalty is to Andrew, not you."

"Part of me is him," he purred.

Ellen wanted to believe him. She wanted desperately to believe him. But she knew doing anything with Randolph would be a mistake. A big mistake.

"You're not him. You're just a stranger who looks like him."

"And you're a tease. You're no better than her." He jerked his head toward the picture.

"You don't know me. You don't know the first thing about me."

"And I don't want to." Randolph's words were acid.

"Oh, you wanted to *know* me a minute ago."

He stared at her, shocked.

He's not used to women talking this way, she thought as she waited for him to respond.

"Please, you're a child. You're not half the woman Olivia is."

"I wouldn't want to be the woman Olivia is," she shot back, trying to sound defiant.

The insult still hit its mark.

Child.

Schoolgirl with a crush.

Two men, same insult.

"As soon as we dock in Celephais, I want you off my ship," Randolph commanded. "Until then, I don't want to hear you or see you. If I do, I don't give a damn what Kuranes wants. I'll throw you overboard. Do I make myself clear?"

"Crystal." She sighed as she sat down on the bench. She thought their conversation was over, so she was confused when he lingered. "Aye, aye, Captain. I understand. I get it."

He gave her a curt little nod. Then he was gone. Back to the helm. To guide his ship toward the city of dreams.

Chapter Twenty

The smell of spice drifted out from the harbor of Celephais. Ellen breathed in the rich, exotic scent. After days of languishing below deck, she found a way around Randolph's demand that he neither see nor hear her. As the ship approached Celephais, she noticed the nightgaunts donned long, monk-like robes. Ellen cornered the nightgaunt Randolph called Mr. Poe. Through sign language and basic psychic communication, she managed to borrow a spare robe from him. Even before she put it on, she knew she would look ridiculous. She was much shorter than the average nightgaunt. And Mr. Poe was far from average. The robe dragged behind her like the train of a wedding gown. But it satisfied Randolph's requirements.

The moment Celephais appeared on the horizon, Ellen forgot all about her ridiculous appearance. She'd never visited a city in the Dreamlands. All her previous trips were to the wilderness, to the outskirts of the parallel world. She was unprepared for the brilliance of it, the sheer, unmitigated perfection.

Celephais was a magnificent walled city. Its limestone ramparts climbed the hills and spilled onto the floodplain below, spreading to the very edge of the Cerenarian Sea. The city was a crazy quilt of culture. Tall minarets stretched toward the sky, their slim forms competing with the spires of cathedrals; the onion domes of a Russian Orthodox church; the clean, elegant lines of Jewish synagogues. She saw evidence of older forms of worship—Greek temples, Assyrian altars, stone formations that looked like Stonehenge. Every religion, every cult, had a place here. What impressed her was how balanced the city was. Celephais should have been a hopeless jumble, a jarring mix of competing beliefs.

Instead, the city blended competing cultures and made it look effortless.

Randolph joined her at the railing.

"Give me one good reason why I shouldn't throw you in the water."

"Because not letting me see Celephais would be heartless. And even you aren't that cruel."

"Are you sure?"

"If a part of you is my Carter, then yes. I'm sure," she replied.

Randolph fell silent.

Ellen slipped out of the robe. She saw no point in keeping up the charade.

Her eyes swept the horizon.

"What do you think of Celephais?" he asked.

"It's beautiful. Absolutely gorgeous," she replied. "It reminds me of Istanbul."

"Istanbul? What's Istanbul?"

"Oh God, what was it called before? Istanbul not . . . Constantinople," she sang the last words, a verse from her favorite They Might Be Giants song. "That's what it's called now. Constantinople."

Randolph smirked. "I suppose that's not a coincidence. William loved Turkey."

"William?" Ellen asked.

"King Kuranes. He was a citizen of the world. He squandered his inheritance as he searched for the central truth behind mythology. The universal theme underlying all religions."

"Your grandson does the same sort of thing. I mean, searching for the central truth behind things, not squandering his inheritance. He teaches art history at Miskatonic."

"Does he really?" Randolph replied without much interest. He watched a small boat sailing out of the harbor. It was a small Greek war galley with painted eyes on the bow.

As Ellen watched it approach, it winked at her.

Ellen's breath caught in her throat. She backed away, feeling a tingle of unease. She studied the men on board. They wore floppy hats and brightly colored uniforms.

Their outfits looked familiar.

"Who are they?"

"The harbor police."

"Harbor police?" She remembered where she saw the uniforms. In Vatican City. At Saint Peter's. "You mean the Swiss Guard."

"I beg your pardon?"

"They look like the Swiss Guard. You know, the soldiers who protect the pope?" Ellen wondered whether the Swiss Guard existed in 1928. She was about to explain when Randolph smiled.

"And William was supposed to be a lapsed Catholic," Randolph said.

"I guess he's not lapsed in his dreams."

His smile vanished when the police headed toward his ship.

Ellen withdrew from the railing and dropped to her knees.

"What are you doing?" Randolph demanded.

"Permission to come aboard, sir?" a voice hailed from the boat.

"Don't let them. It's a setup," Ellen hissed from her hiding place.

"What's the nature of your business?" Randolph called to the other vessel.

"Just a standard inspection."

"They're lying. Don't let them on the ship," Ellen pleaded.

"I have no choice."

"You're the captain. You can do anything you want."

"I'm not jeopardizing my ship for a Flatlander!"

Ellen moved away from him. She spotted an axe embedded in the deck. She grabbed it and scuttled behind some crates.

She listened as Randolph tried to negotiate with the men.

"I have papers from King Kuranes granting me special passage."

"Those privileges have been suspended. Permission to come aboard, sir?" the official said again. This time, there was only the illusion of civility.

Ellen heard Randolph hesitate, then let out a long sigh.

"Permission granted."

"Heave to!" the captain of the other boat shouted.

Ellen watched as the vessels slid into place.

Ropes were thrown between the ships.

A ladder was attached to the deck, and three large men marched on board.

Randolph tensed as the men approached him. This was *not* standard procedure. Still, he offered the officials a thick stack of papers.

"I hope we can get this cleared up quickly. I'm already late coming from Inganok," Randolph said.

The officials refused to take the papers Randolph offered.

"We have reason to believe that you have an illegal passenger aboard this ship," one of them announced.

"My entire crew is illegal."

"We demand that you surrender her."

"Her? The Flatlander? The one who landed on my ship? I threw her overboard. She stank like rotten fish." Randolph sniffed the air in disgust. "God, you can still smell her."

"Search the vessel," the leader of the guard ordered.

For a moment, Randolph considered resisting.

He shrugged and stepped back.

"Fine."

The moment he gave permission, men swarmed the boat. Ellen knew it was only a matter of time before she was discovered. She might elude one or two of Kuranes's men, but not ten. And she wouldn't be able to hold them off with an axe. She peeked around the corner at Randolph. He stared at her with open hatred. *He won't help me. The only thing he cares about is his cargo. And maybe his crew.* The thought was enough to send her racing toward the ship's railing. *If I jump into the sea, maybe I can swim to—*

King Kuranes's lead guard popped out in front of her. He held out his arm and smacked her into the deck.

Ellen's vision swam.

The creature that peered down at her was huge, with a tiger face and long tusks. Its glowing yellow eyes burned into hers.

Ellen knew what it was. They haunted her dreams when she and Joshua lived in India.

"Rakshasa."

The creature offered her a leering smile, a twisted expression that reminded her of . . . of . . . *Solomon.*

Solomon.

The name bounced in her brain.

These are Solomon's men.

The creature licked its bloodred lips.

"Oh, I wish I could eat you. You would be a tasty little morsel. But the boss wants you in one piece."

Ellen scrambled backward on the deck, reaching for the axe.

The creature kicked it away.

"Come, come, my little morsel," it clucked. "Let's be friends."

The creature lunged for her. Just as she felt heat searing her skin, there was a blur of movement. The demon tensed. Surprise lit up its yellow eyes. Then it began to twitch. The thing turned and raised its claws, trying to ward off the attack. It was no use. An invisible force tore the thing apart. As she watched the demon thrash, Ellen remembered her first adventure, when she found a whistle that summoned an army of the dead. Her enemy perished in a flurry of rage.

Now, the same thing was happening here.

Am I doing this, she wondered, *or is someone—*

Randolph hauled her to her feet.

Ellen turned and smacked him in the chest.

"Don't touch me!" she spat. "You betrayed me! You set me up!"

"Traitor? Set you . . . I have no loyalty to you, you Flatland—"

Randolph stopped mid-rant.

More demons boiled off the ship.

She scrambled for the axe. Just as her fingers closed on it, she was hit from behind.

Ellen felt like a weed being torn from the ground. Suddenly, the deck was too far beneath her. Her feet hung in space. She felt funny. Not funny *strange*, just . . . funny.

Out of the corner of her eye, she saw a swishing tail.

"Mr. Poe?" she whispered.

A buzzing filled her head, a soft vibration that tickled her brain.

A giggle burst from her lips. *I'm Peter Pan,* she thought as she spread her arms. For a moment, she savored the pure joy of flying.

Then the nightgaunt threw her into the rigging of the ship.

Ellen hit the rope ladder. Her fingers scrabbled for a handhold as she dangled between the world of air and sea.

Once she was secure, Ellen glanced over her shoulder and looked at the deck.

The rest of Solomon's men shape-shifted into Rakhasa. The nightgaunts rushed forward to engage them. So did

Randolph. He picked up her axe and plunged into the fray. Ellen scrambled up the rope ladder to the crow's nest. She kept her eyes fixed firmly on the horizon, away from the battle below. She didn't like Randolph Carter, but she didn't want to see him die.

Other ships sailed toward Randolph's vessel. They blew their horns, trying to draw attention to what was happening just outside Celephais.

War, she thought as she tumbled into the crow's nest. *This is a declaration of war.*

She just reached safety when the voice in the sky spoke.

"Jump."

"What?"

"*Jump.*"

Ellen peered at the deck. It was at least fifty feet below her. And wide. If she failed to clear the ship, she would be a grease spot on the deck.

"Jump! *Now!*" the voice screamed.

Ellen scrambled onto the lip of the crow's nest.

"God help me," she whispered as she hurled herself into space.

She felt a sudden jerk.

Then nothing.

Chapter Twenty-One

The world slammed into her. Hard. Ellen curled into a tight ball, trying to protect herself as she hit the ground. She smelled trees and flowers. The pungent mixture of compost and fertile soil. Her mind stuttered with hope. *The jump. The jump from Randolph's ship. It must have been enough. It must have been enough to send me back to the waking world. To the Pine Barrens.*

It took a moment for her rational mind to catch up.

You left the Barrens in the winter. This is not the Barrens in winter.

She tried to negotiate, to tell herself that maybe enough time had passed that it was spring in the . . . what did Randolph call it? The Flatlands.

She opened her eyes.

A nightgaunt loomed over her.

So did an old man. He had a sweet elfin face. Like a lovable uncle all the kids adored. A man who never forgot the joy of being young.

"Thank you for bringing her to me, Mr. Poe," he said.

"Mr. Poe? Does he—"

Belong to you. The words almost spilled from her lips.

"Does he work for you?"

He chuckled. "In a way."

"Is he the one who told me to jump off the ship?"

"No. *I* did. Mr. Poe caught you and brought you here. To my palace," he said.

She suddenly realized who stood in front of her. "You! You're King Kuranes!"

She scrambled back, alarmed.

"Your men stormed Randolph's ship. They attacked him. And his crew. Right on the edge of the harbor."

"Please, dear, please. Settle down," Kuranes urged her. "Those weren't my men. You were right. It was a setup. They were creatures sent by . . . what does he call himself now?"

"Solomon Reye?"

The man wrinkled his nose. "Yes. Solomon Reye."

"Oh my god, Randolph! He needs your help! The last time I saw him—"

"I assure you, he's fine. He's a very resourceful man." He knelt beside her and brushed off dirt and shards of broken pottery. *A garden,* she thought. *Mr. Poe must have dropped me onto a rooftop garden.* "Do you think you can stand?"

"I think so."

The man grabbed her arm and helped her to her feet. He peered at her curiously, as if she were an exotic animal. "What's your name, my dear?"

"I'm Ellen. Ellen Logan." She offered him her hand. A piece of a rubbery plant fell from her arm. "Oh God, I'm so sorry. I've ruined your garden."

There was a commotion on the stairs. Kuranes motioned for her to get behind him. A moment later, Randolph burst into the peaceful oasis—with a pair of nightgaunts on his heels. Ellen assumed they were Kuranes's men.

Kuranes's real men, she corrected herself.

"Goddamn it, Will, what's the point of living in your little kingdom if you can't protect your own city?" Randolph shouted. When he saw Ellen, his face turned red. He marched up to Kuranes, standing toe to toe with the leader of Celephais. "My ship was seized. My crew threatened. And all for some little Flatland—"

"Her name's Ellen," Kuranes interrupted.

"I don't care what her name is."

Kuranes grabbed Randolph by the collar of his shirt. In an instant, the king no longer looked like a mild-mannered gardener. He seemed to expand, filling the space around him.

"I asked you to do two simple things," he thundered. "Bring her to me. And treat her well. And you did neither."

"She's here, isn't she? And she's fine."

"You think she's fine? Look at her!"

Ellen examined herself. Bits of plant hung off her. She was smeared with dirt and blood. And one of her shoes lay on the floor a few feet away. Ellen scurried over and grabbed it. She didn't know why, but she felt naked without it.

"She's fine," Randolph insisted again.

He sounded less sure.

Ellen thought she heard a glimmer of sympathy.

It means nothing, she told herself as she put on her shoe. *He's just scared of Kuranes.*

The leader of Celephais turned to her.

"Why don't you clean up and get some rest? We'll talk later. Over dinner," Kuranes offered. It wasn't a suggestion. He was telling her what to do. She saw no point in resisting. When she stood, more clods of dirt spattered onto the floor. Ellen was mortified. "God, I'm sorry. I'm so, so sorry about your plants."

"No need . . . Ellen, right?"

"Right."

"Ellen, Jeffrey will show you to your room."

Ellen jumped as one of Kuranes's servants materialized. She looked at Randolph. He didn't bother to hide his thoughts.

Go away. We have serious business to discuss.

"Fuck you, you arrogant prick," she spat before she realized Kuranes might misunderstand. "I meant him, not you."

Kuranes smiled.

"Oh, I know who you meant. We'll see you at dinner, my dear. You can catch us up on everything that's happened in the waking world."

⟡

Ellen studied herself in the mirror and cringed. *I look ridiculous.* Kuranes not only demanded her presence at dinner, but he also decided what she would wear. When she got out of the tub after a much-needed soak, a gorgeous purple gown was spread out on the bed. Its embroidery was intricate and fine. The floor-length skirt reminded her of the outfits she wore where she worked. *Or where I used to work,* Ellen thought with a twinge. She would give anything to be back at Mote It Be. Selling New Age trinkets to gullible tourists.

Her fingers brushed the dark velvet. The moment they did, a flickering figure appeared before her. This time, it was an older woman. An attendant. As the woman helped her into the gown and braided ribbons into her hair, Ellen wondered whether her attendant was real. Was she a lost soul, trapped in the Dreamlands? Or did Kuranes dream her up, like the rest of his strange city? She wanted to ask the woman, but when she looked up, the servant was gone. Ellen was struck by how oddly time behaved, how it seemed to ripple and distort. As she drifted to the balcony of her room to look out at the city, she wondered if it was something people got used to.

"You do. Eventually. It's like seasickness. If you spend enough time on a ship, you get used to it," a voice answered.

Andrew Carter stood beside her. He was dressed formally, in black-tie attire. He looked as uncomfortable as she felt.

She rushed to him, throwing her arms around his neck.

"Oh my God, Andrew, I'm so happy to see—"

The man tensed beneath her.

"Not lovers, huh?"

Ellen realized her mistake. She backed away slowly, like a hiker who'd crossed paths with a bear.

"I . . . I didn't know . . . You look just like . . . You shaved your beard," she spluttered.

"All for King Kuranes's command performance. That and wearing this ridiculous monkey suit." Randolph watched her as she struggled to recover. "Do I really look that much like him?"

"Yes."

She studied him, searching for something, anything, to tell the two men apart.

"Your eyes," she blurted.

"What?"

"Your eyes are different. Andrew's are blue, but they're darker. And your mouth is thinner. Tighter."

He rolled his eyes. "Fascinating."

Ellen felt a rush of anger. It didn't last long. She wondered how she would feel if a crazy woman showed up, prattling on about knowing her grandson.

"Can I ask you something? About this world?"

"Sure," Randolph replied.

"King Kuranes wants me to tell him about all that's happened. Since he left the waking world."

"Yes?"

"Can I?"

"What do you mean?"

"Are you familiar with science fiction? With the idea that you can go back in time and change the future?"

"You mean like H. G. Wells? *The Time Machine*?"

"Yes. Yes. Exactly," Ellen replied, feeling the first moment of traction since she entered the Dreamlands. "Is that possible here? That I could tell King Kuranes something about the future and he could change it?"

"The world doesn't work that way."

"How does it work?"

"I don't know."

"You mean you won't tell me."

"No. I mean I don't know. It's all a mystery to me."

A nightgaunt walked into the room before Ellen could ask Randolph anything more. This time, she didn't flinch when she saw the creature. She recognized Mr. Poe. She didn't know how. Nightgaunts had no facial features—no eyes, nose, or mouth. She just knew it was him. Maybe it was his body language—the way he casually flicked his tail.

"Hello, Mr. Poe," she greeted.

The creature acknowledged her with a nod and turned to Randolph. Ellen moved closer, trying to understand how he communicated with the nightgaunts.

"It's time," Randolph announced before she could figure it out.

He offered her his arm.

Ellen hesitated.

"I'm scared," she admitted.

His eyebrow spiked.

"You jumped off the top of my ship. What could you possibly scare you?"

"I don't like this. Being all dressed up. I feel like I'm being set up. I'm not going to find myself walking into some sort of shotgun wedding, am I?"

"No."

Ellen saw something stir in his eyes.

Olivia, she thought. *He's remembering his wife.*

"William likes to dress people up, but as far as women are concerned, he's not interested."

"He's gay," she blurted.

Randolph frowned.

Ellen thought he didn't understand.

"He likes to have sex with other men," she offered.

He looked at her, shocked.

"Are all women from your time as blunt as you?"

"I'm about average."

"God help me. If all women are like you, I'd be gay, too."

"That's a terrible thing to say!"

"Yes. I know. That's why I said it," Randolph replied.

Ellen looked down at her feet. King Kuranes's wardrobe choices didn't extend to her feet. They were bare.

She longed for Dorothy's ruby slippers so that she could click her way home.

"Ruby slippers?" he asked.

"Forget it. It's nothing."

When he offered her his arm a second time, she took it. She had no other choice.

Chapter Twenty-Two

"My dear, you look absolutely splendid!"

Ellen thought dinner would be a grand affair, a multiple-course meal served to a roomful of subjects. She expected a Versailles in the Dreamlands, a place where she would have to compete for King Kuranes's attention. But when she walked into the dining room, it was small and unassuming. A simple wooden table sat in the middle of the room, with three places set. A few tapestries hung from the walls. Hand-woven rugs carpeted the floor. A fire blazed in a stone hearth.

That was it. No fancy decorations. No ornate place settings. No courtiers slashing at each other with razor-sharp tongues. Just a cozy, pub-like room.

And King Kuranes. Dressed in an immaculate pearl-gray tuxedo, he waited for her at the head of the table.

He was a far cry from the humble gardener she'd met in the greenhouse.

"Thank you for inviting me," she said as she let go of Randolph's arm.

She bowed to her host.

Randolph snickered at the gesture.

Kuranes shot him a sharp look. "Is something funny, Randy?"

"She's never been that nice to me."

"I wonder why," he replied dryly.

Kuranes rounded the table, pulling out a chair that placed Ellen between the two men.

"I hope you like hearty food. I don't get to entertain as much as I'd like, so when I get the chance, I like to indulge. Roast beef, potatoes, haricot verts. How does that sound?"

"Wonderful."

Randolph and King Kuranes sat on opposite ends of the table. Once they were settled, shimmering servants appeared with the first course. Ellen wanted to ask Kuranes about these strange creatures. They looked like ghosts, but they were capable of handling objects. And when one of them bent down to serve her, its arm brushed against her. Ellen shivered. She thought of Charles Montgomery, the fleshy ghost that haunted her attic room in Arkham. She'd had sex with him (or thought she had) one lonely night. Was Charles a creature like these servants? Was he more than a ghost?

Her speculation didn't last long. The moment she saw the bowl of creamy soup in front of her, she surrendered to her hunger.

"My goodness, Randy. Did you even bother to feed the girl? Don't you know that if you don't feed Flatlanders, they die?" Kuranes scolded.

Ellen's spoon froze in midair.

He's talking about me like I'm some sort of pet.

"She can take care of herself. She doesn't need me to feed her," Randolph insisted. For the first time, Ellen saw him as a progressive man. "Will, I need a word with you about my ship."

Kuranes ignored him.

"So tell me, my dear, what's been going on in the waking world since I left?"

Randolph sat back in his chair and grumbled.

"I don't know. When did you leave?"

"Let's see . . . I . . . um . . . I think it must have been . . . the year that big ship sank. In the North Atlantic. It ran into an iceberg."

"The *Titanic*?" Ellen offered.

"Yes, yes, the *Titanic*. That would make it—"

"Nineteen twelve," Randolph said to speed things along. Ellen turned to him.

"And you left the waking world in 1928. After World War I, right?"

Randolph grew still.

"World War I?" He frowned. "You mean the Great War."

Dread crept through her. "Oh my God. You don't know," Ellen whispered.

"Don't know what?"

"There was another war. Twenty years later."

"Who did we fight?"

Ellen hesitated.

"It was the Germans again, wasn't it?"

She nodded.

Randolph jumped up and slammed his fists on the table.

Utensils clattered across the surface.

"Goddamn it! How could you let that happen? Again?! After everything we—"

"Randolph, enough! It's not like she started it!" Kuranes shot her a wry look. "You didn't, did you?"

Ellen shook her head. "Way beyond my abilities."

"You'll have to excuse my friend's . . . passion. Randy was in the French Foreign Legion in the . . . um . . . World War I."

"No need to apologize for him," Ellen replied. "I'd feel the same way, too, if I made the sacrifices he did."

"I'm so glad! I'm so fucking glad I have your permission to be upset!" Randolph raged. He was so mad, his entire body shook.

"Look, I hate to be the one to bring you such terrible news. Really, I do. But you need to understand . . ."

"We need to understand what?" Kuranes pressed when she hesitated.

"World War II ended in 1945. Way before I was born. Before my parents were even born."

"When are you from?" Kuranes asked her.

"When am I . . . ? You mean when did I leave the waking world?"

"Yes."

"When I left, it was January of 2019."

The two men gawked at her like she was some sort of fantastic creature. *At least I'm no longer a pet,* she thought as she ran her fingers along the worn table.

"Twenty nineteen? How old are you?" Randolph demanded.

"Randy, you never ask a woman how old she is," Kuranes scolded.

"Twenty. I'm twenty years old. Almost twenty-one." She felt a sharp pang. When she left the waking world, her birthday was only a few months away. She wondered if she missed it.

"That means you were . . ."

Now it was Randolph's turn to struggle with numbers.

"I'm a millennium baby," she offered.

"What?"

"The year 2000. I was born just before the turn of the millennium."

Randolph turned pale.

He clutched his head and bolted from the room.

"Don't," Kuranes advised when she rose to follow him.

"What's wrong? What just happened?"

"Randy feels things more. He's one of our more recent arrivals. You remind him how long he's been gone."

Ellen felt her own stab of longing.

What about Tom?

Will he still be there for me if . . . when . . . I return?

"He hasn't seen his wife in ages. He misses her. I don't know why." Kuranes's lips curled into a sneer. "The woman was a *nightmare* in the waking world. Here, she's even worse."

"Here? You mean she crossed over as well?"

"Leads him around like a dog on a leash. Teases him, then runs off." Kuranes sniffed. "Can't you see the look in his eyes? The man is starved. He wants you."

"Oh, come on. The man despises me."

"You can want the thing you hate." His face darkened as he remembered a distant storm in the waking world.

He clapped his hands, and the clouds quickly dispersed.

Servants swooped down with the main course.

"Now, my dear. Please. Tell me what else has happened in the world."

Ellen spent the rest of dinner teaching King Kuranes modern history. Between bites of roast beef and velvety potatoes, she told him about the gap between the world wars—the global economic crisis and the rise of fascism in Italy and Germany. Randolph returned just as she started talking about World War II.

She hesitated, unsure whether she should go on.

Kuranes motioned for her to continue.

Ellen told the terrible tale. World War II was ancient history to her, an event whose outcome was so well known, it no longer shocked her. Watching these two men hang on her every word as she told them about the fall of Berlin and Hitler's suicide, well, it was an experience she would never forget. She guided them through the postwar years—the Cold War, the Cuban Missile Crisis, the cultural revolution of the 1960s.

The 1960s fascinated King Kuranes. He listened intently as she told him about the freedom women fought for. How they worked outside the home. Managed money. Enlisted in the military and served in public office. The thing that interested him the most was sex. Kuranes listened in mock horror as she told him about the liberties women had in the bedroom.

"Wait, wait, you mean when women go to their wedding night—"

"*If* women go to their wedding night," she corrected him, which only deepened his delight.

"You mean *if* they get married, they're already . . ."

"Experienced, yes. In most cases, they've already slept with the men they've married."

Kuranes sat back to consider the idea. "Can you imagine that, Randy?"

"Yes, I get it, Will. I got the picture twenty minutes ago." Randolph drummed his fingers on the table. He hadn't shown much interest in modern history since World War II. "Only some women are like that, right?"

"What do you mean?"

"You're not like that. *You've* never slept with a man."

"Randy, that's none of your—" King Kuranes started.

"Yes, I've been with a man. Several."

"Goodness," Kuranes blurted.

Randolph's eyes locked onto hers.

His lips curled in disgust.

"Do you know what they called women like you in my time?"

Ellen held his gaze. "As a matter of fact, I do. And you know what? I really don't care. Because freedom means more to me than what *you* think."

Kuranes clapped his hands.

"Good for you, my dear. Good for you. I wish I had that attitude when—" He stopped.

Once again, a haunted look crossed his face.

This time, he froze.

Ellen rushed to his side.

"Mr. Kuranes? Mr. Kuranes?"

She put her hand on his shoulder and caught a quick glimpse of a college boy. He had the same cruel mouth as Randolph's wife. Kuranes's next words were soft. Dreamy. "You know, I went into the water because of him."

"William," Randolph called out.

He pulled Ellen away from Kuranes.

"What's happening? What did I do?"

"You didn't do anything," he replied. "He always drifts off when he thinks about Danny."

"Danny?"

"His lover. The one who drove him into the Dreamlands. Go to the window and tell me whether there are any black spots in the city."

"Black spots?"

"Yes. Do it!"

"There are no windows in here."

"Oh, for God's sake, make them up!" he snapped. "The way you did when you were a child. When you pretended to have a tea party with your dolls."

"You mean like D&D?"

"I have no idea what you're talking about," Randolph replied.

Ellen didn't hear him. She closed her eyes and imagined a large picture window, one worthy of the Empire State Building.

When Randolph looked up, his eyes widened. "Dear God—"

"Like that?" She smiled, delighted by her work.

Randolph didn't respond. His attention was fixed on the city below. Most of Celephais was bright, but on the outskirts, thin tendrils of darkness crept into the city.

"What are those?" Ellen asked.

"Kuranes has been in the Dreamlands for a very long time. He came here the same way I did. In physical form. It eliminates the problems of leaving your body behind, but there is a new set of complications."

"What kind of complications?"

"Whatever problems you have in the waking world, you bring here." Randolph's eyes locked on hers, and she felt a crawling sensation. The same gnawing panic she felt right before Solomon Reye's men stormed his ship. "The dark spots are where he's stopped dreaming. Where his mind has failed him."

"What happens to those spots? To the people? And the buildings?"

"What do you think?"

"Gone," Ellen whispered as she looked out across Celephais. She wondered how many people William Kuranes blinked into nonexistence. How many lives this well-intentioned, dangerous man destroyed. "And he's the only one who dreams about Celephais? The only one who keeps it going?"

"Yes."

"This place is a dictatorship. A benevolent dictatorship," she murmured.

"Finally. You're finally getting it."

Ellen glared at him.

"You know, it would help if you stopped treating me like I'm an idiot."

Kuranes stirred.

"Randolph?" he called out.

Ellen looked out the window. She saw distant points blink back to life. *How often?* she wondered. *How often do the lights flicker before they finally go out?*

"Where is she? Where's the girl?" Kuranes asked.

"I'm here." Ellen tried to kneel in front of him, but the gown got in the way. After a few attempts, she gave up. "King Kuranes?"

"William."

She swept her hand down the tight-fitting bodice of her dress. "Can I change out of this?"

"You don't like it?"

"It's not really me."

"Well, I suppose. I guess dress-up time is over," he said with a sigh. Ellen nodded and started to head back to her room. "Where are you going?"

"To change."

Kuranes smiled at her.

"You can do it here," he encouraged her. "Just imagine what you want to wear."

"Right here?" She looked around the room. There were no places to retreat. And worse, the picture window she'd just created. "What if I make a mistake and end up half-naked?"

"I can assure you you're safe with me. Randolph?"

"I have no interest in her. She's revolting."

Ellen looked away, stung.

Even though she just told him his opinion didn't matter, it did.

Kuranes rose, his demeanor dark and threatening. "Miss Logan is a guest in my house. You will *not* speak to her that way."

Randolph scowled at her.

He hates me. He hates the very fact I exist, she thought.

"I'm going to change," Ellen mumbled as she headed for the door.

"Just be yourself, dear," Kuranes called after her. "Show me what women look like in your time."

It didn't take her long to imagine herself into a set of more comfortable clothes—jeans, a soft gray sweater, hiking boots. She found it ironic that all the hours she devoted to Dungeons and Dragons (time Uncle Joshua dismissed as "wasted") served her better here than Latin. *Joshua,* she thought with a sigh. She wondered what he was doing in the waking world. Had he ventured out of his study to find her? Was he part of the search party she saw in the woods? She could imagine him in his wheelchair, commanding volunteers at the crisis center. Was Andrew Carter with him? Were they working together?

"William sent me out here to apologize," Randolph announced as he drifted into the hall. He'd changed into more casual clothes. He now wore a black shirt and a pair of gray linen pants. Ellen didn't want to admit it, but he looked good.

"Don't bother. I know you wouldn't mean it." She leaned against the wall. "We'll just stand here for a minute and then go back. I'll tell Kuranes you fell on your knees and begged for mercy."

His mouth hinted at a smile.

"He'd never believe that. He knows me too well," Randolph said, studying a tapestry that flapped in the wind.

His eyes flickered between her and the curtains.

"Am I really revolting?" she asked when his eyes drifted over her one time too many.

"You're different."

"In other words, yes."

"I didn't say that. God, you're as bad as—"

"Your wife?"

He changed the subject. "You missed a spot."

"What?" She looked down at her clothes, trying to figure out what was wrong. He grabbed a few strands of her hair. They were still braided with ribbons and beads. "Oh God. Thanks."

"Here. Let me." He grabbed a ribbon before she had a chance to object. "My sisters used to get their hair all knotted up and then came running to me for help."

"How many sisters do you have?"

"Had. How many sisters *did* I have," Randolph corrected. "Four."

"And brothers?"

"One."

"The two of you were outnumbered," Ellen teased.

"A couple of my sisters died. When they were young."

"Oh God, I didn't mean—"

He kept his eyes fixed on her hair. "I know."

Kuranes stuck his head into the hall.

"Randy? Are you done apologizing to the lovely girl?"

"Almost," he answered.

He unwound the last of the ribbons and pressed them into her hand.

Ellen felt a warm pulse when he touched her, a deep surge of connection.

Randolph flinched.

There was a strange glow in his eyes.

He yanked his hand back, as if he had been burned.

"What's wrong?"

"Nothing," he insisted.

"Come, children, please. We don't have long," Kuranes urged.

Randolph made a sour face. "Yes, let's. Let's take our seats before His Majesty gets mad."

They returned to a different room, to a place of dark wood and bookshelves. *A gentleman's library,* she thought as she settled onto a buttery leathery couch. She felt a stab of nervousness, the sense she didn't belong. She wondered whether it had been a good idea to change into her street clothes.

Kuranes stared at her when she sat down. Randolph took the chair next to him and pretended to straighten his pants.

Ellen felt like she was at a job interview.

"Hmm. In a strange way, it works," Kuranes said after a moment of contemplation. "Your men's attire actually makes me more aware you're a woman."

"It also has the added advantage that no one can look up my skirt," Ellen quipped.

"Like anyone would want to," Carter said as he plucked at his pants.

"Yes, I think we get it. I'm not your type," Ellen snapped. "Can we move on, please?"

"How do you know the thing that calls itself Solomon Reye?" Kuranes asked.

Thing. Ellen shivered. "I first saw him when I was ghost hunting with friends. He showed up the next night to give a lecture at Miskatonic University."

"Oh, that's rich," Randolph said with a snort.

"Randy—" Kuranes warned.

"Andrew and I were in the audience."

"Andrew?"

"Andrew Carter. *His* grandson." Ellen nodded at Randolph. "Solomon Reye showed a video of a nightgaunt. The nightgaunt that abducted one of Carter's students."

"Video?" Randolph echoed.

"You mean moving picture?" Kuranes asked. "Like *The Musketeers of Pig Alley?*"

Ellen shrugged. "Um. I guess. Ever since then, he's been chasing me. And then there's this strange ring. A ring that dropped out of the sky and drove my friend Martha mad. Solomon kidnapped her from the mental institution when I dropped by to see her."

"Oh, my." Kuranes sighed as he sat back. "That's not what I intended. That's not what I intended at all."

"What do you mean?" Ellen frowned, but Kuranes's attention was focused on Randolph.

"I have a confession to make, my boy. I took one of your family rings and threw it into the waking world."

Randolph leaped to his feet.

"You *what?*" he thundered. "Are you nuts? Are you completely nuts, you senile old man?"

"I thought it would help," Kuranes replied in a small, boyish voice.

Randolph turned, his eyes blazing. "Do you have it?" he demanded. When she didn't respond quickly enough, he grabbed her by the wrist and yanked her to her feet. "*Do you have it?*"

"Randy! Let go of her!" Kuranes roared.

"I don't. I swear to God, I don't," she answered as she squirmed against his iron grip.

He grabbed her sweater and started to undo the buttons.

Strip search, she thought. *The bastard wants to strip search me.*

"Randy, stop! Stop this instant!" Kuranes tried to pull him off her, but Randolph refused to let her go.

She stomped down hard on Carter's foot. He yelped and released her. When he did, Ellen punched him in the face.

Randolph staggered into Kuranes.

Blood trickled from his nose.

The two men stared at her in disbelief.

"She has it," Randolph said softly.

"My dear, maybe you should—" Kuranes started.

"Fine," Ellen blurted.

She unlaced her hiking boots and kicked them at the men. Then she took off her clothes, pulling her pockets inside out so that they could see there was nothing in them. She stripped down to panties and a bra. Kuranes looked away, at the clothes pooled on the floor. Randolph watched her the entire time. His eyes never left her body, not even when he snatched up her clothes and rifled through them.

"There. Are you satisfied? Or do you want to me to keep going?" she demanded.

He threw her jeans at her so hard, she felt the bite of the buttons. "Whore!"

"Hypocrite!" she spat back. "You may be married, but that didn't stop you from taking a good long look, did it?"

He lunged at her.

Once again, Kuranes restrained him.

"Sit down," Kuranes ordered. When Randolph continued to struggle, Kuranes shoved him into a chair with a strength that surprised her. "*Sit down*! And you, put your clothes on. You've proven your innocence."

"I wouldn't say that," Randolph growled.

"Randy, I swear. One more word . . ." His threat trailed off as Ellen slipped into her clothes. "Honestly you two, you're . . . operatic."

"Operatic?" Ellen replied. "Is that your way of saying we're drama queens?"

"I am *not*—" Randolph started.

"It's not what you think it means," she shot back.

The room fell silent.

Kuranes broke the sudden stillness. "Please, my dear, tell us. We need to know. Where did the ring go?"

"I gave it to Carter."

"No, she didn't—"

"I gave it to *my* Carter. Andrew Carter." She silenced him with a glare. "I showed it to my uncle, and he recognized the Carter family crest."

"What?"

"The Carter family crest."

Kuranes handed her a piece of paper and a pen. "Show me."

She sketched the strange symbol.

"I think the motto is 'The only way out is through.'"

Carter pulled away. He looked sick, the way he did when she told him about World War II.

"How did you know that? How could you possibly know that?" he demanded.

"The crest was on the ring. And the motto . . . I've heard it before. In my dreams. When I realized it belonged to Andrew, I passed it on to him."

"Why?" Kuranes asked her.

Ellen shrugged.

"Because it would have been wrong to keep it."

Kuranes eyes narrowed. "You didn't put on the ring? Not even once?"

"No."

"Why not?"

"I wasn't sure what would happen. I'm not going to just put on some magic ring without knowing what it might do."

"Well, you're certainly smarter than most humans."

"Most . . ." Her throat closed around the words.

Ellen scrambled to her feet, trying to put distance between her and Kuranes.

"You and Solomon—"

Kuranes smiled at her. "We are of a type."

She turned to Randolph. "Are you one of them, too?"

Randolph scowled and looked at the floor.

Kuranes exploded with laughter.

For the first time, Ellen felt bad for Randolph.

"I'm sorry. I didn't—" she started to apologize.

"That's it! I've had it." Randolph stood to leave. "I've got better things to do than listen to some Flatland bitch."

"Randy, sit down."

"I've got a ship to—"

"Goddammit, boy. *Sit down!*"

Randolph flopped into the chair with a surly glare.

"You know what, Will? You're a pain in the ass," Randolph groused. "Even for an *Eminence*, you're a pain in the ass."

"Eminence?" Ellen echoed. "What's an Eminence?"

King Kuranes looked to Randolph for help.

Randolph studied the floor.

"When humans started venturing into the Dreamlands, things were different," Kuranes explained. "Flatlanders were much more imaginative. And the border between the two worlds was easily crossed. There were opportunities for humans to interact with creatures from another world. From another dimension. Eminences are the products of those, um, meetings."

"Meetings?"

"Sexual contact. He's talking about sexual contact." Randolph spared Kuranes the embarrassment of making the connection explicit. "Eminences are the product of human and nonhuman sex."

"*Hentai*." Ellen remembered a book a boyfriend brought back from Japan. It had an old painting of a woman making love to an octopus. "Like *The Dream of the Fisherman's Wife?*"

"I'm afraid I don't know," Kuranes admitted.

Randolph did. His eyes burned into hers.

Ellen tried again. "You mean like those Greek myths where Zeus disguises himself as an animal and goes chasing after women?"

Kuranes snorted.

"Close enough," he replied. "Most contact is like that. Isolated encounters and nothing more. But Solomon . . . Solomon is more ambitious. He wants a stronger, more permanent connection. He wants to keep the door between our worlds open. And just leaving a door hanging open is dangerous. Very dangerous."

Ellen thought about Lovecraft's stories, his warning about crossing dimensions, of letting things into this world that didn't belong. Her eyes drifted to Randolph. Lovecraft wrote about him, too. How he returned to the waking world in an inhuman form . . .

"For God's sake, I'm not one of them," Randolph growled.

Ellen turned back to Kuranes.

"Would there be any difference physically? Between a human and an Eminence?"

"No. Not really," he replied after a moment's hesitation. Kuranes clearly didn't like talking about his own kind. "I need you to do something. And Randy, you need to help her."

"What?" Randolph's voice was a dead monotone.

"Solomon can't get to the waking world on his own. For years, he's relied on magical objects. He tries to hide them. Sometimes, he pretends he's doing complex incantations. He scribbles symbols in a magic circle, but it's all an illusion."

Kuranes smiled.

He likes playing the trickster, too, Ellen thought.

"I think he's found something that's given him better access to your world." He turned his attention to Ellen. "You probably had it when you fell. My guess is that you left it on Randy's ship."

"You little—" Randolph started.

Kuranes silenced him with a lethal look.

"She didn't know she had it, so don't start in on her again."

"How am I going to know what it is?" Ellen asked.

"Oh, I think you already know. You just don't remember yet." Kuranes offered her the maddening smile of a Zen monk. "Find it. Find it and take it back to the waking world."

"And where do *I* fit into all this?" Randolph demanded.

"You're going to take her to Solomon's temple and help her look for it. You need to go there anyway, to petition him for the return of your ship. It's the perfect cover."

"Solomon's temple?" Ellen announced in disbelief.

Kuranes shook his head. "Yes, I know. I suppose it's Reye's idea of a joke."

Ellen moved to her feet.

"No," she blurted. "I'm not going there with *him.*"

"You have to," Kuranes insisted.

"Why can't you take me?"

"I've got a city to dream, my dear. I can't just leave it."

"What about Mr. Poe? Or a map? Just give me a map and point me in the right direction. I can get there on my own," she said.

"No, you can't." Kuranes looked between them. "What is it with you two? Why are you so afraid of him?"

"*She's* afraid of *me*?" Randolph exclaimed.

"Because the moment I'm outside the city gates, he's going to strangle me," Ellen insisted.

"Oh, come on—" Randolph started.

She nodded at the hands he'd been flexing for most of the conversation. "Look. He's already practicing."

Randolph tried to hide them, but he wasn't fast enough. Kuranes glared at him.

"It's not his fault," Ellen insisted. "And it's not mine. Sometimes people just don't get along."

"You get along with Andrew Carter," Kuranes pointed out.

"Yes, but he's a different person."

The men looked at each other in a way that made her feel helpless. Out of her element. "Please, promise me you'll at least consider it."

"All right, my dear," Kuranes relented, but it was an empty victory. Ellen already knew what the answer would be. "Now if you'll excuse us—"

"You have important business to discuss. Yes, I know." She felt the deep sadness that comes with exclusion. *It's a man's world,* she thought as she favored Kuranes with another bow. *I think it always will be.* "Thank you for dinner."

Chapter Twenty-Three

Ellen couldn't see, but she knew she was underground. There was a rich, earthy smell undercut by the stench of decay. *I'm in the mine again,* she thought. *On my first adventure with Carter. My* Carter. She looked for him, trying to hold back a wave of panic. *Where is he? Did we ever escape the mine? Or have I been here all this time, dreaming these strange dreams?*

After what seemed like an eternity, her eyes adjusted.

Cracks of light trickled from above. Dust motes danced in the thin rays. Ellen lay at the foot of an unknown set of stairs. People were sprawled on the ground all around her. Their shadowy shapes reached out to her. Some were still alive, but others had crossed the invisible line.

It was only a matter of time before they died.

Ellen forced herself to move, to climb toward the light.

She thought of Emilio Carranza dragging his broken body away from his plane. Ellen crawled up the cold stairs. When she reached the top, she saw a wooden door. Ellen pounded on it with her fists. With each blow, she heard a metallic clang.

A lock, she thought as she peered through the thin gaps in the door. *Someone's locked me in a cellar.*

"Not someone. Something," a voice above her said with a chuckle.

Ellen lost her balance and tumbled down the stairs.

"Oh no. Please," she pleaded in the gloom. "Please, please, please."

When she opened her eyes, Martha Pickman lay next to her. Her friend's eyes were dark with death.

She hissed at Ellen.

"He's coming for you. Don't you feel him? He's coming for you. Do you hear me? *Get out of here!*"

Ellen woke to the sound of her own scream. She scrambled out of bed and onto the cold marble floor. It took a moment before her mind filled in the blanks. *The Dreamlands. Celephais. King Kuranes's palace.* Ellen groaned and sat up. A breeze blew in from the harbor. Ellen gulped the moist, salty air. Slowly, the intensity of the dream faded. She wasn't sure when she noticed Randolph Carter in the room. She just knew he was there. She could *feel* him.

He joined her on the floor.

"Are you all right?" he asked.

"I had a nightmare," she said as she rubbed her neck. "Did I wake you up?"

"I'm right next door," he replied. "I suppose it's Kuranes's idea of a joke. Or an experiment. Maybe both."

"Throw the mortals together and see what happens?" She shook her head. "Does he really think we're that predictable?"

He stared into space. "Most humans *are* that predictable."

Ellen wondered whether he was thinking about his wife.

"The answer is no, by the way," Randolph announced.

"What?"

"King Kuranes insists I accompany you to Solomon's temple."

"That's his final word?"

He rested his head on the side of the bed. "I'm afraid so."

"There's no way around it? Couldn't we just split up once we get outside the city walls?"

"He'd know," Randolph insisted.

"How about—"

Randolph cut her off. "Look, this isn't an ideal situation for me either. Going to a demon stronghold with an inexperienced Flatlander—"

"Stop! Would you please just stop?" she pleaded. Ellen thought about the bodies in the cellar and shivered. "Let's start again."

He frowned. "What do you mean?"

She offered him her hand.

"Hi. I'm Ellen. Ellen Logan."

He looked at her and snorted.

"Do you really think we need to go back that far?"

"I think we should." She continued to hold out her hand.

He shook it. His hand was warm and calloused, not at all what she expected.

"I'm Randolph Carter."

"What should I call you?" Ellen asked.

"What do you mean?"

"Randolph is a little long. How about Randy?"

"Only Kuranes calls me Randy," he replied quietly.

"Because you're friends?"

"Because he can."

"Benevolent dictatorship," she murmured.

"You know, if I were you, I wouldn't say that too loudly."

"I said it before. Right in front of Kuranes."

Randolph waved his hand in front of his face. "Yes, but he wasn't really there."

Ellen looked around the luxurious surroundings. She thought about the less benevolent dictators in the waking world. The ones who created fantasy worlds on the backs of their people.

Same politics, different world.

Ellen shivered.

"Can we get out of here?" she asked.

"We can leave anytime you like. Just get changed."

"In front of you?"

Randolph looked at her and burst into full-throated laughter. "Oh, now you're modest? After you stripped down to your underwear in front of me? I'm sorry. I can forget most things, but I can't forget that."

"Can you at least turn around?"

He stared at her for a long time before he obeyed. Ellen imagined a set of clothes like the ones she wore after dinner—jeans, sweater, and a pair of hiking boots. She added a backpack, filled with items she thought she'd need.

"I'm sorry for, um . . ." He gestured at her clothes. "But when I found out that Kuranes tossed my ring into the waking world, I . . . It was too much."

Ellen sat on the bed and laced her hiking boots. "Can I ask you a question?"

"Maybe."

"I know you won't tell me what the ring does, and to be honest, I really don't want to know," Ellen assured him. "But is it dangerous?"

"Dangerous?"

"To Andrew. Is the ring dangerous to Andrew?"

"Nothing I possess would harm my family members." Randolph paused. The hostility crept back into his voice. "Look, it sounds like there are a lot of rumors about me."

"Rumors are all we have," she admitted. "That and what Lovecraft said."

Randolph looked at her in disbelief. "But I wrote books. Lots of books."

"Most of them lost to time, I'm afraid," King Kuranes announced as he wandered into the room.

Two rust-colored robes were draped over his arm.

Ellen started to rise, but he motioned for her to stay where she was.

"Lost? How?" Randolph blurted.

"You can't just walk away from the world without there being consequences," Kuranes informed him. He turned to Ellen before Randolph could say anything. "I've come to say goodbye. And to give you these."

"Oh, come on. You've *got* to be kidding!" Randolph protested.

Kuranes ignored him.

"I can't guarantee your safety outside Celephais. Things have deteriorated in the countryside." He paused. For a moment, Ellen thought he was going to lapse into one of his "absences."

"If you wear these, people will think you are religious pilgrims," Kuranes continued. "And that might be enough to get you to Ilek-Vad."

"Ilek-Vad?" Ellen asked.

"It's a city east of here. Solomon's temple is on the outskirts," Kuranes informed her.

"How far away is it?"

"A day or so on foot," Randolph replied. "It would have been a shorter journey if I had my ship."

"Well, we don't always get what we want, do we?" Kuranes's voice dripped with malice. Once again, Ellen caught a glimpse behind the mask. She could picture Kuranes as a vengeful god. Torturing mortals the way children teased ants.

"We've taken up enough of your time," Ellen announced, trying to break the tension between the two men.

"Yes. You have," Kuranes agreed as he handed her a robe. In an instant, he was back to being a sweet middle-aged gardener. "I'm sorry we had to meet under such unfortunate circumstances."

"So am I." She sighed. Even though she'd just seen his inhuman side, King Kuranes had been kind to her. Fatherly. Ellen pulled him into a hug. "Thank you for your help."

"You're welcome, my dear." Kuranes wrapped his arms around her and took a deep breath. "God, you smell so much like the waking world."

Ellen jerked, her face flushing. "Is that bad?"

Kuranes smiled as he pulled away.

"No, not at all. What do you think, Randy?"

Randolph refused to take the bait. He stood there with his arms crossed. He was eager to leave. To salvage his ship and what was left of his cargo.

"Well, now that that's settled, I'll send you on your way."

Kuranes patted her arm.

"Have a safe trip home."

Chapter Twenty-Four

A storm drifted through Celephais as they started their journey. Rivulets of rain streamed off the oddly shaped roofs. Small pools gathered at the jagged junctions where buildings met. The city reminded Ellen of the strange drawings of M. C. Escher. The ceilings and stairs fed off each other, twisting and turning and defying normal physics.

I wish Andrew was here to see this, she thought as she walked through the town square.

Randolph kept a close eye on her. At first, she thought it was because he didn't trust her. She soon saw the reason why. The streets that appeared so broad and easy to navigate from the palace were different on the ground. They were dark and narrow, medieval alleys where people and animals jostled for space. It would be easy for a Flatlander like her to get lost. The vendors only added to the chaos. They bellowed at the passing crowds as they tried to attract customers.

Randolph warned her not to look, not to show any interest in their surroundings. They were disguised as religious pilgrims, part of a group devoted to preserving the spiritual purity of the

Dreamlands. They were not interested in material goods. Still, Ellen couldn't resist. One glance was all it took to satisfy her curiosity. Strange creatures hung from hooks in a nearby stall. Some still twitched. Ellen turned away, bile rising in her throat. She wondered why King Kuranes allowed such things in his city.

"He has little choice. You have to give the people what they want. At least *some* of what they want," Randolph explained, his low voice almost lost in the din of the crowd. "It keeps them satisfied. Happy."

"Are you going to be doing that a lot?" she asked him as she shrugged off the grip of a more aggressive merchant.

"Doing what a lot?"

"Getting in my head."

Randolph stepped to the side, allowing a man and his cart to pass.

"Only when you're interesting," he said with a sniff.

"Look, I'm not saying it's bad or anything. It's just that in my time, most people aren't able—"

"Yes, I know. It was that way in my day, too," he shot back. Even though she didn't look at him, she could hear the anger in his voice. "I'm not a fossil, you know."

"I never said you were."

Ellen tugged down her hood as they approached the city gates.

She welcomed an excuse to withdraw, to pull into a protective shell.

Kuranes's special guards flanked the entrance. When Ellen saw their bright Vatican-style uniforms, her heart raced. She flashed back to the encounter on the ship. To the fierce battle with demons pretending to be Kuranes's men. Her hands trembled as she remembered scaling the mast, her feet dangling over the Ceranian Sea.

Randolph pressed his hand into the curve of her back.

Be still, he commanded her.

Ellen shivered. The caress reminded her of their first encounter in the Dreamlands.

He stepped forward and handed the head guard their papers. The two men jabbered in the language of the Dreamlands. Ellen had never heard it before. She leaned forward to listen. No matter how hard she concentrated, the words slithered away from her. They drifted through her mind like smoke. The conversation didn't last long. Almost all the people passing through the gates were heading *into* Celephais. The guards weren't very interested in those who left.

Your funeral, she heard one guard think as she passed him. Another one smacked her on the ass. *Good luck getting back in. I won't make it so easy on you.*

Ellen turned, feeling a rush of anger. She considered confronting him.

There wasn't much point.

This isn't your world.

The wave of resignation that pressed down on her was as thick as the gray sky above.

"Shit," Randolph muttered once they were outside.

He stopped so suddenly, she ran into him.

Ellen followed his gaze.

A line of people stretched to the horizon. All of them were headed toward Celephais.

"Refugees," she whispered.

"'Things have deteriorated in the countryside.' That's rich," he said as he studied the road. "His world's falling apart."

"Have you ever seen anything like this?"

"I travel by ship. I've seen a couple of refugee boats. But this? No." Randolph rubbed at the beard that was already growing back.

Taking Andrew with him, she thought with a pang of regret.

"We can't take the main road. It's too dangerous," he decided. "And we look too suspicious."

"But Kuranes said—"

"I don't care what he said! The old man has lost it!" Randolph waved at the scene around them. "He probably doesn't even know this is going on!"

Ellen noticed he was attracting attention.

She grabbed his arm and pulled him off the road.

"What do we do?" she asked once they were safely out of earshot.

"There's another road along the coast. It's more rugged. Remote. But we have a better chance of getting to Solomon's temple undetected."

"Remote."

The idea was not appealing.

"You don't trust me," he said.

"Does that surprise you? I mean, does that *really* surprise you?"

"Can I give you some advice? Some brutal, honest advice?"

"Please."

Randolph stared at the grim parade of refugees.

"I'm all you have, so you might as well come with me."
He waited for her to reach the same conclusion.
Ellen shook her head. "Terrific. Just fucking terrific."
She followed Randolph into the wilderness.

<hr>

They said almost nothing for the rest of the day. The rain pursued them as they wound their way up the coast. Since they were no longer on the main road, Ellen was tempted to ditch the massive robe. She wanted to think up something more practical, like a lightweight raincoat or a poncho. Randolph Carter refused to let her. He told her that now that they were outside the city, it was no longer safe to imagine things. If she pictured a change of clothes here, she would send out a beacon to anyone (or anything) nearby.

Ellen thought about summoning a demon just because she wanted fresh socks.

Not worth it.

As she walked over the rough terrain, Ellen wondered about the backpack she carried. She'd dreamed it up in King Kuranes's palace, almost as an afterthought. Now she wondered what she was carrying. Did she remember to bring a blanket, a first-aid kit, a change of clothes? Food? Ellen bit her lip. She depended on Randolph. What if they were separated? Or even worse, what if he abandoned her? She was pretty sure she had a compass. But what good was a compass without a map?

Did compasses even work here?

"We're here," he announced.

Ellen blinked and realized she'd missed the last half mile of the trail. They stood in front of a cabin. A snake-like arrow shooting through a square was carved on the door. *The Carter family crest,* she thought as she studied the building.

"This is your family's place."

When she looked over at him, she could see the pride on his face.

"Not bad, is it?"

"Not bad? This is great!" She beamed at the sturdy structure. "I thought we would be camping out in tents."

"Tents? Out here? Um . . . no."

He lifted the mat in front of the house.

A key lay underneath it.

Ellen snickered. "You're kidding, right?"

He shot her a sharp look.

"What did you expect? Some sort of magical spell?"

He opened the door and motioned for her to pass.

The cabin was basic—four beds, a table, chairs, and a fireplace. Someone in the Carter clan (she assumed it was a woman) tried to spruce the place up by adding curtains and a throw rug. Ellen smiled as she set her backpack on the floor. She remembered a story her friend Ashley told her. How her parents almost divorced when her mother tried to "soften" her father's hunting lodge. The final straw came when Ashley's mom brought in a style consultant to look at the place.

"Style consultant? Is that like an interior decorator?" Randolph demanded as Ellen slipped off her robe and draped it over a chair.

"Yes." She was so happy to be out of the rain, she didn't mind that he was peeking into her head again.

"God, I hate that. I hate it when women take over. They always ruin things."

She fixed him with a level stare.

"If you expect me to go anywhere near that comment, you're mad."

"That's it? That's all you're going to say?" He snorted. "You were a lot more entertaining last night."

"I had to be entertaining. I was trying to keep myself alive by charming the emperor," she murmured. Ellen loved *One Thousand and One Nights* when she was a child. Living it was an entirely different story. "I know what I am."

"Do tell."

"I'm a pawn. An insignificant little nobody caught between a demigod and a demon. And being led into the darkness by a man . . ." She hesitated, unsure how to finish. What did she really know about Randolph Carter?

"Nothing. You know nothing about me. Just what Lovecraft told you, and most of that is wrong."

Ellen bowed her head.

She drew in a shuddering breath.

"God, Andrew. I need you. I really, really need you."

"I'm right here, Ellen," Randolph replied after a long pause.

"What?"

"I'm right here." This time, his voice was softer.

All her fear and frustration finally boiled over. Ever since she arrived in the Dreamlands, she managed to hold herself together. Now, she crumbled.

"*You're not him*! Jesus, why are you doing this?" she wailed.

Randolph looked around at the cabin. There was a change, an almost imperceptible shift in body language that made her think—

"God, where are you? In some sort of cabin?" he asked.

"Andrew? No! That's impossible!"

She leaped off the bed and embraced him.

"Hey, girl," he said, the greeting low and affectionate.

Ellen pressed her face into the curve of his neck.

The ring, she thought. *Is he using the ring?*

"Andrew, I'm trapped. I'm trapped in the Dreamlands. Solomon Reye kidnapped me. I managed to escape, but I'm not sure how I can—"

He stiffened in her arms.

"Get away," he growled.

"But I need your help. Find me a way out."

"I said get away. Get away from me."

When she pulled back, Ellen saw the foreign fierceness in his eyes.

Randolph Carter had returned.

He looked at her. For the first time, she saw doubt. Fear.

"I said get away from me." He shoved her, hard enough to make her stumble. "Who are you?"

"I told you. My name's Ellen Logan."

"That's not your real name," he snarled. She felt the hairs on the back of her neck stand up. "Your real name's not Ellen Logan."

"Ellen's my adopted name."

"What's your real name?" He fixed her with a frighten-ing glare.

"I don't know."

Randolph grabbed her by the arm and shook her. "*What's your name?*"

"I said I don't know!"

It was a half lie. She knew her first name, but she refused to tell him.

Names are power, she thought. *And I'm not giving this ma-niac any more power than he already has.*

"Tell me now or so help me God . . ."

He paused in the middle of the threat and closed his eyes.

Randolph pulled back, struggling to regain control. "You know what? I really don't care. Because you're right. You're a pawn. An insignificant little nobody. And the sooner I get rid of you, the sooner I can get on with my life."

"And the sooner I can get out of here," she added.

Her words were heavy with doubt. She knew the chances of returning to the waking world dropped with every passing minute. *I shouldn't even waste time sleeping,* she thought as she stared at the bed. But she was tired. More than tired. *I'm so out of it, I see Andrew Carter in the eyes of my enemy.*

"I'm not your enemy," Randolph insisted.

"Yes, you are," she replied as she crawled onto the bed and surrendered to her exhaustion.

Chapter Twenty-Five

Ellen opened her eyes and peered into the gloom.

I'm in the cellar. Shit, I'm locked in the cellar again.

The nightmare was the same. Dead bodies lay all around her. *His children,* she thought. *No, not his children. His raw materials.* A woman thrashed on the ground beside her. Ellen pressed her hand to the woman's clammy forehead. There was one long convulsion, then peace. She remembered running after Emilio Carranza's doomed plane. As the fireball bloomed in the forest, she could think only one thing.

Witness.

I must be his witness.

"You must be Randolph Carter's witness, too," a sandpaper voice announced.

Martha Pickman stood before her.

Ellen stared at her friend.

"I don't understand."

Martha Pickman pointed to the far corner of the room.

The space expanded, stretching beyond the normal dimensions of a cellar.

"Deeper. You must go deeper. Find him before he is lost."

"I can't."

"You must."

"I don't want to go."

"Randolph Carter needs you," Martha insisted.

Ellen sighed.

The thought that her Carter, any Carter, needed her help was enough for her to fight her fear.

Ellen headed into the darkness. The walls closed behind her; the floor reached for the ceiling. At one point, the passage became so narrow, she was forced to squirm through a tight opening.

I'm being reborn, she thought as she pushed her way through the earth.

God, I hope I make it this time.

Ellen laughed. The manic sound bounced off the walls. Her giddiness quickly turned into panic. The passage tightened around her body, squeezed her like a snake. Ellen remembered her first adventure with Andrew Carter, when they discovered the bodies of men who had been trapped deep inside a mine. Wedged into the earth.

Forever entombed.

Is this what dying is like? she wondered. *Is this what it feels like to be buried alive?*

"No," she panted. "Not going to happen. Not going to happen."

Ellen could see the end of the passage. She slid her body forward and grabbed both sides of the opening.

Please, she prayed as she pulled herself through, *please, please.*

Ellen popped out of the narrow passage and landed in mud.

Slow, ominous thunder rolled in the distance. A dirt wall towered over her, fortified by sandbags and beams of wood. *Trenches,* she thought as she struggled to her feet. *World War I. I've landed in World War I.* She wasn't alone. A man was with her. He was slumped against the wall of a trench. A lit cigarette burned between his dead fingers. His helmet spun like a top on the ground beside him.

Ellen wasn't sure what had happened. Maybe the young soldier had gotten cocky and had taken off his helmet to smoke. Maybe a sniper got off a lucky shot. Or maybe the man stopped caring. *Different reasons, same result,* she thought as she strained to read his name. Private Kevin Nelson. Ellen reached out to close his glassy eyes. Just as her fingers brushed his eyelids, she heard a scream.

She had never heard Randolph Carter scream before, but Ellen knew it was him.

She donned the dead soldier's helmet and ran toward the sound. She kept her head down. Private Kevin Nelson made her all too aware of the dangers of being seen. A sickly greenish-yellow haze drifted overhead. *Poison gas?* Ellen pressed her sleeve against her mouth and nose. A few feet away, she saw the opening to the command post. Randolph rushed out and almost collided with her. He slammed into the wall, his face twisted in mindless horror.

A telephone cord was wrapped around his leg.

Blood seeped through his pants.

Ellen scrambled to free him. But every time she touched the cord, it dug deeper into his leg. Screams of agony filled her ears. He tumbled to the ground. His eyes rolled back. His lips stretched to a bloodless grimace.

And she could do nothing.

You are a witness, a voice commanded. *Only a witness.*

"No. Let me help him. Please, let me help him," she pleaded as she grabbed the wire, trying to relieve the pressure on his leg.

The cord cut deep into her hands.

Their blood mingled.

"You can't help me. It's too late," Randolph insisted, his voice hoarse with terror.

Ellen felt something rise behind her. She fought the urge to look.

"I'm not leaving you."

"Goddamn it, man. Leave!" he screamed.

Man? She looked at her bloody hands. They were large and calloused, the nails chipped and black with grime. *No, it can't be.* Her hand drifted down the front of her pants. Then she felt it. The thing she knew shouldn't be there . . .

Ellen woke up gasping. Her hand dove for the curve of her crotch.

She sighed.

A dream. Thank God. Oh, thank God.

She turned her head and saw Randolph lying on the floor. He thrashed from side to side, writhing and kicking, battling an unseen enemy.

He's still trapped.

She crawled over to him.

Even in the waking world, Ellen didn't know the best way to bring someone out of a nightmare.

She could only imagine how complicated it was here.

With shaking hands, she reached out and gently nudged his shoulder.

"Hey, wake up," she called out. "Wake up!"

Randolph was shirtless. In the dim light, she could see the network of scars that ran along his shoulder and stomach. She thought about the telephone cord cutting into him in the dream.

What unseen force was pulling on the other end? Ellen wondered.

"Listen to me. Open your eyes. That's all you need to do. Just open your eyes."

"I can't," he wailed. "I can't find my eyes. I don't have eyes."

"Yes, you do. Don't be silly!" she scolded as she pressed her fingers against his eyelids. His skin was hot and clammy. "These are my hands. My hands are on your eyes. All you need to do is open them."

"I'm scared."

"I know," she said softly. Randolph reminded her of how she felt at the asylum, lying motionless while a nightmare raged around her.

She took his hand and held it between hers.

"I've just grabbed hold of your hand. Do you feel it?"

"Yes." He sounded faint. Like he was fading. Losing ground.

"I'm going to count to three and pull. And you're going to wake up. Do you understand?"

"Yes," he responded with little conviction.

Ellen leaned over and whispered in his ear. "Don't make me come in there," she warned him. Randolph laughed and grabbed hold of her, trying to wrestle her to the floor. Ellen's nipples hardened against her thin cotton shirt. *Terrific,* she thought. *This is all I need.* "On the count of three? Ready?"

"Yes."

"*Three!*" She hauled on him with every ounce of strength she had. His eyes flew open, and he sat straight up. Ellen grabbed him to make sure he didn't fall back into the dream.

Randolph pushed her away.

"What are you doing? Get away from me!" he spat.

Ellen watched as he fumbled for his shirt, desperate to hide his wounds.

"It's good to have you back," she said, gasping. "Jesus, you scared the shit out of me!"

"What's wrong?" he demanded.

"What's . . . ? I woke up and found you screaming and rolling on the floor—that's what's wrong. For a moment, I thought . . ." She lowered her voice. "I thought Solomon got to you."

"Not Solomon," he said after a few moments of silence. "I came back from the war with my own demons."

"PTSD," Ellen murmured.

Suddenly, everything made sense. The intense bursts of anger. The way he stood frozen while Solomon's men stormed his ship. The shaking when she told him about World War II.

"Excuse me?"

"You have PTSD. Posttraumatic stress disorder."

"You mean shell shock."

"It's the same thing," she replied, relieved to have something besides the nightmare to talk about. "Were you under heavy fire? Artillery barrage?"

"Almost every minute of the day. Even at night."

"That would explain it." She sighed. His words echoed in her head. *Whatever problems you have in the waking world, you bring here.* "They think the explosions cause brain damage."

"But I wasn't hit."

"You don't have to be hit. Being close to the shock wave is enough to give you PTSD. It's a concussive blast. Like constantly getting hit in the head."

"Olivia says it's because I'm weak," he grumbled.

It took Ellen a moment to remember who Olivia was.

Randolph hadn't mentioned his wife in a long time.

"Well, no offense, but your wife is full of shit. It's not something you can control. My friend came back from Afghanistan with PTSD. And he wasn't weak. He was one of the strongest guys I knew."

"Afghanistan?"

"We're in another war."

"*Another* war?!" He echoed.

"Hey, at least we're not nuking each other." Ellen shrugged, offering what she knew was cold comfort.

Carter frowned. "Nuking?"

Dear God, she thought. *I didn't cover that in my little history lesson.*

She looked away, biting down on her lip.

"Is there a cure? For shell shock?" he asked after a long silence.

"They can treat the symptoms, but as far as a cure . . . I don't know."

"What happened to your friend?"

"He, um . . . he . . ." She stumbled over the words, hoping he would get the message. He didn't. He waited for an answer. "He killed himself."

"Well, aren't you a little ray of sunshine?" Randolph said.

Ellen knew his anger wasn't directed at her. She could see the anxiety on his face, the fear of a future he knew was coming.

"I'm sorry. I've been nothing but bad news since I got here, haven't I?"

"Pretty much," he agreed as he sat back.

"I wasn't much good for Kyle either." Ellen moved to her feet, trying to escape the memory of her friend and his last desperate months. And that day. That final day. "He called me so many times. He wanted to talk, but I . . . Jesus . . . I told him I didn't have time. I was too busy studying for exams." She put her face in her hands. "The next time I saw him was when I went to his apartment and . . ."

She leaned against the cabin door.

Her mind jammed, refusing to let her relive the grim moment.

"That's not the way out," Randolph announced, startling her from her reflection. He stood beside her, prying her hand off the doorknob.

"Where *is* the way out?" she pleaded. "Please, I need to get out. I really, really need to get out."

"I don't know. I haven't tried to leave in a very long time."

A wave of grief washed over her.

"I'm not going back, am I?" she whispered.

"I don't know. I hope so. I really hope so."

"I bet you can't wait to get rid of me."

Randolph reached out and touched her face. "That's not true. That's not true at all."

Ellen wasn't sure what happened next. One moment, he was staring at her, watching her with the stillness of a cat. The next, they were in each other's arms, kissing, tugging at each other's clothes.

Randolph's body was lean and hard. *The body of a soldier,* she thought as she traced the war wounds on his chest. He tightened his grip on her, groaning hunger into her mouth. When her hands drifted to the gashes on his stomach, something broke inside him. He seized her hands and pushed her down on the bed.

"The dream. You were in my dream, weren't you?" he panted as he stripped off the rest of her clothes. Before she had a chance to answer, Randolph was in her.

She cried out, burying her face in his neck.

"Yes. I was. I was," Ellen moaned as she rose to meet him.

He didn't hear her. His eyes were closed, his face twisted in a mask of pure lust. He took her hard, pushing deep inside her. If she had been with anyone else, she would have resisted. Randolph was brutal. Demanding. Ellen didn't want him to stop. She was ravenous, connected to her body in a way she'd never felt in the waking world. She needed roughness. She needed connection. She needed everything this strange, tortured man was giving her. Her mind screamed for her to stop, but the other part . . . the other part urged her on.

Arch your back. Lift your hips.

Wrap your legs around him.

Tighter. Faster. Deeper.

In almost no time, her breathing got heavier. Her body hummed, quivering with a familiar tension. Randolph looked at her with a mixture of desire and fear. He was no longer in control. He was no longer in control, and he knew it.

He shut his eyes.

He tried to back away, to fight the force rising inside him.

"No. Please. Stay with me. I need you," she pleaded as she cupped his face in her hands.

"He can't have you. You're mine. Do you hear me? You're mine," he snarled.

His breath hitched in his throat, and Randolph tumbled into a world beyond words. Ellen fell with him. They thrashed on the bed, groaning and clawing with mindless intensity. Then, slowly, the passion receded. They were left dazed, clinging to each other like two swimmers lost at sea.

He pressed his head between her breasts and let out a long, deep sigh.

"I'm sorry," he said after a long stretch of silence.

"For what?"

"I forced myself on you. You were vulnerable, and I forced myself on you."

She ran her fingers through his hair.

"No, you didn't," she insisted as she stroked his head. "I wanted you."

"I'm a married man," he reminded her.

Ellen said nothing. She never thought she was *that* woman, the type who would sleep with a married man. Yet here she was . . .

"There will be consequences," he warned her.

She had another, more terrifying thought.

What if what happens in the Dreamlands doesn't stay in the Dreamlands?

"Oh God. I'm not . . . I didn't. I didn't change things, did I?" she spluttered. "I'm not Andrew's grandmother or something, am I?"

"What? No! Don't be ridiculous!" He scurried out of the bed and snatched up his clothes. "What, did you think I lied because I wanted to get you in bed?"

"No. I didn't. That's not what I meant." The sheet fell away as she moved to her feet. Ellen didn't bother covering up. She saw no reason to be modest.

He hates me again, she thought, feeling a fresh wave of despair.

Randolph shook his head.

"I don't hate you."

"Then can we not do this right now? I don't want to fight. Can we just be together a little while longer?"

Randolph's gaze drifted across her body. Even though he'd just told her he was a married man, he wanted her again.

"Okay," he agreed in a soft voice.

"We're going to hell, aren't we?" she whispered as they moved toward each other.

"I think we're already there."

Chapter Twenty-Six

Where are we now?

For Ellen, the question had nothing to do with distance. Randolph walked beside her, but he wasn't there. He was trying to forget about what happened. Ellen knew it was impossible. She couldn't stop thinking about their night together. They didn't have sex just once (which might have been forgivable)—or even twice. They made love all night, with the same fervor and passion as the first time. And when they woke up in the morning with the sun blazing down on them, they went at each other again. To see if making love in the daylight made them feel guilty. It didn't. If anything, they enjoyed it more. The sex felt deeper. More profound. When they collapsed that last time, Randolph pulled away.

He pulled away and thought about his wife. Wielding Olivia like she was a magical weapon. Ellen supposed she was. The minute Olivia entered his mind, he disappeared. And she was left alone to wonder what she had destroyed in the waking world by sleeping with Randolph.

The road to Solomon's temple did little to lighten her mood. As they moved away from the coast and headed inland, the landscape grew bleaker. The terrain reminded Ellen of the surface of the moon. *Or Mordor,* she added. She shook her head. Mordor was evil, but it was still an active place. The battle between good and evil had yet to be decided. The war was over here. It had been over for a long time. And it was clear who had won.

Ellen hugged her robe tightly to her body, trying to ward off the poisonous atmosphere.

Randolph turned and glared at her.

"Sorry," she muttered, horrified she'd mentioned poisonous gas in front of a veteran of World War I. It took her a moment to realize she hadn't said a word. She'd only thought it.

Ellen saw no point in telling him to get out of her head.

It doesn't matter. He's already been in you.

Randolph made a strange choking sound.

"What's Mordor?" he demanded.

"It's a place in one of my favorite books. *Lord of the Rings.*"

"What's the book about?" he asked.

"About how a small, insignificant creature changed the world."

"Fiction, then."

Ellen gazed across the sterile land. "What did you mean? When you said 'he' couldn't have me?"

"What?"

"Last night when we were making love."

Randolph glared at her.

"I don't want to talk about last night."

Ellen ignored him.

"Last night, when we were making love, you said 'he' couldn't have me. What did you mean? Were you talking about Andrew?"

"I didn't say that," he said without missing a beat.

"Yes, you did."

"No, I didn't," he insisted, but she saw a flicker of uncertainty in his eyes.

She remembered the dazed look he gave her just before he surrendered. *God,* she thought, *who did I sleep with last night? Randolph or Andrew?*

Did the ring have anything to do with it?

The road rumbled before she could make up her mind. Ellen turned and saw a richly appointed covered carriage heading toward them. The grand vehicle looked ridiculous on the dirt road. Ellen couldn't help but think of the French Revolution, of the king breezing by peasants who were starving.

She glanced at Randolph, expecting him to share her anger.

He stepped off the road to make way for the vehicle.

"You're kidding me, right?"

"Cover your face and kneel," he ordered. When she hesitated, he pushed her into position. The gravel dug into her knees. "Pray."

"What?"

"Pray."

She felt a rush of righteous indignation.

"I'm not going to bow down to some rich bastard."

"We're disguised as monks. And monks pray for all who pass. I don't care who you pray for. Just pray!"

Ellen wasn't sure exactly why she prayed for Randolph Carter. She didn't like him. Sure, sleeping with him felt good. Incredible, really. But it did little to change her opinion of him. Maybe it was the nightmare. She'd experienced psychic bonds with people before. None were as intense. As intimate.

She bowed her head. Words swirled around her, but Ellen couldn't focus on them. All she could think about was the nightmare. The blinding pain that shot through Randolph as he lay on the ground, a telephone cord digging into his leg.

She felt a surge of helplessness, a bubble of panic rising in her chest. *I'm not getting out of here. If Randolph can't escape, what chance do I have?*

"How dare you," Randolph growled.

Ellen looked up just in time to see the carriage depart.

"What?"

"How dare you pray for me," he repeated, his tone darker this time.

"You told me to pray."

"I didn't tell you to pray for me!"

"You were the first person who popped into my head," she explained, even as she realized the absurdity of her situation. "Jesus, it's bad enough you're in my head. I'm not going to let you tell me *what* to think!"

"I don't want your sympathy."

"Well, that's tough. Because you've got it," she said sharply. She thought about the scars that riddled his body. "What happened?"

He stiffened.

"What do you mean?"

Ellen stepped forward and put her hand on his chest. Images rushed through her. The swift current almost swept her away.

"What happened during the war? At Denfert-Rochereau? That was the place, wasn't it? When the nightmare started. It wasn't in the trenches. The nightmare *ended* in the trenches. Everything started in Paris. In the catacombs of Denfert-Rochereau."

"Don't touch me."

"That wasn't a telephone cord wrapped around your leg, was it?" Ellen asked.

A switch went off in Randolph's head. His eyes dimmed.

PTSD, her mind whispered.

Her fingers traced the scars under his shirt.

He smacked her hand.

"I said don't touch me," he snapped. "You mean nothing to me. You understand? You're worthless. You gave me the only thing I wanted last night."

"I feel the same way about you," she replied, determined not to show any weakness. But his words dug deep.

"All I want is my ship."

"And all I want is a way out." Her eyes welled as she thought about the things waiting for her at home. "So, nothing's changed between us?"

"No."

"And we understand that?"

"Yes."

"Then let's go. The sooner I'm out of here, the better."

❖❖❖

Solomon Reye's temple loomed over them. It was a monstrosity, its walls so high, they seemed to punch the sky. Made of the same material as the granite cliffs around it, the building blended perfectly with its surroundings. The place reminded Ellen of the Anasazi ruins in Arizona. Slit windows let out tiny rectangles of light. A worn stone door waited on the other side of a creaky rope bridge. Ellen knew the grim features were meant to intimidate, to discourage all but the most devoted followers. But there were no followers. The place looked worn down. Forgotten. All she could see was sadness. As she looked at the empty bridge swaying in the wind, she couldn't help but wonder, *What sort of powerful demon lives in a crappy place like this?*

Randolph chuckled beside her.

The sound startled her. He'd been so quiet, she forgot he was there.

"What do we do? Knock?" Ellen asked. "Or is there a key under the mat?"

He pointed to the side of the cliff. "We're going down there. Where Solomon keeps his treasures."

Ellen crept to the edge and saw stairs carved into the rock. They wound their way down the canyon in narrow switchbacks.

She recognized them.

"This is where I first met you," she blurted.

"I know," Randolph said. "I should have just left you."

Elle gazed into the darkness below. She hoped the trail would look less intimidating than it did in her dreams.

It looked worse.

He grabbed her arm. "All right. Enough time being sentimental."

Ellen pulled away.

"Jesus, would you give a girl a moment? I'm—"

"What?"

"I'm scared. I'm scared, okay?" She regretted the words the moment they spilled from her lips. Still, she saw no reason to hide her feelings. *I think he already knows.* "I've been scared ever since I got here."

"Are you scared of me?"

"Yes," she admitted.

He let out a long sigh.

"You shouldn't be afraid of me."

"I'm the one you should be afraid of," another voice broke in.

Someone grabbed Ellen from behind.

A phalanx of guards surrounded them.

"Run! Run!" she screamed at Randolph.

Solomon Reye stepped forward.

He had taken on a new form. He looked like her boyfriend, Tom.

"How sweet. She's trying to protect you," Solomon purred.

"Get out of here. Run!" she yelled, but Randolph stood motionless. She couldn't decide whether he was hypnotized or shell-shocked.

"You honestly thought he was trying to help you? That Randolph Carter was on your side?" Solomon laughed. The scratchy sound reminded Ellen of dead leaves. "Oh, no. He only wanted one thing. And he made a deal with me to get it."

Ellen's stomach churned. She felt wobbly, like a puppet dangling from a single string.

She looked over at Randolph, sick with realization.

"You traded me for your ship."

"He traded you for his *wife*," Solomon Reye corrected her.

A pale woman emerged from the crowd.

Ellen's knees buckled. Somehow, she managed to stay upright.

"Liv!" Randolph rushed forward to embrace his wife. Olivia looked shaken, but Ellen couldn't miss the malicious glow in her eyes.

She only allowed her husband a quick hug before she turned to Solomon. "*That's* your queen? She's the one you've been chasing all this time?"

"Yes. Isn't she wonderful? My beautiful golden girl." Solomon ran his fingers through Ellen's hair.

Ellen's response was quick, almost automatic. She kicked Solomon Reye in the balls. The demon howled. For a moment, she felt a surge of satisfaction. It didn't last long. Solomon backhanded her across the face, hitting her so hard, she crashed to the ground.

A warm trickle of blood streamed from her nose.

Stay down, Randolph commanded her. *For God's sake, girl, stay down.*

She spat a bloody wad at his feet.

"The mighty Randolph Carter. What a joke."

"Don't talk to my husband that way," Olivia hissed.

Ellen rose and stared down Randolph's wife.

"I'll talk to your husband any fucking way I want."

The woman's hostile expression wavered.

"My, aren't you the tough one? I can't wait for our wedding tomorrow." Solomon sounded like a child contemplating Christmas. "I look forward to breaking your spirit."

"Tomorrow?" Ellen echoed.

"I know it's a bit of a rush, but you do have a nasty habit of getting cold feet," he said drolly. His guards snickered. "But don't worry. Everything is arranged. I have a priest. A wedding gown. I even have someone to give you away."

"Give me awa—"

The guards parted. King Kuranes was shoved into the middle of the circle. One of the soldiers stuck out his leg. Kuranes stumbled and fell.

"William!" Randolph started to move toward them, but Olivia held him back.

Ellen helped Kuranes to his feet.

Ellen exchanged a quick glance with Randolph.

Celephais, she thought. *If Kuranes is here and being held captive, what's happening to Celephais?*

For a single, fleeting moment, they were together again.

United by fear.

Kuranes stared at her with unfocused eyes.

He looked like he was emerging from one of his trances.

"Who are you?" he asked in a weak voice.

Ellen straightened his clothes and smoothed down his hair, trying to restore some of his dignity.

"My name is Ellen. Ellen Logan. We had dinner the other night, remember?"

"No, you're not," he insisted with the firmness of a two-year-old child. "Your name's not Ellen. It's Jessica. Jessica _____."

"What?"

"Your name is Jessica _____," he repeated.

Ellen concentrated, but she couldn't catch the last name. Randolph did. He stared at her in wide-eyed disbelief. He looked afraid. The way he did when they were making love. Just as they reached the edge . . .

"You're lying, old man. You're lying."

"Am I?" he asked Randolph with what she now knew was mock innocence. "She looks a little like Etti, don't you think?"

"No, she doesn't," he insisted.

"You're pretending not to see, Randy."

"No. You're the one who's pretending!" he shot back. "Do you honestly expect me to believe you? You'd say anything right now to get out of this."

"Would I?"

"What the hell is going on? And who's Etti?" Ellen demanded, tired of being tossed back and forth like a tennis ball.

Solomon shifted. "I was about to ask the same thing. What are you doing, Kuranes?"

"Nothing. Just watching Randy break a promise to an old friend."

"I am not breaking a promise! *She's not*—"

Solomon Reye interrupted.

"All right. Enough," he commanded. The two men fell silent. "Randolph, you and your lovely wife can leave *after* the wedding—we need guests to help us celebrate." It was clear it wasn't a request but an order. "Until then, you're free to wander the castle. In fact, you're all free. As long as you stay within certain boundaries."

"And if we don't?" Olivia challenged.

The demon fixed her with a level gaze. "You die."

"How will we know where the boundaries are?" Randolph asked.

"Oh, you'll know. Your weak little human bodies will tell you."

Ellen tightened her hold on Kuranes. "I want to stay with him. Please let me stay with him."

"He won't be able to help you."

"I know."

"Then why do you want to stay with him?"

"Because I don't want to be alone." Her voice caught on the last word.

Solomon just stared at her.

He doesn't understand, she thought with a shiver. *He takes a human form, but nothing about him is human.*

"All right. If it makes you feel better. But just for one night. After that, you're mine."

"How could you betray me like this, Randy?" Kuranes croaked as Ellen put her arm around him. "You were like a son to me. I was ready to give you my kingdom—"

"I don't want your kingdom. I want my own."

Olivia smiled.

It's Lady Macbeth, Ellen thought, *Lady Macbeth and her husband.*

Randolph's eyes shifted to Ellen. "You have something to say to me?"

"You're an awful man. A truly awful man. And I wish I left you trapped in your nightmare." Ellen wanted to do more. Scream. Hit. Bite. Leave a mark on him.

Kuranes tugged her sleeve.

"Come on, my dear. He's not worth it."

"You're right. He's nothing. A coward," she sneered as she led Kuranes away. She gave Randolph one last glare. Then she turned and followed Solomon Reye into the heart of his kingdom.

Chapter Twenty-Seven

Ellen expected to be tossed into a prison cell or locked away in a tower like Rapunzel. The room she and Kuranes were confined to looked like a suite in a grand hotel—huge bed, gorgeous rugs, modern bathroom with all the amenities. Despite the opulence, everything was wrong. When Ellen approached a table, she saw the reason why. The table was larger and higher than it needed to be. Not enough to create problems—she could still reach things—but enough for her to notice. Enough for her to realize she didn't belong in this world.

Ellen remembered the hamster she had as a child. She built what she thought was an ideal environment. Her pet died after only a few weeks.

Did I do the same thing? she wondered.

Did I create an alien world that made it curl up and die?

Her eyes wandered across the room.

There was a name for that kind of death.

"Failure to thrive," she murmured.

Ellen struggled to remember the hamster's name. *Howard? Harvey? Henry?*

"Hannah. Your hamster was a girl named Hannah," Kuranes offered.

She took a deep breath and was about to ask how he knew. It didn't matter. Nothing in the waking world mattered anymore.

"Is Celephais still there?" Ellen asked.

"It's safe," he reassured her. "I've dreamt it for so many years that it's etched a groove in my brain. Even if something did happen to me, others would take over. Despite what Randy thinks, I'm not a dictator."

"No, he's the one who wants to be the dictator."

"That surprised me. That really surprised me," Kuranes admitted in a soft voice. He was only half-human, but the human side hurt. "You slept with him, didn't you?"

"Excuse me?"

"You slept with him," he said again.

"How did you know?"

"Because your smell is all over him. He must have rolled in you like a dog."

Ellen held her tongue.

"His wife noticed, you know. I'm sure his reunion with Olivia is not going to be a pleasant one."

She rolled her eyes.

"Gee, that makes me feel *so* much better. I'll remember that when the demon is raping me." Ellen immediately regretted her words. She didn't want to think about it. "That's what's going to happen to me, isn't it?"

Kuranes sighed. "That's what happens to all Persephones."

"Persephone*s*?"

"You know, Persephone. The queen of the Underworld? The earth maiden the god of death kidnapped?"

"Yes, I know the myth. But . . . Persephone*s*?"

He shook his head.

"God, you Flatlanders are so narrow-minded. Always thinking about yourselves as individuals. Persephone isn't a single person. It's a role. Part of a ritual that joins our worlds. That keeps things connected."

"A sacrificial ritual."

"A sacrificial ritual," he agreed.

A cold trickle ran down her spine. "Oh God," she croaked. Another terrible thought followed. "Did he know?"

"Did who know?"

"Randolph Carter. Did he know he was giving me up to be sacrificed?"

"Does it matter?"

"It matters to me."

"You're in love with him."

"No, I'm not."

"You just found out you're going to be raped and killed, and your first question is whether Randy knew?" Kuranes fixed her with an appraising stare. "That sounds like love to me."

"Did. He. Know?" She pronounced each word like it was a sentence.

"No. He. Didn't," Kuranes replied after a long pause.

Only then did Ellen breathe.

"Why didn't you tell him?" she asked.

"There's only so much meddling I can do," he admitted with a shrug. "That's both a good thing and a bad thing."

"So what now? Am I just supposed to wait while Solomon sharpens his knives?"

"I don't know what to say. I did everything I could. I thought I could stop him this time. Rob him of the sacrifice that gives him power. But Randy betrayed me and. . . ." A pained expression crossed his face. "There's only so much I can do. And no matter how much I want to help you—"

"The needs of the many outweigh the needs of a few," she said wearily.

"Who said that?" Kuranes asked.

"S'chn T'gai Spock," she replied as she twisted her hair.

Logic is cold, she thought. *It's so fucking cold.*

Kuranes spread out on the bed. "Then you understand. I'm sorry, my dear. Truly I am. But—"

"You have a city to dream."

The next time she looked at him, he was asleep.

⁕⁕⁕⁕⁕

Andrew. I'm never going to see Andrew Carter again. The thought ran through Ellen's head as she searched for a way to kill herself. She didn't think about Uncle Joshua. Or Tom. Or any of her friends. She didn't even think about her missing family. But *Andrew Carter*—he mattered. He was the central point of her universe. She knew now that what she felt for him wasn't a schoolgirl crush or a passing physical attraction. This went far beyond anything she expected. Miss Cummings's words echoed in her head. *You two have a connection. A powerful connection. He feels it, too.* She'd doubted the director of the

Eibon Institute at the time. But now . . . the world she knew before the Dreamlands was gone. Everything was different. She didn't even feel like the same person.

She pulled a blanket away from King Kuranes.

The monarch shifted, muttering in his sleep.

"I have to get away. Any way I can," she whispered to herself.

Daylight had softened the sky by the time Ellen finished the noose she made from the torn pieces of the blanket. Even though its purpose was grim, she paused to admire her work. She was hopeless with arts and crafts. It was the only class she ever failed. But when it mattered, when it really mattered, she pulled it off.

Uncle Joshua would be so proud, she thought.

Ellen's eyes blurred with tears.

She bit down on her lip, unsure whether to laugh or scream.

The doorknob to the room rattled.

Ellen reeled in her homemade noose and dove under Kuranes's bed.

A pair of shoes marched up to the bed.

Kuranes stirred above her.

"You came to see me," he greeted the stranger. "I knew you would. I knew you were better than—"

"Is it true? Is it true, old man?" Randolph demanded.

"It's not for me to say. You need to decide for yourself."

Ellen could hear the smile behind his words.

"I think you already know," Kuranes purred. "Why else would you be here?"

"Where is she?" Randolph demanded after a few moments of silence.

"Under the bed. Where all scared little girls hide."

Ellen crawled out from the other side of the bed and kicked the bed frame.

"Goddamnit. God fucking damn it! Do you have any loyalty? Any loyalty at all?"

King Kuranes's eyes were open, but he wasn't listening.

He's back in Celephais, she thought as she looked at his blank face. *Holding his world together.*

Randolph nodded at the noose draped around her shoulders.

"What's that?"

"My escape plan."

"That's not the way out," he replied.

"I'm not looking for a way out. I'm trying to kill myself."

"Why?"

"Because I'm a Persephone," Ellen said.

"*What?*" Randolph demanded in a low, level voice.

"I'm a Persephone. I'm going to be—"

"I know what a Persephone is." He turned to Kuranes. "You can't let this happen, Will."

Kuranes lapsed out of his trance. "It's out of my hands, my boy," he said with a shrug.

Randolph rounded the bed and grabbed her arm. "Then I'm taking her. He can't have her."

Ellen recoiled and wrenched free from his grip.

"Get away! Don't touch me!"

Pain flared in his eyes.

"Look, you have no reason to trust me, but you need to do it," he pleaded. "You *have* to do it."

"You said that before, and things didn't turn out so well."

"I got you here, didn't I?"

"Only to deliver me into the arms of a homicidal demon. Thank you a *whole* fucking lot."

Kuranes laughed.

"You two are hopeless. Utterly hopeless." Kuranes looked between them. "Randy, shut up. And Jessica, look into his eyes."

"What?" Ellen blurted.

"Look into his eyes," Kuranes commanded.

"No!"

"Jessie."

Ellen's anger flared. "Stop calling me that! It's not my name!"

"That *is* your name. You just don't know it yet."

"I don't know what sick little game you're playing, but it ends now," Ellen insisted.

"*I* decide when the game ends."

Ellen heard the inhuman coldness in Kuranes's voice.

She refused to let him scare her.

"We're all little playthings to you, aren't we? '*Oi chusoi Dios aei enpiptousi.*'"

Randolph jumped, as if he'd heard a sudden gunshot.

"What did you just say?" he demanded.

"The dice of God are always loaded," she replied. "It's an old—"

"Yes, I know what it is, thank you very much!" Randolph stammered, his words crashing into each other.

Kuranes leered at him.

"You still think I'm lying, Randy? That I'm making it up?"

"Shut up, old man," Randolph snarled.

Randolph's eyes locked on hers. Ellen expected to see hostility. But there was warmth. For the first time since entering the Dreamlands, she felt warm.

She moved toward Randolph.

Kuranes's smile spread.

"What the hell is going on?" Ellen whispered.

Randolph held out a shaking hand. "I don't know how you're going to do it, but you have to trust me."

"I can't."

"Please."

This time, it was a plea.

Uncle Joshua's words came back to haunt her. *The world you're in requires split-second decisions. Decisions the head and heart can't make.*

She took his hand.

He pulled her into his arms and held her tight.

Ellen slumped against him, burying her face in his chest.

"My girl, my dear, sweet girl," he said softly, the words warm on her head.

"You need to get her out of here, Randy," Kuranes said after a few moments of silence.

"How?"

"I told you the truth when I said there was an object that would help her cross over. You need to find it. It's got to be on your ship."

"I don't know where my ship is." Randolph finally let her go. "Solomon took it, remember?"

"There's an underground lake at the base of the mountain. That's where he keeps his earthly treasures. I'm certain your vessel is among them," Kuranes insisted.

"Can I ask you a question, King Kuranes?" Ellen asked.

"Will."

"Will," she corrected. "How do you know all this? About Solomon Reye?"

"I was about to ask the same thing," Randolph chimed in.

"Believe it or not, we were once allies." He paused to let the words sink in. "Solomon and I were repulsed by the Persephone ritual, by the violence of it. But over time, Solomon developed a . . . taste for your kind. He came to appreciate human beings in a very dark, twisted way."

"The way a serial killer appreciates his victims," Ellen offered.

Kuranes frowned. "A serial what?"

"How do we get to his collection?" Randolph asked.

"I don't know. I've never tried to get there. I suspect there's a path somewhere. You should be able to find it. Assuming you can keep your hands off her long enough, Randy."

Randolph whirled to face her. "*Did you tell him?*"

"She didn't have to tell me." Kuranes tapped his nose. A flush spread down Randolph's neck. "Now, run along, you two. I need to find a way out, too."

Chapter Twenty-Eight

"What are we looking for?" Ellen asked.

"Smelling for," Randolph corrected. "It's better to smell for things here. Smell is harder to hide."

"What are we smelling for?"

He shrugged. "The smell of a ship, I suppose."

"And you're sure we're safe? Being out here like this?" She hugged her arms to her body. The hallway they were in was warm, but she still shivered. She couldn't stop thinking about Solomon's warnings about boundaries.

"As sure as I can be." Randolph paused to study a door. "I think Solomon established his boundaries outside of the castle, not inside."

"And why are you sure the path to the ship is inside the castle?"

He let out an exasperated sigh. "Think about it. You want to look at your collection. To take pleasure in what you've plundered. Are you going to go outside and hike down a dangerous canyon trail every time you want to do that?"

"Why would he even have to do that? He's a demon, right? Can't he just wish himself there?"

"He's only *half*-demon. There are limits to what he can do. And I'd bet money he takes the easy way whenever he can. I mean, he may be powerful, but that doesn't mean he's not lazy."

Ellen smiled.

"You've got a point there," she admitted.

Randolph stared at her with burning eyes. He stepped forward and pressed his fingers to her lips. Almost as if he were trying to catch her smile before it fluttered away. Ellen tilted her head back, offering him her mouth. She was ready to go under. She wanted to go under.

Her eyes snapped open.

"Dirty fuel," she blurted just as his lips brushed hers.

For a moment, she wasn't sure if it was even her thought. "What?"

Ellen pulled away. She didn't want to let go. Letting Randolph go felt like sliding out of bed on a cold winter morning.

"Dirty fuel. I smell dirty fuel," she insisted. "You know, that awful mix you get on fishing boats when the fuel line is clogged up. I think you're right. The path to the cave is around here somewhere.."

"You don't have to sound so surprised," he grumbled.

He turned his attention to the task at hand. He felt along the wall, searching for any hidden levers or springs. Ellen did the same. She didn't expect to find anything, so she was surprised when her finger sank into a hole.

She felt and heard a click.

Her heart surged in her chest.

"Oh shit," she whispered.

Carter looked up, his face darkening. "Don't move. It's a trap."

"Yeah, I kind of assumed that. I *do* play D&D, you know."

"You mentioned D&D before. What the hell is it?" he asked as he rummaged through his pockets.

We're in the middle of it right now, she thought.

"Dungeons and Dragons. It's a game," she replied, chatting to keep her mind off her situation. "You invent characters and take them through various adventures. They go on quests, get into battles. Oh, and you roll dice to figure out what happens."

"Sounds ridiculous."

"It's not ridiculous. It's wonderful. You get together and play with your friends. There's lots of beer and pizza. You know what pizza is, right?"

"I know what beer is, too. I'd be with you on the beer part," Randolph replied.

"You don't like pizza?"

"No."

"Randolph Carter, you are downright un-American."

For a moment, for one fleeting moment, he smiled. Then he pulled out a Swiss army knife and returned to the task at hand.

She frowned at the weapon. "How can you even have that?"

"What do you mean?"

"Solomon Reye lets people run around his place with weapons?"

"He doesn't think humans are very smart. Most Eminences are arrogant that way." He knelt in front of her and peered into the opening. "Besides, he's older. He has a very short attention span. I mean, how many times have you managed to get away from him?"

Carter slid the cold knife blade between her finger and the wall.

"Kuranes has been around humans more. He knows us better. He knows we can be simple and complex at the same time." He fiddled with the knife for a little longer. "There! I think I've jammed it. Pull out your finger."

Ellen yanked so hard, she lost her balance.

She landed hard on her butt.

There was a sickening snap, followed by the sound of grinding.

"Are you hurt?" He demanded.

She held up her hand, too afraid to look.

Randolph counted her fingers and pulled her to her feet.

"Do you fall on your ass a lot in D&D?" he asked as she brushed off her clothes.

"More times than I'd like." Now that her eyes were open, she could see that the wall had opened, revealing a set of stairs that snaked into the darkness. "Well, at least it worked."

"It almost cost you a finger."

"I suppose Solomon would consider that a small price to pay to look at his collection." Ellen inched closer to the passage. The smell of diesel was distant but intense. She took off her coat and waved it over the threshold.

"What are you doing now? Bullfighting?"

"Trying not to make the same mistake twice," she said, too distracted to register his sarcasm.

They crossed the threshold together. The moment they cleared the door, it ground shut behind them.

Ellen jumped, startled by the sudden movement. She looked grimly at her companion. "Well, I guess there's only one way out now."

The path to the cave was a medieval cliché—uneven steps and stone walls punctuated by flickering glass lanterns.

The only thing this place needs is a dragon, she thought.

"Don't be so sure there isn't one," Carter replied. "We haven't gotten to the bottom yet."

They spiraled down. And down. And down. They walked down the stairs for so long, Ellen forgot there were other directions. She thought about a Buddhist temple she visited in Nepal. Perched on a mountain, it required its visitors to climb an endless set of stairs. She remembered how excited she was when she reached the top, how beautiful the sunrise over the mountains was. But here, on *this* staircase, she felt only dread. There would be no sunrise. There would be no sense of accomplishment. There would only be desolation. She pictured the lowest ring of hell—a frozen lake with Satan hovering over the landscape.

Randolph paused on the stairs.

An eerie glow spread out to meet them.

"I think we're here," he announced. "Wherever *here* is."

After a few more turns, the spiral stairs ended. A huge beach spread out before them. In the distance, a lake flashed like an emerald in the darkness. Solomon Reye's treasures were spread out on the smooth black sand, as far as the eye could see. The demon didn't just collect ships. There were trains, cars, planes, buses, even golf carts. Ellen recognized the items, but Carter struggled to understand what he was seeing.

Most of it was too modern for him.

Ellen wished she had time to introduce him to her world.

"Look." Randolph pointed at the ceiling.

Ellen followed his gaze to the object suspended above them.

"That's a helicopter."

"No. Look *inside* it."

Every muscle in Ellen's body tightened as she moved in to get a closer look. The helicopter was from a news station. Its call numbers were splashed garishly across the roof. *KRCW*, Ellen read. *Where is KRCW?* Her focus drifted to the cockpit. The pilot was still at the controls. He was snatched from the waking world so recently, she could still see the shock in his dead eyes. In his last moments, he'd tried to free himself from his restraints. He'd only gotten halfway out and strangled himself with his safety harness.

"Oh God. Do you think there are—"

Others. The word died in her throat. Something struck her from behind. Ellen fell forward, crashing into the sand. She rolled on the ground, groaning. She tried to get back up but couldn't find her feet. Her mind was stuffed with cotton; her legs were jelly. Out of the corner of her eye, she saw shadowy figures darting around her. More blows pelted her body. They were so quick that she didn't have time to react. All she could do was curl into a ball and try to protect herself.

"*Ajsadahom tazija*," a voice called out.

The attacks stopped.

Randolph shouted at her, but his voice was distant.

Just let go, a voice urged her. *You knew you wouldn't make it. Stop the pain.*

Ellen closed her eyes.

She melted back into her warm spring day—grass pressing against her back. Tom teasing her with a flower.

"Get up." Randolph shook her, his voice gruff.

"No."

He prodded her like a stubborn horse. "I said get up."

"I can't."

His next words were a menacing whisper. "You know, they'll feed on you while you're still alive. They'll rip your face off, just like a hyena."

Ellen sat up, spitting sand out of her mouth. The world spun around her.

For a moment, she thought she would throw up.

Carter pressed his cold hand to her forehead.

The wave of nausea passed.

"Better?" he asked.

"Sort of. I feel like I've been in a car crash."

"You're lucky. If one of the ghouls hit you full force, you'd be dead." The last words caught in his throat. "You'd be dead," he repeated faintly.

"Ghouls?"

Randolph lifted his hands from her eyes. They were still in Solomon's graveyard. The pilot in the news chopper still swung from his safety harness. But they were no longer alone. Four creatures surrounded them, crouched on their haunches. They had grayish-blue skin. Long arms and legs. Their faces were a cross between a pit bull and a wild boar. And they had dead, black eyes. One creature leered at her, baring yellow teeth.

Ellen curled against Randolph for protection.

"Oh my God. Ohmygod. Ohmygod," she chanted, her teeth chattering.

"You've never seen a ghoul before?" he asked as he helped her to her feet.

"No."

"Richard Pickman painted nothing *but* ghouls," he declared.

"He's lost to history, too, I'm afraid."

Just like you, Randolph Carter, a voice whispered in her head.

"*Damnatio memoriae,*" he replied.

"What?"

The creatures stirred before he could respond. A huge ghoul marched into the middle of the circle. It sported tattoos all over its grayish-blue face. *Marks of status,* she thought as she studied the intricate designs. Then she noticed the ghoul also wore a three-piece suit. Ellen wondered where he found such formal clothes.

You know the answer, her mind taunted. *Graves. They scavenge clothes from the bodies of the dead.*

"*Masaa el Kheer, Assayed Jinn.*" Randolph greeted the creature.

Jinn.

Ellen realized why she couldn't understand him earlier, back on the beach.

The creature spoke Arabic.

"*Hal anta men aalam al 'ejram?*" the ghoul demanded.

The creature turned to face her, studying her with milky white eyes.

All Ellen could do was stare.

"I-I-I'm sorry. I don't understand," she spluttered.

"She doesn't speak Arabic," Randolph explained. He put his hand on her shoulder. *Just be honest with him,* he urged her. *Tell him the truth.*

"Are you the one from the underground?" the ghoul asked, feeling its way over the foreign words.

Ellen was so shocked by his English, she didn't notice his awkwardness.

"Part of the underground?"

"He wants to know if you're a Persephone."

"Solomon Reye seems to think so."

The ghoul hissed at the name.

"What do *you* think?" the creature pressed.

"I think he sees things in me that aren't there," Ellen admitted.

"He's getting old, *Assayed*. Old and desperate," Randolph offered as he moved forward. His eyes glittered with excitement. "Now's the time for us to strike."

"I'm not interested in human politics. I'm only interested in freeing my pack," the creature said.

"This is your time. You must take it," Randolph insisted.

"Freeing your pack? You're trapped?" Ellen blurted.

The ghoul shifted his attention back to her. Even though he had a thick, rubbery face, she could see his anger.

"That demon put his palace on our land. He traps us inside his magical boundaries. Keeps us from our hunting grounds in the waking world. Then he tries to make up for it by tossing us his leftovers." He sneered at the body dangling from the helicopter. Then he nodded at the other ghouls, clad in jeans and old football jerseys. "My pack is a shadow of what it once was. Look at them. They're like zombies. Weak. Slow. Dressed in human rags."

"Slow? You could have fooled me," Randolph observed.

The alpha ghoul turned and eyed him coldly.

"If we were in our prime, you'd be warm in our bellies now," the creature growled.

"For a ghoul is a ghoul and, at best, an unpleasant companion for man," Randolph said.

The leader flashed him a wide, predatory smile.

"Don't you forget. Don't you ever forget that."

He looked over at Ellen, offering her the same unsettling look.

"Now, tell me, humans. How do we defeat the demon?"

Chapter Twenty-Nine

The ghoul ferried them across the glowing water. Ellen studied the creature as he steered the boat. The creature shed his jacket before they left. The tattoos on his face and arms were different. The ghoul's face and neck sported abstract designs, colorful patterns that reminded her of the carvings on totem poles. His arms were marked with black squiggles and dashes. Ellen leaned in for a closer look. She tried to memorize both types of tattoos, so she could reproduce them if she got home. *When I get home*, she corrected herself. The thought still burned. Ellen had done everything she could to stay optimistic, but as they sailed between the ships in Solomon's "collection," the stench of death overwhelmed her.

"You have a boyfriend," Randolph Carter announced.

"What?" Ellen asked, only half-listening. She couldn't take her eyes off Solomon's collection.

"You have a boyfriend," he muttered. "I saw him, just as you were about to go under. Your mind was full of sunlight. I haven't felt warmth like that in a very, very long time."

Ellen turned to him, surprised by the sadness she heard in his voice.

"Are you going to tell him? About us?" he asked her.

"I don't know. I haven't really had time to think about it."

"Are you going to tell Andrew?"

She shook her head. "You cast a long enough shadow over him as it is."

"You're very protective of him."

"Yes, I am."

Randolph's ship emerged in the twilight.

For the first time, Ellen saw the name of the ship.

The *Olivia*.

She looked away, blushing. "Do you regret sleeping with me?"

He stared into her eyes with an almost unbearable intensity. "I regret nothing. Not a single moment. Do you?"

"I wish we were in bed right now," she admitted.

The expression on his face darkened. Suddenly, Randolph looked as fierce and hungry as a ghoul.

An angry howl pierced the sky.

The sound rolled toward them like an approaching storm.

Carter grimaced.

"I think your future husband might have a problem with that."

"That's not funny," she scolded.

"I'm not trying to be funny."

He nodded at the ladder that dangled over the side of the other ship. "Get on board."

Ellen examined the fraying rope. The rope ladder looked unstable. She turned to Randolph, to ask him if there was another way, when a large wave slammed into the boat. Ellen lost her footing and stumbled toward the edge. Her body reacted instantly, instinctually. She leapt across the narrow space between the vessels. She managed to grab onto the rope ladder, lifting her body just as the ghoul's boat slammed into the *Olivia*.

A second roar shook the air. Ellen trembled. She wanted to give up. To let go and plunge into the deep, dark waters. Then she thought of losing Andrew Carter. And Tom and Uncle Joshua. She would never see Miskatonic University again. She would never know if she had what it took to graduate. Ellen hooked her feet on one of the rungs and scurried up the side of the ship.

This is the only thing you can do, she thought as she climbed onto the deck of the *Olivia. Either that or wait for a demon to rape and kill you.*

Out of the corner of her eye, she saw Randolph haul himself aboard.

"I told you, that's not going to happen," he gasped as he joined her. "I'll kill you first. Drive a knife straight into your heart."

"Well, that's a relief," she quipped. Ellen meant the words to be sarcastic but realized that dying at Randolph's hands was a better option. A *much* better option.

A low sound spread out from the shore. The deep, sub-sonic throb reminded her of a digeridoo. At first, it competed with Solomon Reye's war whoops and the rattle of his approaching guard.

The sound soon overwhelmed Solomon's army.

Randolph pointed to the horizon. "Look!"

Ellen couldn't see much, just the narrow flow of Solomon's men as they streamed through the junkyard. A blur of motion hit Solomon's forces. Followed by another. And another.

A cloud of sand rose from the beach.

"The ghouls," Ellen said softly.

"They're rising up," Randolph blurted.

"What?"

"They're attacking Solomon's men."

He stared at her with wide-eyed wonder. Then he grabbed her wrist and pulled her toward the cargo hold. "They're helping us, but we don't have much time. If we're lucky, we can . . ."

His words died at the foot of the stairs. Ellen assumed the *Olivia* would be empty, that between Solomon Reye and the ghouls, the place would be picked clean. But Solomon had converted it into a storage space. A place to put his treasures. The ship was stuffed to the rafters with souvenirs from every human era. They stepped onto a floor coated in coins. All around them were statues, paintings, piles of ancient scrolls and books. Full suits of medieval armor guarded the collection.

Under any other circumstances, such priceless treasures would thrill Ellen. She'd spend countless hours sifting through them.

Ellen picked up a battered crown.

She saw a brief flash of a hunchback on a horse.

Useless, she thought as she tossed it back on the pile. *Totally useless.*

"How am I supposed to find what I need to get back?" she asked.

"I don't know," Randolph replied.

He eyed a menacing dagger.

Probably Jack the Ripper's.

He snorted and looked away.

Her eyes drifted to the hatch that led to the deck.

Dust motes danced in the light.

"Oh my God," Ellen said.

She spun around, half expecting to see Martha Pickman sprawled among the treasures.

"Cellar door," she whispered. "All this time, I thought it was a cellar door."

She ran up the stairs and grabbed the door to the deck. She slammed it shut, fumbling for the padlock she knew was there.

She snapped it into place before Carter could stop her.

"What the hell are you doing? You cut off the only way out!"

"This is my nightmare. Trust me. That's not the way out."

A thud came from overhead.

The wood buckled with the impact.

Ellen stumbled backward down the stairs, slipping on the rich carpet of coins.

Randolph caught her.

"Focus. Do you hear me? Focus," he hissed in her ear.

Another powerful blow splintered the wood. The door hatch held firm, but Ellen knew a few more hits would destroy it.

She looked at the dagger lying on the floor.

Tired, so tired.

Randolph shook her.

"My cabin. That's where I took you when I fished you out of the sea. Maybe what we're looking for is there."

"But what if—" she started to protest.

He shoved her in the direction of his cabin.

"*Move!*"

They fought their way through a narrow passage that ran through the ship. The path reminded her of the hedge mazes that popped up around Halloween. Ellen always laughed when she went through them, playing along with her friends. But they terrified her. This was much worse. Trapped in an enclosed space, in a foreign world, with a demon on her tail . . . The only thing that kept her going was Randolph Carter. He was behind her, shielding her from Solomon Reye. If she stopped, if she gave into her fear, Randolph would die protecting her. So she kept moving, even though the walls closed in around her, even though the space grew tight and constricted.

When they reached the cabin, Ellen fell to her knees in the middle of the room. She scrabbled through Solomon's collection, searching for the item that would return her to the waking world.

"Dark. Too dark in here," she muttered.

She reached for a flashlight lying on the floor.

The air around them grew heavy.

"It's too late," Randolph whispered.

Ellen looked up.

A shadowy figure stood at the foot of the stairs.

"I'm through," Solomon Reye said in a dead voice. "I'm through *playing* with you."

Randolph grabbed her and yanked her head back.

Ellen felt the bite of cold steel.

The dagger, she thought dimly. *He picked up the dagger.*

"I'm done playing with you, too," Carter rasped.

"Please, no! Oh God, please, no!" she pleaded, even though she knew it was pointless. Randolph *had* to kill her. He needed to stop Solomon Reye.

Ellen tightened her grip on the flashlight. She wanted to die holding on to something from the waking world.

LA CLAVE.

The words blazed across her eyelids.

ESTA ES LA CLAVE.

She saw it all again. Emilio Carranza's plane flying into the storm, the nightgaunt attack, how Carranza freed her by swinging a flashlight at Solomon Reye's magical barrier.

"Key! This is the key!"

Carter hesitated for a moment.

It was all she needed.

She flipped the switch of Carranza's flashlight.

Light flooded the room, bathing them in searing white. Then, just as quickly, the world disappeared.

Chapter Thirty

Ellen woke to a soft, feathery sound. She rolled onto her stomach. Cold seeped through her clothes. She opened her eyes and found herself face down in a snowbank. Flurries twirled in the air around her. A few feet away, a flashlight shined a sickly yellow light into a tree.

Am I dead?

She gasped. Her hands groped for her neck.

There was no cut, no sign that Randolph had slit her throat.

She moved to her feet, brushing the snow off her clothes. King Kuranes had told her that Solomon's object would return her to the waking world. Was he telling the truth? She looked around. Nothing looked familiar or Earth-like. What if the flashlight transported her to another part of the Dreamlands? To a place that was hostile to humans? Ellen shivered. She didn't want to think about being abandoned, left to die in an icy wasteland.

A moan came from nearby. Randolph lay motionless on the ground. Ellen wasn't sure which Carter it was. Then she saw the knife.

She reached down and pried it out of his hand.

"Randolph? It's Ellen," she said.

He rolled on the ground in agony.

Ellen knelt beside him.

"What's wrong?" she called out. "Hey, what's wrong?"

"Too much. It's too much," he moaned, turning away when the sun popped out from behind a cloud.

The waking world. He's not used to being in the waking world.

She straightened.

"Oh God. I'm back. I'm back," she cried out in disbelief.

The fog around them thinned.

She could see a cabin in the distance.

"Uh . . ." Randolph's eyes rolled back.

Ellen moved closer and cupped his face in her hands. The way she had that night in the cabin. Right before they . . .

"Stay with me. Do you hear me? Please, stay with me," Ellen pleaded.

"Leave. You have to leave."

"No."

"I said leave."

She punched him in the shoulder. "And I said no!"

Randolph's eyes flew open.

He stared at her in disbelief.

A huge, drunken smile spread across his face.

"You're Etti's girl. Oh, you're definitely Etti's girl."

"Who's Et—?"

"You left the flashlight on." The voice seared the snow.

Ellen didn't have to look to know it was Solomon Reye. She could see the dread in Randolph's eyes. A moment later, the flashlight bounced off the tree. The light flickered and went out.

"Oh God." Ellen exhaled, her breath thick in the air. She felt all the fight drain out of her. The sensation was so sharp, so visceral, she looked at the ground, half expecting to see blood on the snow.

"Why are you doing this? She's crossed over. She's useless to you now," Randolph croaked with all the defiance he could muster.

The demon chuckled. The malignant sound filled the air.

"I don't like losing."

She heard a rasp of metal on the ground. Ellen turned to see what form their death would take.

Randolph pulled her to the ground and shielded her with his body.

"What are you doing?"

"Protecting you."

"I don't want to watch you die."

"Then close your eyes."

Ellen wrapped her arms around him.

Even now, in the shadow of death, she could feel Randolph's desire pressing against her.

Pop! The sound was not what she expected. Pop! Pop! Pop! Each sound followed by a sharp, metallic clang. Randolph gasped. His body tensed. *A gun,* she thought numbly, *Solomon's shooting us.* She tightened her grip on Randolph, waiting for the bullets to rip into her.

There was nothing.

Randolph looked down at her, confused.

"My, my. Look at you, Randy. The noble knight protecting the maiden. Who would have thought?" King Kuranes observed as he lowered his gun.

Randolph scrambled off Ellen.

Solomon Reye lay on the ground, his hands wrapped around a battle-ax.

Blood bloomed underneath him.

Carter stared at the body.

"What . . . what the fuck! What did you just do, old man?" he spluttered.

"What did I do? I took your advice. I struck Solomon Reye when he was weak. Vulnerable."

Kuranes smiled at Ellen as he helped her to her feet.

"I should have listened to you, my dear. Do you remember what you said to me when we first met?"

Ellen shook her head, unable to speak.

"You said you'd had enough of that fucking moron. Well, truth be told, I felt the same way. In fact, he was such a nuisance, I almost killed Solomon *and* you when you crossed into the Dreamlands."

He paused to let the point sink in.

"I'm glad I waited. It worked out *so* much better this way," he cooed.

"What do you mean?" Randolph demanded in a husky voice.

"Let's not discuss it here." Kuranes pulled up the collar of his coat. He nodded to the cabin in the distance. "Do you think you can get us into your family's cabin, Randy?"

Randolph's eyes were glassy. Fixed on the dead demon at their feet.

"Randy?"

"Yeah. Sure," he agreed.

"What about *him*?" Ellen gestured at Solomon Reye. She knew better than to turn her back on a maniac. She'd seen too many horror movies to make *that* mistake.

Kuranes waved off her concern.

"He's no longer a danger. You have other things to worry about."

"Other things to—" Ellen stopped, feeling a stab of dread. "I'm not in the waking world, am I? I'm still in the Dreamlands."

Kuranes held out his arm. "You don't have much farther to go, my dear. You're very close to the end of your journey. But the last steps are the most dangerous."

Ellen looked at Randolph.

"Please don't leave me," she pleaded.

Kuranes's eyes glittered in the twilight.

"Oh, he won't," he assured her. "He has no choice."

———————— ✦✦✦✦✦ ————————

King Kuranes flopped into the worn leather chair. A puff of dust rose from the cushions. He ran a finger across the grimy surface.

"Really, Randy. You should think about cleaning up a little," Kuranes chided.

Randolph said nothing.

He drifted to a far corner and leaned against the wall.

Putting as much space between us as he can, she thought with a sigh.

Ellen looked around the room. She found it hard to believe she had been there a few days ago. The place was dusty, thick with cobwebs. Parts of the ceiling sagged. It had aged a hundred years in only a few days.

Ellen looked to Kuranes.

"Did you do this?"

"What?"

"Did you trash Randolph Carter's house?"

"Me?" Kuranes replied in mock indignation. "No, *time* did this. Time and neglect."

"I have no reason to keep this place clean. I'm no longer part of the waking world," Randolph announced from the corner.

Ellen perked up.

"Waking world? You mean this—"

She rushed toward the grimy windows.

Kuranes grabbed her before she could reach them.

"I said you were close. You're not there yet." He put his hand on her shoulder and steered her to the couch. "Please, my dear, sit. Randy, join her."

"No."

Kuranes shot him a sharp look.

Randolph plopped onto the couch.

His sudden change of mood bothered Ellen. If there was anyone she considered an ally in the Dreamlands, Randolph was it. And now . . .

"Why do you hate me all of a sudden?" she blurted.

He folded his arms and glared at her.

"You don't know?"

"Not a clue."

"You seduced me."

"Seduced you?" Ellen echoed.

Kuranes snickered. "Oh please, Randy. That's not true. Everything you did that night was of your own free will."

Carter's mouth curled into a sneer.

"What did you do, old man? Watch us the whole time? I didn't think that was your kind of thing."

Ellen leaned forward and buried her face in her hands.

"Oh please . . ." she groaned.

"She didn't set you up. And she didn't seduce you," Kuranes replied. "Look at her. She's horrified by what happened that night. She wished it never happened."

"Don't put words in my mouth, old man," Ellen mumbled through her fingers.

The atmosphere in the room changed.

Kuranes suddenly towered over her.

"*What* did you just say, girl?" he hissed.

Ellen rose to her feet. A strange electrical energy coursed through her body. She didn't know what was happening. All she knew was that she was fed up. She was tired of being afraid all the time, of expecting to die every second of the day. Most of all, Ellen was tired of being trapped between these two men, of being a pawn in their elaborate game of chess.

"I don't care who you are. You do *not* speak for me!" Ellen growled in a voice she didn't recognize. "You do not put words in my mouth. Do I make myself clear?"

Kuranes gazed deep into her eyes.

He searched for any weakness, any fault line he could exploit.

A look of wonder spread across his face.

"My God, you are. You're a true Persephone. *Kore memagmeni.*"

"I'm not a Persephone! Persephone isn't real!" Ellen exploded. "It's just a myth. A stupid myth about the seasons!"

She turned to Randolph for help.

His eyes were locked on King Kuranes.

"A *kore memagmeni*? Are you serious, Will?"

"Think about it. Has crossing back and forth into the Dreamlands diminished her in any way? She's just as strong here as in the waking world. Maybe even stronger. You just saw her stand up to me. That took some serious goddess energy. For a moment, even *I* was scared."

"That certainly explains why I slept with her," Randolph offered.

Kuranes rolled his eyes.

"Yes, she overpowered you. Whatever you say, Randy."

"Is somebody going to tell me what *kore megalomaniac* is?" Ellen asked.

Kuranes let out a hearty laugh.

"*Memagmeni*," he corrected.

"What is it?"

"The Persephone myth isn't what you think. It's not an explanation of the seasons. And it's not about kidnapping, rape, and domination, although Solomon wanted you to believe that. Persephone is a powerful deity. A *kore memagmeni.* The mixed daughter who passes between the two worlds. Guards the borderlands—"

Ellen felt something pulse behind her eyes.

"Thin place," she whispered. "You're talking about thin places."

Kuranes wrinkled his nose.

"Thin places? Is that what they call it now? Not very poetic." He sighed. "But the name doesn't diminish your power. Or your responsibility."

Your responsibility. The words sounded like a death knell.

"Don't worry, my dear," Kuranes reassured her. "You'll have someone to help you. Someone who will patrol the border on this side. A partner, if you will."

His eyes settled on Randolph.

"What?" Randolph's voice was as heavy as lead.

"You bound yourself to her that night. Don't you feel the connection?"

Carter launched himself off the couch.

"What? But I'm already . . . I have a . . . Olivia's my wife!"

"Have you consummated your marriage with Olivia?" Kuranes asked.

"Of course I have!"

"In the Dreamlands?"

Randolph froze.

Kuranes nodded in Ellen's direction.

"You slept with her first, didn't you?"

"No!"

"I think you'll find you did."

Kuranes brought Carter and Ellen together.

She tried to pull away.

"I don't want to be with him!" she protested.

"It doesn't matter what you want," Kuranes insisted.

"This is ridiculous!"

"Would you rather be with Solomon Reye?" Kuranes growled. "Because that can still be arranged."

"Ellen, stop," Randolph said softly.

She looked at him, stunned. It was the first time he'd ever called her by name.

"We can't—"

He let out a long, weary sigh. "We have no choice. Everyone has to contribute a grain of sand."

"What?" Ellen frowned.

"It's a gloomy little saying Randy brought back from the war," Kuranes offered.

"The *First* World War," Carter corrected.

"So does this mean you're going to keep your promise?" Kuranes pressed him. "Are you going to honor your obligations?"

Randolph's shoulders slumped.

"Yes."

"What?"

"Yes, I will."

"You mean, I do," Kuranes purred.

He grabbed their hands and brought them together.

"No, I—" Ellen spluttered.

Randolph silenced her with a stern look. "Don't fight it."

The old man bowed his head and mumbled.

After a few moments, he released their hands.

Married, she thought, *I think we just got married.*

"So, what happens now?" Ellen asked.

"Well, normally you would have your wedding night. But you put the wedding night before the wedding, didn't you? Such a modern girl."

"You're exiling me," Randolph grumbled. "You're sending me to Siberia. To patrol the Wastelands."

King Kuranes's face darkened.

"Just be thankful I'm not making you pay a higher price for your betrayal. You left me to Solomon Reye. You abandoned me. All for that hussy of a wife. That hussy of a *first* wife."

Randolph stared at the warped floor. Biding his time. Waiting to escape from Kuranes. And her.

Ellen suddenly wished Solomon Reye had hacked her to death.

"I can't do this," she said in a tight voice.

"You have to," Kuranes insisted. "You made an oath."

"Do you know what I am in the waking world? I'm a starving student. Between work and scholarships, I barely have enough to survive. Being a Persephone is about . . . it's about traveling, right? It's about going anywhere a thin place causes trouble."

"Yes."

"I can't do that! I have no money!"

"I'll take care of that, my dear. You worry about the other things." Kuranes moved closer. His eyes were still full of wonder. "She's an incredible girl, isn't she, Randy?"

"She's not a girl, Will," Randolph muttered.

"You would know, my boy." Kuranes circled around Ellen three times and stopped in front of her. "I'm sorry."

"For what?"

"Your landing is going to be a little rough, but I'm sure you'll manage," he assured her. "I've left you a little something. Show him what you are."

The room rose like a cyclone around her.

Randolph's eyes widened in horror.

"Wait, what are you . . . Don't just . . . No. *No!*"

Randolph rushed toward her. Just as his hands settled on her shoulders, he disappeared.

King Kuranes vanished with him.

Chapter Thirty-One

"I thought I lost you."

Ellen Logan jerked on the cold dirt floor. Pain shot through her arm, a thunderbolt so intense, it took her breath away.

The stench of decay filled her nostrils.

Basement, she thought. *I'm in the basement again. And it's real this time.*

Ellen rolled onto her stomach. A man lay beside her. His head was half-scalped. A fleshy flap hung over his ears like a bad toupee.

She gagged, fighting the urge to vomit.

A shadowy figure stirred on the stairs above them.

"You disappeared. Solomon brought you to me, and you just disappeared," he said.

The man's voice sounded familiar.

She gazed at him through the gloom.

Her stomach dropped.

Leonard. Calvin Leonard. Solomon's accomplice. The man who tried to kidnap me during the lecture.

"I can't tell you how embarrassed I was," he continued. "He brought me all this wonderful material for my work, and I *lost* it."

As her eyes adjusted to the dark, Ellen saw more evidence of his "wonderful" material. Bodies were strewn all over the floor. Some people were dead, but some . . . She remembered her nightmares in the Dreamlands. Some reached out for her. She tried her best to comfort them as she witnessed their final moments.

Kore memagmeni.

The one who passes between the two worlds.

The strange energy she felt with King Kuranes rose inside her again.

She saw a baseball bat lodged under one of the bodies.

Minnie Mouse peeked out at her.

Kuranes's words reached out to her from the Dreamlands: *I've left you a little something. Show him what you are.*

Ellen crawled toward the weapon.

When she got closer, she gasped. Martha Pickman rested on her bat. Leonard hadn't gotten to her yet. She was still beautiful. Untouched.

Ellen reached out and touched her friend's cold face.

"I'm sorry, Martha," she whispered. "I'm so sorry."

The wood creaked as Calvin Leonard moved to his feet.

"What are you doing?" he yelped. "Don't touch my things!"

Things...

Ellen scurried to her feet, hiding the bat behind her back.

She waved at the pile of bodies.

"What exactly is the point of all this?"

"The *point* of all this? I'm helping these people," he insisted. "I'm taking the people Solomon gives me and shaping them into something new. I'm *transforming* them."

Ellen closed her eyes.

Energy filled her body like a balloon.

"You're not transforming them. You're nothing," she said. "Just a little boy playing with dolls. Working with the scraps Solomon throws you. If he thought you were worth anything, he would have given you more."

Calvin Leonard snarled and thundered down the stairs.

He had a knife in his hand. A sharp, *bloody* knife.

Ellen didn't care.

She was beyond fear.

Leonard skidded to a stop. His face clouded with confusion.

"Wait a minute. You're not in your gown. You aren't dressed the way—" he spluttered.

"That's because I changed. I don't need your help to transform," she replied. "And you didn't lose me. I was somewhere else. Do you want to know where I was?"

Leonard stared at her, speechless. He was used to being in control—directing all the action.

"Do you want to know where I was?" she asked again, her rage filling the room.

He shook his head.

Ellen felt her mouth spread into a wide smile. "I was watching Solomon Reye die. You see, your master wasn't as tough as he thought he was."

Leonard let out an inhuman shriek.

He charged her with the knife.

Ellen dodged the weapon and struck him in the back of the head. Even though she hit him full force, she wasn't sure it would be enough. She expected him to be hard and strong, like a nightgaunt.

She crushed Leonard's skull with the first blow.

His body plummeted to the floor, blood spreading out like a halo beneath him.

There was no lingering in the twilight. Death was nothing for him. A simple flip of the switch.

Just like that, she thought, *after everything he's done. After all the misery he caused, he gets off that easily.*

"You . . . *fuck!*" Ellen snarled.

She raised her bat and delivered another blow. And another. And another.

Blood and brains flew off the bat, bathing Ellen in gore.

Out of the corner of her eye, she saw movement.

A figure stirred in the pile of victims.

Ellen froze.

Alive, she thought in disbelief, *someone's still alive.*

She struck Leonard one last time. Then she kicked the knife away from him and knelt beside the body.

"Listen to me," she announced to the survivor as she rifled through Leonard's pockets. "I'm going to get help. You stay here."

A weak voice popped into her head.

What else do you expect me to do?

Ellen wasn't sure if she imagined the voice or if it was one of the victims. She didn't care. It made her laugh. It was a harsh cackle, the sound of darkness.

It was enough for now.

She snatched Leonard's keys and was halfway up the stairs when she stopped. She didn't want to escape through the house. Solomon Reye had an accomplice. What if Calvin Leonard had an accomplice? What if that accomplice had an accomplice with an accomplice? Ellen could see Solomon's evil spreading out like an endless set of Russian nesting dolls.

No, she decided, *there is only one way for a Persephone to leave.*

Weak rays of sunlight trickled through the cellar door. The passage led to the outside world, to the end of her long journey. Ellen was sure of it this time. She swung the blood-soaked bat. The wood splintered with the same ease as the killer's head. She pounded on the door until she opened a space wide enough for her body.

Ellen Logan clawed her way out of the darkness and into the cold winter air.

◆◆◆◆◆◆

Ellen ran down a narrow two-lane road. Even though she was exhausted, her lungs burning as she gulped the icy air, she knew she had to keep moving. The clouds were chunky with snow. She didn't want to escape from Calvin Leonard's lair only to die in a blizzard. She had to stay strong. Not only for herself but for the others she left behind.

She came upon a beat-up truck parked by the side of the road. Ellen threw herself onto the hood. The metal was warm. The engine still ticked. She spread her arms and embraced the heat.

Fresh snow was beginning to fall when two men emerged from the forest, guns slung over their shoulders. *Hunters,* she thought with a smile. They were always the ones who dealt with strange things. Children wandering, abandoned and lost; witches searching for ingredients to poison and destroy; monsters hiding deep in the wilderness.

They stopped when they saw her clinging to their truck.

One of the men took a piece of paper out of his coat pocket and studied her.

"You're that girl." He held the paper out for her to see.

It was a picture from her freshman year. She was at some forgotten party, red-faced and drunk, with her friends at her side.

MISSING, a headline screamed above her head.

"How long?" Ellen croaked. "How long have I been missing?"

The man glanced at his watch. "About two weeks."

She was overwhelmed by a flood of relief. She had no idea how much time had passed. A month? A year? A decade? Anything seemed possible.

"Where've you been all this time?" the other man asked.

Ellen flashed him a weary smile. "I wish I knew. I really, really wish I knew."

⋅⋅✦✦✦⋅⋅

Concussion. Dehydration. Hypothermia. Broken ribs. Cuts and bruises.

Not bad, considering what could have been.

The police kept a guard outside her hospital room. Whenever she felt up to it, they interviewed her. She told them as much as she could, carefully avoiding any mention of demons or the Dreamlands. The detectives seemed particularly interested in her relationship with Andrew Carter. They brought in a CSI to collect physical evidence. The technician took DNA and ran a sexual assault test.

Sexual assault? The thought shocked her. She was pretty sure they would find nothing. Still, she wondered. Were any signs of Randolph Carter still inside her? If there were, would such an impossible piece of evidence be enough to implicate Andrew?

"Goddamn it. I missed the wake-up," a voice announced, interrupting her thoughts.

Tom stood in the doorway, holding flowers and a teddy bear.

A wave of guilt crashed down on Ellen.

I cheated on him with Randolph Carter. Our relationship just started, and I've already cheated on him.

She began to cry, the sobs coming out thick and ugly. "Tom," she cried.

He abandoned the gifts at the foot of the bed and flew to her side.

"Hey. Hey, hey, hey."

Ellen threw her arms around him, wincing as stabbing pain shot through her. "Oh, Tom. I tried so hard. I tried so hard to fight. But he—"

He pulled back to look at her.

"You survived. That's all that matters. Do you hear me? That's what counts."

He doesn't understand, she thought as she ducked his gaze. *He doesn't understand what I'm trying to tell him.*

Another voice in her head chimed in.

Did you really expect him to?

"You know, you're a hero. The beauty who killed the beast."

Ellen's heart lurched in her chest. "What?"

"That's what they're calling you. 'The beauty who killed the beast.'"

"Who calls me that?"

Tom stared at her in wide-eyed disbelief.

"You don't know. Oh my God, you don't know."

"Please tell me what's going on."

He glanced over his shoulder at the man guarding her room.

"I don't know. The police—"

"The police already talked to me. I told them everything I knew," she replied.

When he continued to hesitate, she did something she thought she would never do. She played the pity card. "Please, Tom. I need to know. No one will tell me what happened, and it's driving me crazy."

"Solomon Reye. You know, the weirdo who came and showed that fake video of a monster attacking some guy?"

"It wasn't fake," Ellen blurted, but Tom didn't seem to hear.

"He was a serial killer. And he had a partner. They kidnapped and murdered a guy named Victor Ramsey. They took Martha Pickman. Then you. They locked you in his house in the Barrens, and they . . . they . . ." He stuttered to a stop. "They did terrible things to the others, Ellen. Some of them were alive when they did it. You escaped just as his partner was about to start on you. And when he came after you, you beat him to death with a bat. That's why they're calling you the beauty who killed the beast. You're a hero."

"Martha Pickman is dead."

"Assumed dead. They haven't found her body," Tom explained.

Haven't found her...

Ellen shook her head.

She put the information aside to process later.

"What about the others? The ones who were still in the cellar?"

Her boyfriend's face darkened. "They didn't make it."

"None of them?"

"They were too far gone. I'm sorry."

"Where's Solomon Reye?"

"He disappeared. But the police are hot on his trail."

"They won't find him." Ellen looked at the bedspread. She didn't voice her next thought. *Is he even dead? Can you kill a creature like Solomon?* "I don't feel much like a hero, Tom."

"You killed a madman. You stopped him before he could hurt anyone else. That makes you a hero in anyone's book."

"Does Andrew know?" she asked after a long silence.

"Andrew?"

"Carter. Does he know what happened?"

"Oh, Carter." Tom winced. "Yeah. I owe him a *big* apology."

"Why?"

"We got into a fight. A knock-down, drag-out fight."

"Why?" she asked again.

Tom gave her an incredulous look. "Think about it. His student, Victor Ramsey, disappears. Martha Pickman is kidnapped when he visits her in the asylum. And then you vanish into thin air while the two of you are in the middle of an investigation."

"You thought he did it?"

"*Everybody* thought he did it."

"But he . . . he's innocent. He didn't have anything to do—" she spluttered, throwing off the sheets.

"Relax. Relax. They know. They know." He soothed her before she could climb out of bed and rip out her IV line.

He smiled as he pulled the blankets back over her.

"I'll tell you this much. Carter's a good fighter. For an old man."

"Tom, that's not funny. Andrew Carter's very powerful. He could get you kicked out of Miskatonic."

"He won't."

"What makes you so sure?"

Tom shot her a sour look. "Are you really that naive? He likes you."

"I like him."

"No. He *likes* you." Tom gestured in a way that made his meaning perfectly clear. "He wouldn't do anything to hurt you. Unlike all the other poor souls who've been with him."

"What's that supposed to mean?"

"Oh, come on, Ellen. You've heard the rumors. A lot of people have died when they were with him."

Jonah, she thought.

"You have no idea what happened," she whispered. "No one does."

"Except Carter."

"There are going to be a lot of rumors about me, too. Are you going to believe them?" she snapped, feeling a hot rush of helplessness.

You may have escaped, but you're never going to be free of this. Never.

"Ellen?"

"Who are you to judge? You have no idea what it's like until . . . until you're put in a situation that . . . where you . . ."

"Ellen," he said.

The tenderness in his voice did little to calm her. She felt dirty. Dirty and deceitful and . . . doomed.

Above all, she felt doomed.

"Get out. Go find someone else. Someone who deserves you."

"Ellen—"

"I said go! *Go away!*" she cried out, clamping her hands over her ears to block the brittle sound of her own voice.

A nurse suddenly appeared at the door.

"Sir, you're going to have to leave now."

Tom looked at her one last time. Then he did as he was told.

Chapter Thirty-Two

Two days later, after enduring another round of tests and a psychiatric evaluation, Ellen was released from the hospital. She thought she was in Arkham, at Herbert West Memorial, so she was stunned when she saw *Atlantic City Regional* on her discharge papers. She was about to open her mouth to ask why she was there when she remembered. *The Barrens*. Atlantic City was the closest major city to the Barrens.

As Ellen signed the release forms, she wondered how she'd get back to Arkham. She hadn't seen Tom since she threw him out of her room. She assumed they were history. Andrew Carter wouldn't be there. He had only just been cleared as a suspect in her disappearance. To be seen with her would seem, at the very least, unwise. And Joshua . . . Where the hell was Joshua? Did he even notice she was gone? It was easy for her to imagine him in his study, oblivious to the drama outside his door. Ellen bowed her head. She was just beginning to feel sorry for herself when a bright voice pierced the dark cloud that surrounded her.

"I always knew you'd be a celebrity. It was only a matter of time."

She looked up and saw Marshall Dunphy. He was a driver for Arkham Paratransit, the company Ellen used whenever she needed to take Joshua to the doctor.

"What are you doing here?"

"What am I doing here?" he repeated. "I'm here to give you a ride home."

"All the way from Atlantic City?"

"Yeah," he replied, shooting her a stern look. "Your Uncle Joshua sent me. And I hope you're better company than he is. We've got a *long* trip ahead of us. I'm not above locking you in the trunk."

"I promise I'll be good."

Marshall plopped a small bag on her bed.

Ellen frowned. "What's that?"

"A change of clothes."

"Oh God. Joshua didn't pack this, did he?"

"No. I did," Tom offered. He hovered in the doorway.

Marshall eyed Tom suspiciously. "This guy says he's your boyfriend."

Ellen's eyes filled with tears.

"Yes. Yes, he is."

Chapter Thirty-Three

When Ellen returned to Miskatonic, she was put into what was called the "reentry program." She was removed from the general student population and assigned individual tutors, so she didn't have to attend classes. Once a week, she met with a psychiatrist to "process" what had happened. She told the strange tale again and again. With each telling, her adventures seemed more distant, her encounter with King Kuranes and Randolph Carter more unlikely.

Her psychiatrist celebrated her progress. He told her that her adventures were nothing more than a coping device, a way of escaping the horrible things that went on in the cellar. Ellen wasn't convinced. All she knew was that with each day in the waking world, her memory of the Dreamlands faded. And she still had to tell the story to one more person.

It took her almost a week to work up the courage to make the call.

"Hello." Andrew Carter picked up his office phone after two rings.

Ellen immediately heard the difference in the voices of the two men. Andrew's voice was lighter than Randolph's. Less husky.

"Andrew? It's Ellen."

"Yes?" he replied after a long silence. He sounded wary. And tired.

"Look, I know things have been intense for you, but once things settle down, will you come and see me?"

"Intense? Things have been *intense* for me?" He mocked her, but beneath the sarcasm, Ellen could hear fear.

She closed her eyes and forged ahead.

"I really need to see you. It's important."

"No."

"Please, I—"

"I'm not coming over to visit," he spat, his voice curling around the last word. "I've gotten into enough trouble because of you."

"Yes, I know. And I'm sorry." Ellen took a deep, ragged breath. "You're not a Jonah. You know that, right?"

"What?" Andrew's voice was quiet, full of steel.

"I survived. I'm the one who came back."

"Am I supposed to congratulate you? Throw you a party? Is that what you want?"

Ellen gasped. She felt like she had been punched in the gut.

"When?" she blurted.

"When what?" he shot back.

"When did you become so cruel? Were you always this way and I just didn't notice, or did—"

Did something happen when I was gone?

"Did what? Or did what?" Carter pressed.

She hung up before the thought had a chance to form.

Chapter Thirty-Four

Winter refused to release Arkham from its grip. It was a week before Easter, and Ellen trudged home through sludgy snow. Clouds gathered overhead, threatening to dump another thick blanket on Miskatonic. Hugging her coat to her body, she tried to avoid the stares of the people who passed her. Almost two months had gone by since she'd returned to the waking world. Ellen was still a celebrity, but her star was fading.

Solomon Reye and his partner rose in her place.

The interest in them was academic at first. Officials at Miskatonic University brought in experts to "analyze" the two men. They conducted the research for noble reasons (or so they said), to stop such monsters from being created again.

The response from the students was murkier.

They lingered with almost morbid glee on the slaughter, looking for clues in the slow, Inquisition-like torture, the flaying of the victims' skin, the fashioning of crude "wings" on the bodies. When the police found Calvin Leonard's journal, it was leaked on the internet. Ellen tried to avoid looking at it, but she was drawn to it like everybody else. One night, with Tom sleeping nearby, she read the entire thing. It was terrible, the product of a mind so twisted, she wondered whether the man had ever been sane. As she turned onto her street, a passage from Leonard's journal blazed in her head.

> I am only helping them realize their true potential. Revealing their divinity. Oh, they struggle. They scream. They cling to their weak human bodies. But when the moment comes, when they surrender, when they let go of the burdens of the flesh, they understand. I love them. You must understand. I am their friend. I am preparing them for their future. I am their Tailor.

Ellen stopped at the gate of her house. Even though her address was supposed to be secret, it had found its way onto the internet, too. People no longer threw beer bottles at her house. They left notes, flowers, and candles. Ellen wasn't sure why. Was it a memorial for the Tailor's victims or just for her? Did they think she was special? That there was a reason she survived?

There was a new bouquet on the sidewalk. A sprig of artificial flowers, bloodred and black.

She plucked out the note attached to them.

"I am so proud of you, my dear. My kore memagmeni."

Ellen's breath caught in her throat.

She hadn't told anyone about being a Persephone.

Only two people knew.

And a demon, her mind whispered. *Don't forget the demon.*

Ellen wasn't sure how she made it into the house. One moment, she was in the cold, with snow flurries brushing her cheeks. The next, she was inside, shoving furniture against the door. She stripped off snow boots, gloves, her coat—anything that might have touched the flowers.

She backed into the hall and waited for someone to break the door down.

Not someone. Something. Because demons don't die, do they?

A flicker of movement caught her eye.

Her eyes dropped to the floor.

"Oh no. Please, please. No," she wailed.

"Ellen?"

"Please, please. Just kill me. Get it over with," she begged.

"Ellen. It's Carter. Andrew Carter."

Ellen looked up.

Even though it had only been a couple of months, it felt like a lifetime since she'd last seen him.

"Is it really you? Is it really, truly you?" she whispered.

He frowned. "Who else would it be?"

Ellen's knees buckled.

She sank to the floor in relief.

◆◆◆◆◆

The plastic flowers dribbled snow onto the coffee table. As soon as she told Andrew what happened, he insisted on retrieving her "gift." Ellen didn't want to be left alone, so she had no choice but to follow him. The note was gone. Carried away by the winter wind. She stared at the flowers. Ellen hated the way they made her feel. She hated the way *Carter* made her feel.

He sat across from her, gazing at her with distant eyes. Observing her.

"Why are you here?" she finally demanded.

"I didn't like the way you sounded on the phone."

"I didn't like the way *you* sounded either, but I didn't break into your house and terrorize you."

Andrew raised his eyebrows.

"You gave me the keys to this house, remember?"

Ellen looked away. She *did* remember. She'd given them to Carter at Christmas and urged him to visit Joshua more often.

"Why are you here?" she asked again. This time, her voice was softer.

"I was worried about you. And I—" he looked around, noticing the stillness of the house for the first time. "Where's Joshua?"

"He's at an art conference in New York."

"Uh-huh," he muttered, as if he didn't believe it. "And that boyfriend of yours?"

Tom's voice echoed in her head. *He likes you.* She studied him, searching for any sign that what Tom told her was true.

Andrew betrayed nothing.

"He had to go home to Oregon," she replied. "His mother's in the hospital. Cancer."

"At least he has a decent excuse."

"I wasn't aware Tom *needed* an excuse." Ellen paused to let the point sink in. "He said the two of you got into a fight."

Carter shrugged.

"He was the only one with the balls to say what other people were thinking. And he backed it with his fists. I have no problem with that."

"He said he won," she teased.

He smiled and plucked at his pant leg.

"Well, he would say that to his girlfriend, wouldn't he?"

They fell into a comfortable silence. Which made Carter's next words shocking. They rushed out of him like a dam broke.

"Look, I know you've been through a lot, and in no way am I comparing myself to you, but I just want you to understand that the last few months have been a nightmare. A total fucking nightmare."

Ellen blinked, startled by the sudden deluge.

"I know. I heard," she reassured him.

"Heard what?"

"That you were a suspect in Victor Ramsey's disappearance. And Martha's. And mine. That the police dragged you in and interrogated you."

"The police? You think I'm worried about the police?" Andrew snorted. "They cleared me a long time ago. It's Miskatonic I'm worried about."

Ellen suddenly felt cold.

"What do you mean?"

"A lot of people have died around me. That's to be expected. It's an occupational hazard, the price we pay for what we do. But when too many bodies pile up, people notice. Especially when you have a lot of enemies."

"Do you want me to talk to them?" she blurted before she realized how absurd it sounded.

"Seriously, Ellen? Do you really think they'd listen? I've already been notified about you."

"Notified?"

"When a student develops an unhealthy fixation on a teacher, the school notifies them as a precaution."

Andrew Carter = Randolph Carter. The math was so simple. Her psychiatrist had suggested it to her countless times: that she had "invented" Randolph as a stand-in for Andrew, as a way of dealing with a traumatic situation.

She didn't realize the theory had found its way into her official record.

Ellen rose from the couch and drifted to the window. Even though the house was warm, she hugged herself.

Carter joined her.

"Do you believe them? That I have an unhealthy fixation on you?" she asked.

"Would I be in an empty house with you if I did?"

Ellen bit down on her lip.

"Thank you," she said hoarsely.

They fell silent, the grandfather clock counting out time. Ellen was full of questions she knew she could never ask. Did Andrew use the ring she gave him, the one that supposedly belonged to his grandfather? Did it work the way she thought it did, as a gateway to the Dreamlands? She remembered that moment in the cabin when she was sure Andrew was occupying his grandfather's body. Did it really happen?

"Here." Carter handed her an envelope.

Ellen winced.

"This isn't more paperwork, is it?"

"Take a look."

She opened the envelope and read the letter.

> To Dr. Charles Hayley
> President of Miskatonic University
> Arkham, Massachusetts
>
> I, Andrew Phillips Carter, request that my student, Ellen Logan, be admitted into the program of Advanced Studies at Miskatonic University. Ms. Logan has exhibited all the qualities we look for in an advanced student—an inquiring mind, an independent spirit, and most important, coolness under fire. Ms. Logan will be a valuable addition to our community.

"Oh my God," Ellen said after she scanned the letter several times. "Is this what I think it is?"

"What do you think it is?"

"Did you just let me into the advanced program?"

"I did. And the president signed off on it. You'll get the formal letter in a few days."

Ellen threw her arms around him.

Carter backed away, wrestling free from her grip.

"Yeah, um. Let's not do that."

"I'm sorry. It's just . . . I mean." Her eyes filled with tears. "No one's ever . . . You've given me . . . You're giving me a chance."

"No, Ellen. *You* gave yourself a chance," he insisted. "You fought your way back here with everything you had. And that needs to be acknowledged. Acknowledged and respected."

Carter fell silent.

His thoughts returned to that lonely road in New Jersey.

"It happened just the way you said it would," he told her. "The last thing I remember was running down the road with you. Then . . . I was alone. Standing by my car. I wasn't sure how I got there. For a moment, I didn't remember *you*. It was like I was abducted by aliens."

"That's not too far off," she offered.

Carter stared deep into her eyes. "What happened to you, Ellen?"

Ellen Logan took a deep breath. Then she told her tale one last time.

Introducing

If you enjoyed
Darkness Below,
look out for

Shadow Zone

Book Three of the Shadows of Miskatonic

by Barbara Cottrell

Available 2024

Chapter One

The creature raised its sword above its head, its jackal-like face twisted in triumph. A crowd gathered at the base of the altar. They leaned forward in anticipation, ears pricked, teeth bared. Gerard Caron held his breath. He waited for the blow to land, the deed to be done.

"Is it real?"

The gallery owner glanced up from the painting.

"There's no way to know for sure," he admitted. "The artist we're talking about is a legend, a myth—"

"A boogeyman," the stranger added.

Gerard Caron studied the man beside him. He rarely met people after hours at his gallery. Dark art was a risky business. He preferred to work through well-worn channels, with people he knew. Even then, he took precautions. He told his friends where he was going. He texted them before and after his meetings. But when this man called and hinted at what he had—*what he might have,* Gerard corrected himself—he relaxed his rules.

A shaft of sunlight hit the canvas with a glancing blow, illuminating two figures in the corner of the painting.

Gerald moved in for a closer look.

They were females. *Human* females. The women wore long robes.

And in the arms of one . . .

A shiver skittered up his spine.

The other man shifted in the gloom. "It *is* real, isn't it?" he said softly.

Glancing at the pile of paperwork waiting on his desk, Gerard didn't respond. He wanted nothing more than to kick the man out, return to his normal routine. Two words held him back.

What if?

"There might be a way of identifying it," Gerald said after a long silence. "The artist never signed his work, but there are rumors he marked them in other ways. I'm not sure what he did, but if we remove the frame and find something, it might add strength to your claim."

The man shifted nervously. "Remove the frame?"

"The frame isn't where the value is. Artists rarely frame their own work," Gerard replied. "I'll be blunt, sir. What you have now is an interesting story. That's all."

"All right. If you must," the stranger huffed, sounding like a petulant teenager.

Gerard popped off the wooden frame. An odor rose from the canvas. He leaned forward and took a deep breath, like a connoisseur appreciating fine wine. The smell was complex— dry, dusty, undercut with the unmistakable smell of rot. A con- tradiction. Just like the man who'd painted it. *The man who'd supposedly painted it.* Gerard struggled to stay professional, but as his eyes drifted across the exposed painting, his excitement grew.

In the corner of the canvas, he spotted a single word. He raised his reading glasses to examine the spidery writing. "*Al-Uqdah*," he read.

"What?" the man demanded.

"I'm not sure, but I think it's Arabic. I have a translation app on my—"

Pain shot through Gerard, so sudden and intense, he thought he was having another heart attack.

Something warm and wet trickled down his back.

Not my heart, he thought. *I'm being stabbed.*

He turned to face his attacker.

The next blow hit him in the chest. He gasped, feeling the grind of metal on bone. When his attacker yanked out the knife, Gerard lurched forward, collapsing into the man's arms.

His attacker lowered him to the ground.

"I'm sorry," he apologized. "But I have to keep this a secret."

The man stepped over him to reclaim his prize. Gerard rolled onto his stomach, crawling in his own blood to reach the painting. "No, please," he wheezed. "Wait, wait—"

A sudden roar filled the air. The man who'd stabbed him collapsed at the foot of the easel. Gerard stared up at the canvas. The creature at the altar loomed over them both. The men looked like they had fallen victim to its sword.

A figure stepped into the room, his gun winking in the sun.

"You . . . you just shot your partner!" Gerard gasped.

"That man is *not* my partner."

Gerard knew he was telling the truth. This man was a professional. Even though it was a sweltering summer day, he wore a ski mask. And he had gloves. White cotton gloves.

He slipped them on to examine the painting.

Gerard moaned his approval. "It is real, isn't it?" the gallery owner whispered.

The man said nothing.

"Can I have another look?"

The intruder's lips twisted into a smile. "Do you think that's wise? I mean, look what's already happened to you."

"I don't care. I must—" His words ended with a wheeze.

The man picked up the painting and held it in front of him. A fresh wave of agony ripped through Gerard as he strained for a better look. The pain didn't matter. *It's him. After all these years, I'm finally seeing something by him.* It wasn't what he expected. The artist's legend was so much larger than life, Gerard expected the work to match. He expected a Rembrandt, a masterpiece measured in feet. The work was modest in size, but the scene crawled with energy. He could hear the snarl of the creatures, the crackle of the altar fire. He could smell the stench of the group as their dirty bodies pressed together. And the creature looking out at him from the bottom of the painting, its eyes red, as if it had been frozen by a camera flash.

Gerard closed his eyes, trying to hold the image in his mind.

"Thank you," he said to the shadowy figure.

The man chuckled. "Not words I usually hear in my profession."

"I mean it. I never thought I'd see one." Gerard kept his eyes shut, waiting for the gunshot.

The man's footsteps retreated.

Gerard blinked, confused. "What? What are—" he spluttered.

"Good luck, Mr. Caron."

The man punched the keypad on the wall.

The burglar alarm howled. Whooping and wailing.

Calling for help.

Chapter Two

here Is Solomon Reye?

The spray-painted words bit into Ellen Logan. They transported her to a cold basement in the Pine Barrens of New Jersey. Five months earlier, she had escaped from the clutches of a serial killer named Calvin Leonard. A man she claimed had a partner in crime, a demon who called the shots: Solomon Reye. The police dismissed the demon angle. *Trauma,* they told her. *That's just the trauma talking.* The reality was horrifying enough. Ten bodies discovered in an abandoned farmhouse—many of them mere piles of flesh. Only Ellen Logan had survived. Bloody Ellen Logan, clutching a baseball bat. She'd killed Calvin Leonard. Solomon Reye . . .

"He's the one who got away," she whispered.

In his absence, the legend grew. Spawned in the dark heart of the internet. Questions began to swirl around her. Why had she survived? Why had she emerged from the basement practically unharmed? What made Ellen Logan so special? She remembered the moment it all changed, when a reporter thrust a microphone in front of her face and demanded, "How did you get out alive? Did you make a deal with Calvin Leonard?"

A few days later, a headline blared from the local paper: "The Pine Barren Blasphemies: Was There a Second Killer?"

The article didn't mention Ellen by name.

It didn't need to.

That's when the whispers started. The sideways looks. The accusation plastered on the wall.

Where Is Solomon Reye?

Even now, she could feel people watching her, their eyes boring into her back.

Ellen turned and fled to the safety of Edgewood Manor.

Edgewood Manor Retirement Home. She'd first visited the Victorian house when she interviewed a resident as part of an investigation. The conversation had grown heated. Intense. A few weeks later, the man was dead. Ellen knew he was living on borrowed time—he had a constellation of health problems. Still, questions burned in her mind. *Did I push him over the edge? Was he another one of my "victims"?* After the funeral, Ellen returned to Edgewood to check on his widow, Lily. And something wonderful happened. What started out as obligation blossomed into friendship.

Ellen arrived at Lily's room just as she returned from her yoga class.

She plopped down on her friend's couch and snatched a chocolate from a candy dish.

"Sorry I'm late," Ellen apologized.

"You know, you don't have to keep visiting me," Lily replied. "I'm sure you're a busy girl."

"I like visiting you."

"You like visiting my sweets."

Ellen smiled as she reached for another piece of candy.

"Are you sure you want to do that? You don't want to gain the freshman fifteen your senior year."

Ellen dropped the truffle and looked down at her body.

"Lily!" she protested.

"Oh, don't get me wrong. There's nothing wrong with you now. But why don't you have some iced tea instead?"

Lily patted a spot on her loveseat.

Ellen cleared away the newspapers on the cushions.

A headline glared at her:

One Man Dead
Gallery Owner Critically Injured in Bold Daylight Robbery

Her friend wrinkled her nose.

"Can you believe it? All that violence. Over *art*."

Ellen couldn't ignore the sneer in her friend's voice.

Her uncle Joshua was an art dealer.

Their lives revolved around art.

"Art is big business," Ellen pointed out as she took her iced tea. "Do you know how much they think the *Mona Lisa* is worth?"

"I can't imagine."

"Half a billion dollars. For something small enough to slip into a duffel bag."

"Nothing but nonsense." Lily dismissed the thought with a wave of her hand.

A nurse entered the room before Ellen could respond. The man was young, good-looking in a boy-band kind of way. His fresh face made her feel old.

"Oh, Justin. Again?" Lily lowered her voice to a stage whisper. "He can't keep his hands off me."

The man blushed bright red.

"Would you give us a moment alone, dear?" Lily cooed.

"Yell if you need help," Ellen told Justin as she walked out of the room.

Edgewood Manor had changed since her first visit. She'd read somewhere that a corporation had recently bought it. They told the usual lies. Nothing would change. Their goal was to make the place more efficient without sacrificing quality. The threadbare furniture and chipped linoleum floors told a different story. Edgewood hadn't just reached a tipping point. It had blown right through it. And then there were the rules. Residents must not . . . residents will not . . . residents are forbidden . . .

The one plastered on the front door bothered Ellen the most.

RESIDENTS ARE NOT ALLOWED ON THE PORCH UNLESS FAMILY OR STAFF IS PRESENT.

The first time Ellen came to Edgewood, the porch was full of residents. They napped. Read books. Argued. Watched people on the street. No one supervised them back then.

What changed? she wondered.

Was someone snatching old people off porches?

A woman joined her at the picture window.

"Would you like to go outside with me?" Ellen offered.

The woman looked at her, stunned.

"Yes. Please," she whispered.

Ellen escorted the woman outside, guiding her to one of the Adirondack chairs. Ellen perched on the railing a few feet away and tilted her head back, closing her eyes and letting the sun warm her skin.

"You're not a staff member," a voice declared.

Ellen groaned and opened her eyes.

A man sat in the corner of the porch, smoking a cigarette, his legs splayed in front of him. He had stringy gray hair and a lanky body. His face tickled her memory. Ellen was sure she had seen him before, but she had seen a lot of guys like him. He was straight out of the movies. An aging cowboy. Tommy Lee Jones in *Lonesome Dove*. Jack Palance in *City Slickers*.

"You're not a staff member either," she pointed out.

The stranger took a deep drag off his cigarette and flicked the ashes into a coffee can.

"You're that girl."

"Excuse me?" she blurted, even though she knew what was coming.

"You're that girl. The one who escaped from the serial killer in New Jersey. God, what was his name?"

"Calvin Leonard."

She hated to say his name, but her psychiatrist insisted on it.

That's how you rob him of his power.

"The Tailor. Isn't that what he called himself?" The man continued without waiting for a response. "He sewed body parts onto his victims. Tried to transform them into divine creatures."

Ellen gave him a hard look.

"Are you one of his fans?"

The man stared at her with intense blue eyes.

"No, I'm one of *yours*," he insisted. "You ended all his nonsense with a baseball bat."

A nurse marched onto the porch, resting her hands on her hips in a classic battle pose.

"What the hell are you doing?" the woman barked at Ellen. "I've seen you around, so I know you're familiar with the rules. No one is allowed on the porch without family or staff."

"This is my daughter-in-law. And we decided to add Lisa to our little family," the man offered, nodding at the woman Ellen had brought outside. "Is there a problem, Miss Worden? Or is the god of liability against random acts of kindness?"

Miss Worden hissed.

"*You*. I should have known you were involved."

The man flicked his cigarette into the coffee can.

"What can I say? I'm diabolical."

Ellen stifled a giggle.

A moment later, Lily popped her head out the front door. When she saw the man on the porch, her expression cooled. "Robert."

"Lily," he replied in a neutral voice.

Lily grabbed Ellen by the arm and yanked her off the railing. "You can come back. I'm done flirting with the new boy."

Robert raised an eyebrow. "You mean there's a time when you're *not* flirting?"

"When I'm with you," Lily cooed.

His lips twisted into a crooked smile.

"It was nice to see you again, Ellen," he said as Lily pulled her inside the house.

Ellen tensed at the sound of her name, at the familiarity in his voice.

See me again?

Lily marched Ellen back to her room. Several residents looked up as the two women passed. Ellen knew she would be the subject of dinnertime conversation. The people at Edgewood Manor loved gossip. And she gave them a steady supply.

When they got to Lily's room, her friend turned on her. "You shouldn't talk to Robert."

"Why?"

"He's not a nice man."

"There are a lot of people around here who fit that description," Ellen joked.

Lily grabbed her arm and squeezed. "I mean it. Don't talk to him."

Ellen jerked free from her friend's grip. "Don't tell me what to do!" She stopped, forcing down her anger. "What's going on, Lil? Are you jealous because I'm paying attention to him? Because you're the one who's my friend."

"It's not that, and you know it."

"Then what is it?"

A horrible thought bloomed in Ellen's head. "Oh my God, he's not taking advantage of you, is he?"

Lily almost choked. "*Him?* That scarecrow? I'd tear him apart if he tried." Lily hesitated for a moment. Then she moved to her nightstand and picked up an envelope.

"He's been bugging me. He wants me to give this to you. To pass on to Dr. Carter."

Andrew Carter. Ellen hadn't thought about him in a long time. There was no point. He had already been warned about her unhealthy "obsession" with him. Now, with the rumors about her spreading . . .

He wouldn't touch me with a ten-foot pole.

Still, Ellen took the letter, if only to relieve her friend of the burden.

"I can't promise you he'll get it," she warned Lily as she tucked it into her bag. "Not that it matters. It's probably just fan mail."

"Fan mail?" Lily echoed.

"People give me stuff for Carter all the time. They think that since I worked with him in the past—" She let the sentence die.

"Are you sleeping with him?" Lily asked.

Ellen stiffened. It was a familiar question, but it caught her off guard every time.

"I have a boyfriend. And he is *not* Andrew Carter."

Lily gawked at her. "Wait a minute. You have a boyfriend? Why haven't I met him?"

"And have you steal him from me? I don't think so!" Ellen quipped.

"I wouldn't stand a chance against you."

Ellen looked at the floor, hiding a smile. Her happiness didn't last long.

"Tom went home for the summer," Ellen explained. "His mom has cancer."

"Oh! I'm so sorry to hear that."

Ellen nodded and looked away, her eyes locking on a spot above Lily's head. There, at the junction between the wall and the ceiling, a purple light pulsed. The glow trickled down the wall like liquid.

Ellen's skin prickled.

Thin place.

It was the gateway Solomon Reye had used to kidnap her, to pull her into the parallel world of the Dreamlands. A moment that forever divided her life into two parts: before and after.

Ellen closed her eyes, hoping to clear her vision.

The spot grew, spreading like a stain.

She leaped off the couch.

"You have to leave, Lily."

Lily turned, looking at the opening Ellen knew she couldn't see.

"What? Why? I don't—" her friend spluttered.

Ellen stepped between Lily and the ever-widening hole. She felt heat on her back, like she was standing in front of an open oven.

She put her hands on her friend's shoulders.

"Please. Trust me," she pleaded. "Leave."

Lily Graham was a tough woman. She didn't like being told what to do. Even so, she fled the room.

Leaving Ellen alone with . . .

What exactly?

Ellen took a deep breath and turned.

A man stood in front of a chalkboard. Ellen blinked. It was the last thing she expected to see. A man—in a robe and pajama bottoms. Books covered every surface of the room.

Papers littered the floor. The stranger didn't notice her. He was too focused on his work. His fingers flew across the board. He filled the black slate with what looked like equations.

Ellen moved closer.

The rhythm of the chalk sounded like an irregular heartbeat.

Bam, bam bam bam, bam bam, ba-bam.

"Who are you?" she whispered.

The man stopped midstroke and turned to face her.

Ellen tensed. *Oh, here it comes,* she thought. *This is when it gets bad.*

The man didn't transform. He didn't grow tentacles or assume an impossible shape. He stayed the way he was— unshaven, with a mop of unruly brown hair and a pinched, boyish face.

His eyes widened when he saw her, and he yanked off his glasses and rubbed his face, his fingers leaving chalky war paint on his skin.

"Who are you?" Ellen asked again.

The man dropped the book in his hand and rushed toward her, stopping just short of the gateway, his eyes climbing the barrier.

Ellen's skin crawled.

He's trying to get to me.

The man grabbed the chair next to his desk.

"What are you . . . Don't, don't!" Ellen yelped.

He hurled the chair at the barrier.

Ellen dropped to the floor to shield herself.

A pair of leathery hands shook her.

"Girl, snap out of it, girl," a man commanded.

"Her name is Ellen," a familiar voice corrected him.

Ellen opened her eyes. The man from the porch knelt beside her. Lily fluttered around him like an anxious bird.

Ellen looked at the wall. The purple light was gone.

"What happened?" she croaked.

"Lily barged into my room. Said something was wrong with you," the man replied.

Robert, she remembered. *His name is Robert.*

"When I got here, you were mumbling and hugging the wall. Trying to sink your fingers into it. Then you screamed and hit the floor."

"I fainted?"

Robert's eyes flicked to the wall. "I didn't say that."

A jolt of energy shot through Ellen. *Had he seen the man?*

"You're lucky he caught you. It could have been much, much worse." Lily shot Robert a grateful look that seemed to annoy him.

"Are you going to get off the floor?" he barked at Ellen. "Or do you want to keep making a scene?"

Ellen looked up.

A crowd of people crammed into the doorway.

"Oh, oh, no," she whispered.

The group parted as Nurse Worden pushed her way through.

"You, again! What the hell have you done now?"

"It's my fault," Lily announced. "I teased Ellen about needing to lose weight—she's been skipping meals. I guess it caught up with her."

"I got dizzy. That's all," Ellen insisted as Robert helped her to her feet.

Nurse Worden shot her a skeptical look.

"You should go to the hospital. Get yourself checked out."

"What she needs to do is eat," Robert offered. "And some old lady needs to stop telling her she's fat."

"I was only giving her some advice," Lily protested.

"Yeah, Lily. We're all familiar with your 'helpful' advice."

Several people in the crowd tittered.

"All right, you two. Enough," Nurse Worden snapped. "I'm not going to referee another fight."

The woman squinted at her. Her face was lined with exhaustion. Ellen wondered how much of her staff had been cut in the name of "efficiency."

"You sure you're okay?" the nurse asked.

"Yes."

"And you'll get something to eat?"

"And if I still feel strange, I'll go to the clinic on campus," Ellen assured her.

Nurse Worden nodded and dismissed the crowd.

"Why do you have to be such a bastard, Robert?" Lily spat when the others drifted away.

He ignored her and turned to Ellen.

"Take care of yourself," he said, departing with a nod.

"That man. That man," Lily hissed as soon as Robert was gone.

She likes him.

The thought hit Ellen like a thunderbolt. Under any other circumstances, she would have teased her friend. But her mind was fixed on the man she had just seen in the room. A man willing to shatter the boundaries between two worlds.

But why?

What was he after?

Ellen stared at the blank wall.

"I should go. I've caused enough trouble for one day," she said, grabbing her backpack and heading for the door.

"Oh, no. Please don't! Don't leave," Lily urged. "Robert's right. Don't listen to an old lady. You're not fat. You can have as many of my sweets as you like."

Ellen smiled at her friend. "I'm sorry, Lily," she replied. "My uncle will want to eat soon, and dinner's not going to make itself. Well, it would if he let me get take-out, but Joshua's not the kind—"

Lily interrupted Ellen's attempt at a joke.

"He pushes you too hard. *You* push yourself too hard."

Ellen shifted under the weight of her backpack.

"Is it because of the others?" her friend asked.

The others. No one ever called the Tailor's victims by their names. They were always lumped together in a homogeneous mass, their identities consumed along with their bodies.

"Ellen?"

"Hmm?"

"Do yourself a favor. Don't let the dead rule your life."

Ellen's breath hitched in her throat. She felt like she was drowning. Being pulled into the icy depths. "I don't think I have a choice," she whispered.

"What?"

"Nothing." Ellen offered her friend a smile she didn't feel. "I should go. Let you get back to your flirting."

"I wasn't flirting with Robert!" Lily protested.

"I wasn't talking about Robert. I was talking about the nurse." Ellen tilted her head. "My, my. Isn't this an interesting development?"

Her friend's face turned bright red. She grabbed Ellen by the shoulders and pushed her toward the door.

"You're right. You should be going. Off you go, bird. Flap, flap, flap."

The front gates to the house were open. That was unusual. Ellen and her uncle lived in a house that was notorious in Arkham. People loved to vandalize it. With the gates closed, the attacks were limited to bottle throwing and the odd piece of graffiti. With the gates open . . .

"Shit!"

Ellen ran down the driveway, her mind churning with grim possibilities.

Broken windows. Toppled statues. Cut cables.

So help me God, if we've lost internet.

Ellen skittered to a stop.

A silver Mercedes was parked in the drive.

Her uncle bought and sold art, but most of his business took place online. Their visitors were usually UPS and FedEx drivers.

Ellen couldn't remember the last time Joshua entertained a buyer at the house.

The headline from the paper popped into her head.

One Man Dead
Gallery Owner Critically Injured in Bold Daylight Robbery

She reached into her bag and grabbed a can of mace.

The door to Joshua's study was closed. Ellen sighed at the sight. Over the past few months, Joshua had shut her out of his life. She wasn't sure why, but she had her suspicions. After all, why should her uncle be different than anyone else? Why shouldn't he believe the stories about her? Still, the rejection stung. Of all the people she knew, she thought he would be the one to defend her.

The sound of angry voices greeted her in the hall.

Ellen froze, unsure what to do.

The voices became heavier, thick with the threat of violence.

Joshua's in a wheelchair. If someone wanted to overpower him, it would be trivial.

She marched toward the study, raising her can of mace.

A man burst out the door at the same time.

He threw his hands in front of his face when he saw her.

"Whoa! Whoa, whoa! Don't shoot," he pleaded.

"It's all right, Ellen," her uncle's disembodied voice reassured her.

Ellen tried to look past the man to get a glimpse of Joshua.

"Are you sure?"

"I'm fine."

"Ellen?"

A smile spread across the man's face.

"Little Ellen Logan?"

Ellen studied the stranger. He had a lean, foxlike face and grayish-blond hair, buzzed business short. He had a regal, vaguely European bearing. The way the man held himself reminded Ellen of stories she'd read as a child, of royalty trying to pass themselves off as regular people.

"Do I know you?" she asked.

"You do, but it was a long time ago—"

"Wait, wait—don't tell me. In a galaxy far, far away?"

The man laughed. "Still crazy about *Star Wars*. You haven't changed a bit. Well, except for the mace."

She dropped her weapon back into her bag.

"Sorry about that."

"Understandable. Especially after what you've been through." The man called out to Joshua. "We'll talk later, yes?"

"Not if I can help it," her unseen uncle growled.

Ellen walked the man to the door.

He paused on the threshold and offered her his hand.

His skin was soft. Like the leather of a reading chair.

"It was good to see you again. I hope you're well," he said.

"I am." *All things considered,* she silently added. "Would you do me a favor?"

His expression flickered before he smiled. "Maybe."

"Would you close the gates when you leave?"

The man smacked his head. "I knew there was something I forgot to do!" he exclaimed, then leaned forward, eyes twinkling. "Locked gates? Passwords at the door? When did Joshua get so dramatic?"

Dramatic?

The word echoed in her head as she watched the man drive away. The crunch of tire on gravel filled her with a deep sadness. She knew it would be a long time before they had another visitor.

"You certainly made an impression on him," Joshua grumbled when she perched herself on the edge of his desk.

"It's called being polite. You should try it," she replied. "Who is he?"

He shrugged. "A colleague."

"Uh-huh," she replied. "Have you been following the news? There was a robbery at one of the art galleries in town."

"I don't do any business locally," he said, cutting her off and flashing her a sour look. "Don't you have homework to do?"

Ellen pursed her lips. Joshua always brought up Miskatonic University when he was mad. Her uncle had opposed the move to Arkham, didn't want her to attend the school. He certainly didn't want her to be accepted into the advanced program. But Andrew Carter made it happen. He'd arranged it after she escaped from the Tailor.

Joshua resented her for "forcing" him to return to Arkham. She couldn't imagine how he felt about Carter.

Ellen continued. "I was wondering if you knew the owner who was hurt. His name was Gerard Car . . . Car-something."

Joshua frowned. "Car-something? Doesn't ring a bell."

His hand dropped to his wheelchair and nervously toggled the brake.

Liar, she thought.

Ellen hopped off the desk and headed for the door.

"Well, when you're ready to tell me the truth, you know where to find me."

Acknowledgments

A lot of people helped me with *Thin Places*, the second book in my series.

To my husband, Lance, who spent a lot of time in the Dreamlands, making sure my first attempt at a split-world plot didn't go off the rails. He also accompanied me on many weird expeditions, including to the site of Emilio Carranza's crash in the Pine Barrens of New Jersey.

To Robbi Sommers Bryant, my intrepid editor, who knew just when to push me and when I needed praise.

To Paul Carrick, who created the original cover art. This was the first project we did together, and I loved the mystery he brought to *Thin Places*. When I asked him why the sky behind the nightgaunt was glowing red, he replied, "You tell me." It was then that I realized a disaster would be central to the plot.

To Ross E. Lockhart, for all his professional support and advice. If you are ever in Petaluma, California, do yourself a favor and drop by his bookshop, Word Horde Emporium of the Weird and Fantastic.

Finally, I would like to thank the man who created the world my characters inhabit: H. P. Lovecraft. I'm not sure he would have approved of what I've done, but he always insisted on leaving his world open so that other writers could explore it. I may disagree with him on a lot, but I am grateful to him for that.

About the Author

Barbara Cottrell gave up her career as a professor to pursue her true passion: writing weird fiction. She is the author of *Darkness Below* and is a lifetime member of the Horror Writers Association. She enjoys presenting her work in unusual venues, like Mystery Writers in the Mausoleum and Word Horde Emporium of the Weird and Fantastic. She also served as a judge on the Redwood Writers anthologies *Redemption: Stories from the Edge* and *Endeavor: Stories of Struggle and Perseverance*, and she helped edit *Remember When* and *On Fire*. She lives in Sonoma County in a not-at-all-haunted vineyard. When she isn't exploring the dark side, she makes wine with her husband, Lance.

To find out more about her and the world of Miskatonic University, visit www.barbaracottrell.com. While there, subscribe to her newsletter to keep up with new releases and access exclusive content.